Labor Day's Revelations

A Larry Macklin Mystery-Book 21

A. E. Howe

Books in the
Larry Macklin Mystery Series
(in order):

November's Past	October's Fear
December's Secrets	Spring's Promises
January's Betrayal	Summer's Rage
February's Regrets	Autumn's Ghost
March's Luck	Winter's Chill
April's Desires	Valentine's Warning
May's Danger	St. Patrick's Cross
June's Troubles	Memorial Day's Escape
July's Trials	Independence Day's Search
August's Heat	Labor Day's Revelations
September's Fury	

ISBN-13: 979-8-9899501-3-3

CHAPTER ONE

I got up for the fourth time since I'd gone to bed and went to the bathroom. I'd started feeling off the day before, and now I was in the midst of a nasty virus that left me feeling simultaneously irritated, pathetic and violated.

"Do you need anything?" Cara asked from the bed as I came back into the bedroom.

"A cure," I moaned. "I'm going into the living room. I'm just keeping you up."

"Drink some water or something. Let me know if I can do anything."

"I just hope I don't give it to you."

I went into the living room and sat down on the couch. Restless, I opened my laptop and figured I'd try to keep my mind off of the fact that I was suffering a slow and agonizing death… or, at the very least, a rotten stomach bug.

I read through various reports and tried to respond to emails, but I wasn't up to doing any thinking. At some point, I fell asleep on the couch.

Cara woke me with a gentle hand on my shoulder and I opened my eyes to see sun streaming through the windows.

"I'm heading to work. Do you want me to pick up anything at the store? I could swing by the pharmacy and bring you some drugs at lunch."

"I've got enough drugs. I think the odds are fifty-fifty that I'll be alive when you get home."

"Overly dramatic much?" She smiled. "Yesterday, Mom said she'd overnight some of her herbal remedies."

"Just what I need to finish me off." I groaned and sat up. "It's the end of summer; I shouldn't even be sick."

"And you say Mauser is spoiled," Cara said, giving me a kiss on the head.

Mauser was my father's one-hundred-and-ninety-pound, almost four-year-old Great Dane, and he was definitely more spoiled then I was.

"I'll take Alvin to the clinic with me," she said, and called our Pug to her side. "You're on your own with the cats."

I managed to stand up and got some crackers and a Coke from the kitchen. Sipping soda and nibbling on a cracker had been my mom's answer to any sickness that involved the digestive system. I was getting ready to sit back down when my phone buzzed with a text alert.

I glanced at the message. It was from Julio Ortiz, one of the investigators who reported to me in my position as a sergeant with the Adams County Sheriff's Office. *Know you're sick. Call when you can.*

With a sigh, I pressed his number.

"Sorry, but the situation is quickly rising above my pay grade," Julio said. "Martel got a call for a welfare check. When he arrived, the door was open. He knocked, yelled, got no answer, then entered the premises to find the owner of the home dead on the floor. Pills on the table. Looks like a suicide or a maybe an accidental overdose."

"Okay." I wasn't seeing the urgency.

"He called me, then I called crime scene and the coroner's office."

"What time was this?"

"The call came in about two this morning. The victim was supposed to have been at work at ten. He works for a painting company that's mostly commercial, so they work at night a lot. They waited for a while, thinking he was just running late or had an emergency, that sort of thing. When he never showed up and they couldn't reach him by phone, they called us."

"His boss called in a welfare check?" I asked, surprised. A lot of bosses would be pissed off the first day, and probably the second, before they started to actually worry about an employee.

"Seems the deceased was a super-nice guy, very dependable. When he didn't show up, the boss was worried, so he texted and called. Said that the guy would always respond when he called. When he didn't, that set off alarm bells for the boss. He had to go out on a job and couldn't go to the guy's house, so he called us."

"Okay." I still didn't understand how this warranted getting me off of my deathbed.

"I haven't gotten to the kicker yet. When Marcus was taking pictures of the scene, he found a box of drivers' licenses, jewelry and other stuff that had spilled out on the floor in one of the bedrooms."

"Did the man live alone?"

"I wasn't sure, but it was odd enough that I went ahead and got a search warrant from Judge Jackson."

"Good. So what about the box?"

"There were six licenses. All belonging to victims of unsolved murders."

My heart jumped and I forgot about being sick. "What murders?"

"About a dozen across North Florida and South Georgia. The FBI has evidence attributing most of them to the same killer. A special agent is on the way. That's why I called."

"Damn it," I muttered. I didn't dislike the FBI, but my past experiences with them had been mixed. I wondered if Elaine Padilla would be the special agent in charge. "Have you told Lieutenant Eccles?"

"Yes, and it's already gone up the chain. Your dad's the one who told me about the FBI." My dad was the sheriff.

"Then this is probably above my pay grade too. Okay, I'm coming out to the scene."

"If you're sick…"

"I want to see it while it's fresh, sick or not."

"There's something else you should know."

"What?"

"Dill's here," Julio said, referring to the office's desk sergeant. Dill Kirby was old enough to be retired, but the sheriff's office wouldn't have been the same without him. Often, he was the first person I saw in the morning and the last before I went home. "He says that the victim is his cousin."

I cursed again. This wasn't getting any less complicated.

"I'll be on my way as soon as I drink a bottle of Pepto Bismol."

I took a long, hot shower, got dressed and told the cats to hold down the fort. With my gut still grumbling, I grabbed my gun and badge and headed for the car.

As I drove, I tried to make sense of Dill's cousin being a serial killer. I wondered if he'd killed himself, died from an accidental overdose or—and this seemed the least likely—if he'd been murdered. In that case, I would have expected a more violent crime scene.

I arrived ahead of the FBI, which made me feel better. I wanted to get a handle on things before the pushy-shovey Feds showed up.

The dead man had lived in a small, ranch-style house three miles outside of Calhoun, set back from the road up a hundred-yard dirt driveway. Julio had set up a police line at the entrance to the driveway, so there were half a dozen cars parked on the side of the road around the mailbox, including a couple from the highway patrol that were mainly there to discourage gawkers. I found a spot and slowly got out of my car, trying to decide if my stomach was going to throw a fit or not.

Julio got there before I'd managed to take a dozen steps. "You look like hell," he blurted.

"Feel great," I lied and forced a smile, stepping back and propping myself up against my car to keep from falling over. "Fill me in."

"Dill's not taking it well. I finally convinced him to sit in his truck and wait for you while Marcus finishes documenting the scene. The Feds wanted me to clear the house, but I couldn't see the point, so I called the captain and he called your dad. Final word was to finish what we were doing but not to move the body or collect any evidence."

"What's your impression?" I asked. Julio had a good eye, and I trusted his judgment.

"I would buy a suicide or overdose. As far as murder, there's an outside chance that someone killed him. He's on the floor halfway between the kitchen table and the sink, which are maybe fifteen feet apart. His head is pointed toward the sink. According to Martel, the body was cold to the touch. No signs of a break-in, fight or another person being present. The house looks lived-in. Not too clean or too dirty, and he didn't have any pets."

"You said there were pills on the table?"

Julio nodded. "Yep, an over-the-counter sleep aid next to a bottle of Jack Daniels. Most of the pills were gone and the bottle of Jack Daniels was half empty."

"What was his name?"

"Davis. Davis Briggs. He was fifty-eight years old."

"Friends or family?"

"His only relative in the area is Dill. I haven't had a chance to dig into friends. The boss who called it in seemed genuinely concerned about him."

"Dill," I muttered. "How did he find out about this?"

"He was nearby when Captain Grant took my call."

"He was going to find out anyway. I just wish we'd had time to prepare him." In an ideal world, Dill would have been interviewed about his cousin before he knew about the box of serial-killer souvenirs, but it couldn't be helped now.

I pulled myself away from the support of the car and was

getting ready to find Dill when I saw him hurrying toward us.

"Larry, I got to talk to you," he said urgently.

"Stay back. I've got some sort of stomach flu."

Dill ignored me. "My cousin isn't a serial killer."

"I understand your feelings."

"They aren't just feelings! Davis was a good man. I don't believe he committed suicide either." Dill was overweight with at least one heart procedure in his rearview mirror, so when I took note of his reddening face and rapid breathing, I knew he needed to calm down.

"Let's talk about it. We can sit in my car."

Once we were inside the car with the air running, Dill looked better.

"Now, tell me everything you can about your cousin," I encouraged him.

Dill sighed. "I owe Davis for my sobriety. Twenty-five years ago, I'd run myself into the ground. My wife had left me, the sheriff had put me on unpaid leave and Doc Spencer told me if I kept drinking the way I was, I'd be dead in five years. At that point, I gave up. Most of my family had washed their hands of me. With nowhere to live, I ran into Davis at the grocery store. He took me to my first AA meeting, convinced me to move into his spare room. He was driving a truck at the time, but he took some time off to stay home, keep an eye on me, make sure I wasn't drinking."

"That must have meant a lot to you."

"It did. He even got Glenda to give me another chance. Funny thing was, he wasn't an outgoing type of guy. Seldom showed up at family get-togethers or went out on dates. Kind of a stay-at-home sort when he wasn't on the road."

"Why do you think he helped you?"

"He never got as deep into the bottle as I did, but when he was in his twenties, he had some close calls with alcohol. He told me that his 'I can't keep doing this' moment came one night when he was at a bar and, the next thing he knew, he was lying in a ditch filled with water. It was only chance that he didn't drown."

"Almost waking up dead can make you reassess your life," I said ruefully.

"Exactly. He went to AA and never took another drink."

I thought about the bottle Julio had said was on the table. Could Davis have fallen off the wagon? Had that led to a downward spiral that ended with suicide? But then how did the souvenirs fit into the picture?

"Did y'all stay in touch?" I asked.

"We saw each other almost every month. He'd come over to our house for holidays and birthdays if he was in town. He drove as many hours as the DOT would let him. About five years ago, he stopped driving a semi and went to work for the painting company. He's a hard worker."

I looked at the modest house and the Dodge truck in the driveway that was at least eight years old. "If he was bringing in a solid income, what did he spend his money on?"

"I don't know. He had a big heart. He probably spent some of it helping other people like… me." Dill's voice caught in his throat and he took a moment to recover himself. "Who's going to be the lead on the case?"

"If the FBI doesn't manage to steal it out from under us, it will be Julio."

"The FBI is really coming in on this?" Dill's face was full of pain and, perhaps, fear. Having someone in the family accused of horrendous crimes could taint everyone related to them.

"The decision is out of our hands. With those IDs and other items Marcus found, even Dad won't be able to keep them out."

"What exactly did he find?"

I shook my head. "You know I can't go into details."

"Larry, this isn't just me thinking that no one in my family could do a bad thing. I *know* Davis was a good man."

I shrugged sympathetically without being convinced. There were people in the world who were true Jekyll-and-Hyde monsters. Seemingly decent people one moment and brutal killers the next. Luckily, they were rare, but they existed. Davis wouldn't be the first person to shock everyone he knew with a secret life as a serial killer.

"Even with the FBI around, we'll still be involved in the investigation. I won't let your cousin have his name smeared if he's innocent," I promised. "When was the last time you talked or texted with him?"

"I talked to him a week ago. Glenda and I are going down to the coast for Labor Day, and I invited him to come with us. He said he thought he'd be working."

"How did he sound?"

"Normal. A hundred percent."

My stomach rumbled. "Look, I feel like crap. I shouldn't even be here. Julio will do a formal interview with you tomorrow. Right now, you need to go home and keep away from the news."

"I haven't told Glenda. She's going to be broken-hearted," Dill said, sounding lost.

"Ah hell!" I said involuntarily as I caught sight of Special Agent Padilla getting out of a black SUV that had just pulled up beside us. I'd secretly hoped that she'd been assigned to another field office.

Dill saw where I was looking. "You've got other problems. Please, don't let them take over this investigation."

"I'll do everything I can for you cousin," I promised, feeling uncomfortable having Dill plead for my help.

Dill and I both got out of the car. He went back toward his truck, walking a little unsteadily. I headed toward Padilla, not feeling much more steady on my own feet. My stomach lurched, and I wasn't sure if it was caused by the virus or seeing the FBI agent again. Probably both.

Padilla frowned at the sight of me and walked just inside my comfort zone.

"You'll want to back up. I might have the flu," I told her.

"No one gets the flu in August," she said, dismissing my illness with a wave of her hand. "Your investigator sent us pictures of the licenses. This is big. We've had a significant task force looking for the Petite Killer."

"Does it help to give them nicknames?"

"Truth is, it's getting harder to come up with unique names. But in this case, the task force has linked ten deaths, with another three probables, all to this guy. Each victim weighed less than a hundred and ten pounds. So the name works. Tell me what you have."

"Are we going to argue over jurisdiction?"

"Are you going to be a royal pain in the ass?"

"At this point, it's hard to say," I said honestly.

"Are you the lead investigator?"

"No, it's Julio Ortiz." I pointed to where Julio was talking with Marcus Brown and the other crime scene techs.

"I remember him. Competent," she proclaimed. "Do you want to fill me in or have him do it?"

"He can. Remember, I'm sick."

Padilla gave me a condescending frown. "We'll want all your people to stand off. We'll bring in our own crime scene techs, forensic experts and pathologist."

"His crimes may be your jurisdiction, but not his death," I argued.

"You can't be serious! Our task force has spent almost five years tracking this guy down."

"And they never found him." I smiled.

Padilla pulled out her phone. "If you're going to act like a juvenile, then I'll treat you like one. I'm calling your father."

When Dad answered, she said, "It's Special Agent Padilla. I assume you got a call from the assistant director? Yes, then tell your son that this is our crime scene."

She handed the phone over to me. I breathed on it before I put it to my ear, hoping to spread my germs.

"I thought you were sick?" Dad said.

"I am."

"This is out of our hands."

"Briggs's death is in our jurisdiction," I protested.

"Let them have it. This is going to be a deep dive that we

don't want to have to pay for. Besides, we don't have any real skin in the game."

I looked at Padilla. I didn't want her to hear what I was about to say, but I didn't have any choice. Reluctantly, I said, "The dead man is Dill's cousin and he's sure that Briggs isn't a serial killer."

There was a long pause from the other end of the phone, then: "We keep the man's death. Our jurisdiction. They get to investigate the other murders all they want. Put me on speaker."

"He wants the phone on speaker," I said, handing it back to Padilla, though I knew she'd already heard Dad's response.

She made a few swipes at the screen, then held the phone out between us. "Go ahead," she told Dad.

"Your choice. You can collect the evidence from the house and then share everything with us. And I mean everything. Or we'll collect it and share with you."

"We'll collect it."

"We keep the body and our pathologist, Dr. Darzi, does the autopsy."

Padilla rolled her eyes in exasperation, then said, "I can live with that as long as we're present at the autopsy and get all the reports."

"Finally, if the man's death is determined to be anything other than a natural death, we are the primary on that investigation," Dad told her.

Padilla chewed her lip and narrowed her eyes as she thought about this. "We can move forward with that assumption, but my superiors may have other ideas."

"He's dead. You can't prosecute your murder cases anyway," Dad argued.

"If Briggs had a partner and they were involved in the murders—"

"Okay. We'll cross that bridge when we come to it," Dad agreed and disconnected the call.

I didn't like that Dad was letting the FBI's forensic team

take control of collecting evidence. Still, I was glad that we would be the lead on the investigation into Briggs's death.

"Since you're dragging yourself into this, then you need to know about another problem which kicks it up a notch," Padilla told me.

"What's the problem if you're so sure that you have your bad guy and he's dead?" I asked. "You don't even have to worry about a trial."

"There was a witness and she's gone missing." Padilla looked uncomfortable.

"You lost a witness?" I asked incredulously.

Padilla sighed. "It's complicated. She wouldn't allow us to put her into protective custody and, frankly, I'm not sure we could have convinced the powers that be to make it happen. We didn't publicize it and hoped the killer didn't know who she was."

"Did she give you a good description of the suspect?"

"She was a possible victim. Grabbed from behind at a park, but she was able to get away. Unfortunately, she didn't trust us. She's an addict and paranoid. We were hoping she would eventually open up to us, but we couldn't even get her into a shelter. She insisted on continuing to live on the streets."

"When did she go missing?" My stomach was roiling madly now, and I decided I really needed to get closer to a bathroom, but I wasn't about to show any weakness in front of Padilla.

"About three months ago. The agent who was keeping tabs on her saw her outside a Fast Mart. That was the last anyone saw of her."

"Where?"

"Eaton County, down by the coast. The killer took another victim in the same area a few years ago."

"Send us her information and we'll get it to all our people. We can circulate her picture and see if she's been seen in the area."

"We're going to search the grounds and any other

property he might have owned."

"Fine. I need to get back to the office," I said, turning and walking quickly toward my car.

"There are a few more things we need to talk about," Padilla said, following me.

"Discuss it with Julio. I'll get back with you as soon as I can." I was moving as fast as I could with my gut swirling dangerously.

"Very soon," Padilla said to my back.

I got into the car, backed it up and was starting to accelerate down the road when Matti Sanderson stepped out from behind her patrol car and flagged me down. Reluctantly, I stopped and rolled down my window.

"I'm sick and I need to go," I told her.

"The victim is Davis Briggs?" she asked, ignoring my urgency.

"That's right. He's Dill's cousin."

"He's also a good friend of my brother's. They work together."

This was news, and I wanted to ask her more questions, but time wasn't on my side. "I'll be back soon. Julio is heading up the investigation and the FBI is involved."

"Why?"

"Talk to Julio." I rolled up the window and gave her a wave as I pressed the accelerator.

CHAPTER TWO

I made it to the pharmacy, used their restroom and bought another bottle of Pepto Bismol. After taking a large swig from the bottle of pink relief, I consulted both Google and the pharmacist. Based on the combined advice, I decided that the virus probably wouldn't kill me.

Back in my car, I thought about what was going to happen with the Briggs case. With the missing witness, the FBI would be chomping at the bit to start digging, literally, through the man's property.

I called Julio. "Did Padilla tell you about the missing witness?"

"We've been talking," he said.

"They need to respect our investigation while we try to help them track down this person and—"

I was interrupted by a text alert. Holding the phone away from my ear, I saw that Padilla had sent a photo and basic stats about the witness in a group text that had included Julio. Her name was Kat Fergusson.

"I'll get the information out to patrol," Julio said, reading my mind.

"If we find their witness, we'll score a few points with

Padilla."

"Sandy said that her brother worked with the victim."

"Yeah, she mentioned that when I was heading out. Some painting company, right? What's the name of it?"

"Sunshine Industrial Paint. According to Sandy, they work all over North Florida and South Georgia."

"Since you're going to be busy at the scene for a while, I'll go talk to the people at Sunshine," I offered.

"Are you up to it?" Julio sounded hesitant to question my fitness for the job.

"I'm feeling better," I said, stretching the truth only a little. I told him I'd call him as soon as I was done doing interviews at Sunshine Industrial.

Before I could get out of the parking lot, Cara called.

"Terry said he saw you at the pharmacy. I would have picked up anything you needed."

"I had to go out anyway for a case," I said, knowing what was coming.

"You can't go to work! You're sick."

"I don't think I'm contagious and—"

"I'm not worried about other people; I'm worried about you," Cara said, her voice rising.

"I wouldn't have left the house if it wasn't a crisis."

"It's going to be a personal crisis if you get sicker. I leave home expecting you to stay inside and take care of yourself, and next thing I know, you're wandering around town." She sounded exasperated.

"Dill's cousin is the victim and there's more to it that I can't talk about right now," I explained. "I need to be on top of this, sick or not."

"I understand wanting to help Dill. But if your fever comes back, I'm putting you to bed and making you take whatever herbal horrors my mother sends up here."

"That is a threat I'll take seriously," I promised.

Sunshine Industrial Paint was in the county's industrial park near the interstate. It was one of several companies housed in a long building with office space in the front and work bays with large roll-up doors in the back.

The sign over the door was nondescript, and it was clear that most of their business didn't involve window shoppers. No one was at the front desk when I came in. I walked down a hallway that led to the work bay, where a man was cleaning plastic fifty-gallon drums with a pressure washer. I waved my hands to get his attention.

"What can I do for you?" the man asked after turning off the machine and removing his ear protection. He was in his late thirties with thick black hair, a square jaw and just a hint of a beer belly. His movements and speech had an entrepreneurial energy that reminded me of some of the best salesmen I'd ever met.

"I'm Sergeant Larry Macklin with the sheriff's office," I said, showing him my ID.

"Is this about Davis?" he asked, his face clouding with concern.

"That's right. And you are?"

He peeled off his rubber gloves and stuck out his hand.

"I'm Joey Zavala, the owner. It was me that asked y'all to check on him."

"He was supposed to come in last night?"

"Yeah. We do a lot of our painting at night when businesses are closed. That way, we don't interfere with their employees or customers. Davis was supposed to be here at ten and is normally early. He's okay, isn't he?" I could tell by the way he asked the question that he'd already figured out that an investigator probably wasn't bringing good news.

"I'm afraid he's dead," I said, watching his reaction.

Zavala looked genuinely shocked. "How?"

"We don't have much information right now. All I can tell you is that he was found dead in his home."

"That's terrible. He was such a great guy. Come on, let's go to my office."

Zavala led me over to a door that opened into a small

room with a desk, a small filing cabinet and two chairs. Piles of pamphlets and paint samples were stacked around the room. On his desk was a high-end computer and monitor.

He sat down behind his desk and gestured to the other chair as he opened a drawer. He pulled out a bottle of bourbon and poured a couple of fingers into a coffee cup printed with the name of his company. He downed the drink in one swallow and turned to me with a shake of his head.

"Sorry. This is just a shock. I guess you don't want any?"

"The days when a deputy could take a drink on duty went out with the truncheon," I said

"With what?"

"Never mind. When was the last time you saw Davis?"

"Yesterday morning around six o'clock. He got back here about five and took his time cleaning his van. Usually takes about forty-five minutes to clean up and restock so you're ready to go out again."

"So he worked Monday night?"

"That's right."

"Where did he work?"

"Umm, I think he did the place they're turning into a Mexican restaurant over in Madison County. Let me check." He turned to his computer and pressed a few keys. "Yep. Buena Fiesta. Miguel Mata is the owner."

He wrote a phone number down on a piece of paper and handed it to me.

"What kind of mood was he in the last time you saw him?" I asked.

"Normal. I mean Davis was an upbeat guy. Quick with a smile. Everybody liked him. In five years, not once did I get a serious complaint from a customer. Occasionally, there'd be small things. You know, like a little smear of paint or a missed spot. Whenever that happened, I'd tell Davis and he'd make things right with the customer immediately. This is horrible to say, but the business will suffer without him."

"How many employees do you have?"

"Eight. Well, I guess seven with Davis gone. I run four

crews, usually two guys at a time. These days you got to overemploy 'cause the kids… Listen to me, I'm thirty-eight talking about twenty-year-olds being kids… but they are. A week doesn't go by that someone doesn't call in at the last minute and say they can't come in. So I sort of divide them up into teams of senior employees and junior employees. The senior employees are the ones who can drive the vans and work on projects alone."

"We'll need a list of everyone that works here."

"That's not a problem." He gave me a quizzical look. "Did someone kill him?"

"We don't know what happened yet, so we're treating it like a violent death," I said honestly.

"Sure. I watch some of those shows. The first forty-eight hours, you have to preserve the evidence. I get it."

"Is the van he used for work here?"

"No. He drove it home."

"I don't remember seeing it." I pulled out my phone and called Julio, who assured me that there wasn't a work van anywhere around the house. I told him I'd get the information on the van so we could put out a BOLO notice.

"You think someone stole it?" Zavala asked as he pulled the registration information out of a file, then he shook his head. "You don't know. I get it."

"Hello?" came a voice I recognized from the front office, followed by footsteps moving down the hallway.

I looked at Zavala. "There's something I should have mentioned. The FBI is also looking into… certain aspects of the case."

He looked completely confused. "What? Why would they… I don't understand."

"I'll let her explain," I said, standing up. I stuck my head outside the office and waved for Padilla to join us.

"I saw your car out front," she said, frowning. There was judgment in her voice.

"We *are* investigating Briggs's death," I reminded her.

"Are you the owner?" She looked past me at Joey Zavala.

"Yeah, that's right. He told me that Davis is dead." He was looking back and forth between Padilla and me.

"That's right, and we believe his death might be connected with other crimes."

"This is crazy." Zavala shook his head.

"Your name is?" Padilla asked.

"Sorry, I'm Joey Zavala."

She proceeded to ask him the same questions that I had. When they got to the part where the work van was missing, Padilla pulled out her phone and told some schmuck working for her to prepare a notice to go out to all agencies to be on the lookout for it.

All I could think was that I wanted to find the van before she did. I had texted the tag and VIN numbers to Julio while she was talking to Joey.

"Did he have a locker or other places where he might have kept personal items?" Padilla asked.

"No, just the van."

"I'll need the contact information for everyone that works here. Do we have your permission to search the premises?" she asked in an offhand manner.

I saw Zavala get ready to agree, but at the last moment he stopped himself.

"I don't know."

"What don't you know, Mr. Zavala?"

"I hate to say this, but I think I want you to get a warrant." He sounded unsure of himself.

"Why wouldn't you want to cooperate with us?" Padilla took a step toward him.

I'd been on the receiving end of her intimidation methods in the past. She was good. Really, she was just testing how cooperative he would be. We were all taught to get a warrant if time permitted, to help avoid questions down the road about the admissibility of evidence. But Padilla didn't really have probable cause. You couldn't search a business just because a bad guy might have worked there.

"I want to cooperate," Zavala said, actual sweat forming

on his brow. "It's just… You always hear people say, you know, make them get a warrant."

"I'll tell you what," Padilla said, sounding like a used-car salesman. "I'm going to ask *you* to search any place that Davis Briggs had access to. If you find something out of place, or an item that belonged to Mr. Briggs, you can point it out to me. I'll just watch."

"I… guess I can do that," he said hesitantly. "Is there anything in particular I should be looking for?"

"Anything out of place," Padilla told him. "Or anything missing."

We watched as Zavala started walking around the open bay, looking in cabinets, shifting machinery and moving five-gallon buckets of paint.

"Nice trick getting him to search his own business," I said.

"Same as asking a homeowner if anything is missing after a burglary."

"Point taken."

"Are we going to be bumping into each other as we interview the other employees?" she asked.

"It's that or we could interview them together," I suggested.

"That seems the better course," Padilla admitted. "We'll take the employees that worked the night shift first."

"They'll love being woken up for that. Any ideas on where the van is?"

"My guess is that he ditched it to get rid of evidence before he killed himself. Probably in a body of water… or maybe burned. That's more likely since he burned his victims' bodies."

"You're sure he's your guy?"

"Are you sure he's not?"

I had no answer for that.

Half an hour later, Zavala came over to us, shaking his head.

"I didn't see anything out of place."

"Let us have that list of your employees and their contact info. Be sure to mark who's currently on the clock," I requested.

Zavala went back to his office and quickly printed out a list. He marked three names and handed the paper to me.

"Like I said, we do most of our work at night when the businesses are closed. These guys are working on some apartments that are under construction. We've got the contract for all the painting, interior and exterior."

"Where is it?" I asked.

"This side of Leon County. I'll give you the address if you want."

"Thanks. We'll talk to them after we've spoken with the guys at home."

CHAPTER THREE

Padilla and I spent twenty minutes in the parking lot, arguing over the best order to interview the seven employees. With a plan finally in place, we headed out with me in the lead since I knew the county better than she did.

The first person on the list was Colson Holloway. He was one of Sunshine's senior employees. He lived in a neighborhood of small starter homes. There were a few toys in the yard and a pickup in the driveway.

We parked on the street, and I followed Padilla up to the front door.

"Ladies first," I said, waving toward the door. She gave me a smirk and knocked loudly.

"There's a doorbell," I pointed out.

"Never use them." She rapped again on the door, even louder this time.

An unintelligible shout came from inside.

Padilla knocked again, softly.

"Who is it?" a man's voice grumbled from the other side of the door.

"FBI," Padilla said, and I could only imagine what went through Holloway's mind.

"Yeah, okay, wait. I got to put some pants on." His voice

was nervous and hurried.

"Maybe one of us should have watched the back," I said after a few minutes had passed.

Padilla rolled her eyes. Humor was not her strong suit.

The sound of the lock clicking over told us he hadn't done a runner. Holloway was looking at his phone as he opened the door. He was a large, muscular man in his mid-thirties, with a tan complexion and short-cropped dark hair.

"Shit," he said and looked up. "I guess this is about Davis."

"You heard about his death?" Padilla asked as she held out her FBI ID toward him.

He turned the phone around so she could see the screen. "A friend texted me. He said Davis was found dead and there're police all around his house. What happened?"

"We need to ask you a few questions." Padilla ignored him and stepped forward as if she planned to walk right through him. Reflexively, he backed away and she stepped into the house without waiting for permission.

Guess that proves she's not a vampire, I thought, chuckling to myself and following her inside.

There was an assortment of toys and abandoned cups and plates scattered around the living room.

"Sorry, the place is a mess. Had the kids this weekend and haven't cleaned up yet," Holloway apologized.

"Did you and Davis get along?" Padilla asked.

"Yeah, I'd say so."

"What would he say?" she asked.

"I think he'd say we were friends. Not like best buds. I mean, we didn't hang out when we were away from work or anything. But we worked together for about five years. First year I was there, we went out on jobs together. Was he murdered or something?"

"We don't have any answers right now," Padilla said. "What can you tell me about Davis?"

"I don't know." Holloway shrugged his shoulders. "He was a good guy. Like I said, we weren't real close, but he helped me when I moved into this house. He was the type of guy who has your back, you know?"

"Did you have *his* back?" Padilla asked, watching Holloway closely.

"I mean, yeah, sure. Not that I'd bury a body for—" He stopped short, and his eyes grew large. "I mean… I… just… wow, I've never been questioned by the FBI before. Can I sit down?"

I almost felt sorry for the guy. He'd been woken up after a long night at work, told that a co-worker had been found dead and was being questioned by the FBI's queen bee all before he'd even had a cup of coffee.

"Sure, sit. We just need to ask a few more questions," Padilla said, letting her good-cop persona take over.

Holloway eased himself down on the couch, half sitting on a child's toy tablet. Padilla nodded to me.

"I'm from the sheriff's office," I said, wanting to put some distance between myself and the FBI. "When was the last time you saw Davis?"

"Yesterday morning before daylight. We were both cleaning out our vans and rinsing off our equipment. You have to make sure to get all the paint out of the sprayers and restock the vans."

"What kind of mood was he in?"

Holloway grinned. "He was smiling. Always smiling. I can count on one hand the number of times I saw him mad or upset about anything."

"What did you all talk about?"

"We didn't. I mean, just 'Hi, how ya doin" sort of stuff. Nothing memorable, which is awful since that was the last time I'll ever talk to him."

"Did he do anything different?"

"No," he said, so fast that I knew he hadn't thought about the question.

"Think about it," I said.

Holloway thought for a second, then shook his head. "No. Nothing that I can think of."

"What about the other employees? Were any of them close friends with Davis?" I asked.

"Doug Sanderson and him were real close. He got Doug the job with Sunshine."

I realized that Doug must have been Matti Sanderson's brother. I was worried about how all that was going to shake out, but I pushed my concerns aside.

"Did Davis have any enemies?" I asked.

"Davis? No. Like I said, the man was always happy. I think you could have slapped him in the face and he would have smiled and shook your hand. With that kind of person, you'd just feel like a creep if you got mad at them, you know?"

"He never had a problem with a customer?"

"Davis did his job, and he did it well. He taught me and several of the other guys how to treat the customer right."

"Including Doug?"

Holloway nodded. "Especially Doug. They spent a bunch of time working together when Doug was learning the ropes. Doug would be working on his own now, except he doesn't have a driver's license. Guess he got in trouble and had it revoked. Seems like a touchy subject, so I haven't asked too many questions."

"What did you do yesterday?" I asked.

"Same thing I always do. Got home around seven in the morning and went to sleep. Got up, I guess it was around two o'clock, then I ate, played games. Went to work by ten."

"And Davis wasn't there."

"Yeah, that was odd. I don't think he's missed a day of work since I've been there. Joey seemed worried. I guess I should have been too, but I kept thinking that Davis was a grown-ass man and missing work wasn't that big of a deal. Everybody has a bad day. This is awful, but I had this thought that it made him seem more normal. I was looking forward to kidding him about being late. Then, as the night went along and Joey kept texting me, asking if I'd heard from Davis, I began to worry about him too."

"Did you do anything about it?"

"I texted Davis. Didn't hear anything back, but that didn't mean much 'cause Davis didn't always respond right away to messages. He wasn't a real techy kind of guy."

"May I see the message you sent?" Padilla held out her hand.

At first, I thought Holloway was going to refuse. Instead, he slowly looked down at his phone, found the text message and held the phone out to her. She took it and read the message, then scrolled up and down for a second before handing the phone back to him.

"Have you ever been over to his house?" I asked.

"Maybe once or twice. Like I said, it wasn't like we ever hung out together."

"What did Davis do when he wasn't working?"

"You'd have to ask someone other than me. He didn't seem to have any hobbies. I guess I heard him talk about hunting a couple of times, and he might have mentioned watching a football game. But he wasn't a fanatic about anything, near as I could tell."

"Did you ever see him take any medication?"

"I think he took sinus stuff sometimes." He shrugged.

"I didn't see a work van outside. Don't y'all take your vans home when you're done with your shifts?"

"All depends. Some days one of us night guys has to leave their van for a day crew, depending on the job. If that happens, the day guys clean and stock the vans back up for us."

I looked at Padilla and she gave me a short nod, letting me know she was ready to move on. We thanked Holloway for his cooperation and headed out for the next interview.

Kian Birch was another of Sunshine's senior employees. He lived in a duplex on the edge of one of Calhoun's rougher neighborhoods. As was typical of many Southern towns, there were places where only a street or two separated the nicer neighborhoods from areas that were plagued with vandalism, drugs and prostitution. The folks who lived in this no man's land were usually good people who had rented or bought the only home they could afford.

Parked outside the duplex were a Sunshine van and a partially restored 1968 Dodge Charger. The front door opened before we had a chance to knock.

"I got a text from Joey that said y'all might be coming to talk to me." Birch was twenty-six years old and was wearing jeans and a sleeveless white T-shirt. His hair was slicked back, giving him a look that went well with the car in the driveway.

"Can we come in?" Padilla asked.

"I'm not going to make you stand out here sweating." He turned and walked into the duplex, leaving the door open for us to follow.

"I've never had the FBI visit me before," Birch said once we were all inside the small living room. "You can sit if you want."

The room was neat and clean, with a couple of loveseats and shelves on the wall full of classic car models.

"No, thank you," Padilla told him, glancing around.

"I might have an obsession," he said with a grin.

"The Charger is nice," I told him.

"She's a work in progress, though I'll admit I'm falling in love with her. Fixing up cars is my part-time job. It's why I took the job at Sunshine. Joey lets me use the equipment in the bay to paint cars. But I guess you don't want to talk about cars."

"How well did you know Davis Briggs?" I asked.

"A little. He wasn't interested in cars, so..." Birch shrugged.

"What *was* he interested in?"

"Your guess is as good as mine. When he was at work, he worked. Joey loved him. The work isn't exactly intellectually stimulating, so it takes the right kind of guy to do the job well. Even my mind wanders from time to time. Not Davis.

He was totally focused on his work. Don't get me wrong. He was always nice and would help anyone who needed it. He stayed late one day to help me tape up a car I was going to paint."

"Was there anyone he didn't get along with?" I asked.

"Not that I know of."

"Did you ever see him doing anything… odd?" Padilla asked.

"Odd?" Birch seemed to think about it. "I thought it was odd that he never talked about anything outside of work. I mean, sometimes he'd say stuff, but I got the feeling he was only doing it 'cause he thought we might want to talk about it."

"What do you mean?" Padilla pressed.

"Like football. He'd mention something about an FSU game, but if you really tried to talk with him about it, he didn't actually know that much. It was like he brought it up just because he figured we'd want to talk about it."

"Any other examples?" Padilla asked.

"Sure. Women, for instance. I never got the impression that he cared one way or the other about them, but every once in a while, he'd talk about how some celebrity was beautiful. It was kind of awkward."

"Do you think he was gay?" I asked.

"Maybe. These days, I don't know why he wouldn't have said if he was. No one cares. Really, it was just he didn't have any interests of his own."

"Or none that he could talk about," Padilla muttered under her breath.

"What?" Birch asked.

"Nothing." Padilla waved it away. "Did you ever think he was hiding anything?"

"Like being gay?"

"Anything. Family problems, drinking problems, gambling, anything."

"Now that you mention it, he *did* talk about AA a couple of times. We have to be careful with all the paint mist and fumes. Sometimes one of the guys will make a lame joke about getting high or something. I remember Davis saying his sponsor wouldn't want him getting high. I didn't think much of it. These days, it seems like half the folks you meet have some sort of addiction or another."

"Did you ever see him drunk or high?"

"Never. And I know all the signs. I've got a brother who's traveled some dark roads."

"Did anyone seem mad when he talked about AA?" I asked.

"What could they be mad about?"

"Some folks don't like people who come across as being better than other people, or judgmental," I pointed out.

Birch shook his head. "No one took it that way. It's horrible to say it now that he's gone, but I don't think most of the guys thought about Davis much at all. He was so dependable that you took him for granted. That's why Joey was so worried when he didn't show up for work. If it had been one of us, Joey would have just sent a text telling us to get our asses into work or plan on picking up our last check."

"Is Joey a tough boss?" I asked.

"He gets keyed up sometimes. I understand 'cause I've tried to run my own business and every little mistake or misstep can drive you crazy. Joey just worries about everything. Guess he's freaking out about losing Davis. A guy like that will be hard to replace."

"When was the last time you saw Davis?" Padilla asked.

"When we went out Monday night."

"You didn't see him when you came back yesterday morning?"

"I got done early and left before he came in. That's the good thing about Joey. As uptight as he can be, he doesn't have a problem with me leaving if I've got my jobs done and the van cleaned and stocked."

"Did you and Davis ever talk on the phone or text with each other?" Padilla asked.

"Only about work."

"When was the last time?"

"Called or texted?"

"Either."

"I'd have to look," he said.

"How about now?" Padilla suggested.

With a shrug, Birch pulled his phone out of his pocket and started scrolling.

"I texted him last week about some paint I needed for a job. I asked him to bring it to me."

Padilla held out her hand and he reluctantly passed her the phone. She looked over the text, then handed the phone back to him.

We asked a few more questions, but didn't learn anything else from Birch. As we were walking toward our cars, Padilla's phone buzzed. She checked it and let out a loud guffaw, which surprised me since she wasn't prone to laughter. She stopped and held the phone out toward me.

"Got a call from your favorite reporter."

Tina Knightly's name was on the caller ID.

"You have her as a contact on your phone?" I asked, disgusted.

"She's been calling me for weeks trying to get some dirt on you and your father."

"And you haven't helped her out?" I said doubtfully.

"When it comes to reporters, I support the thin blue line," Padilla responded as she opened the door to her car.

"Doug Sanderson next?" I asked.

"Did I hear that he's related to one of your deputies?"

"Yeah, he's Matti Sanderson's brother. I don't think it'll be a problem. Rural county like this, there's never more than one degree of separation from anyone."

Doug Sanderson shared a house with a roommate who gave us a hard look when he answered the door. The black man was in his forties with his hair cut in a flattop. He looked like he spent all of his free time in the gym. There was a tattoo of a weightlifter on his bulging bicep with the motto *Lift for Life* printed under it. With encouragement, he said that his name was Javon Hayden.

"Doug left about half an hour ago after his sister called and told him that a co-worker had died."

"You know where he went?" I asked.

"He's taking a walk. When he's upset, he likes to go off by himself."

"Did you know Davis Briggs?"

"He came by a few times. Nice guy." The way he said it made me think there was more to the story.

"Doug and Davis get along?"

Hayden's eyes narrowed and his biceps flexed, making me wonder if Padilla would back me up if the guy jumped me.

"I'm done talking to you." He started to close the door.

"Did we touch a nerve?" Padilla asked.

The big man opened the door wide again. I had to fight my instincts not to take a step back.

"They were good friends. I'm done here, 'cause it's clear y'all are fishing for dirt on Doug," he said and slammed the door.

"Charming," I grumbled.

"Roid rage?" Padilla wondered.

"Best not to find out. I'll catch up with Sanderson later."

"I'd like to be there."

I nodded. "That just leaves us one more employee who isn't currently working. Waylon Bauer."

Our next stop was a rundown block house a few miles north of town. It was set back from the road up a long, narrow driveway that opened into a small, unkempt yard. The house needed painting, and the roof looked like it wouldn't survive the next serious storm. There were several cars parked near the house, all in various states of repair. By the time Padilla parked between an old Ford Bronco and a truck up on blocks, there wasn't much room for my car. I pulled in behind Padilla, effectively blocking most of the driveway.

Padilla was already headed for the house. I caught up with her as she knocked on the screen door. There was no answer, but we could hear footsteps inside the house. With a sigh, Padilla knocked louder, making the wooden screen door bang back and forth against the frame. We heard more sounds from inside, but no one came to the door. Padilla squared her shoulders and took out her ID. She opened the screen door and banged on the inner door, holding her ID up to the peephole.

"FBI!" she yelled. "We want to talk to you!" She enunciated each word as if speaking to a child who was hard of hearing.

"Wait, I'm coming!" a man shouted.

I'll chalk it up to being sick, but by the time I noticed that there was movement off to my left, I was too late to intercept the man who ran from behind the house toward the dirty brown Bronco. He was in his fifties and hastily dressed in cut-off shorts and a half-buttoned shirt. I started to turn and go after him when the front door opened, dividing my attention.

"What do you want?" asked the younger man who stood in the doorway.

Once I was sure that the man didn't pose a threat, I turned toward the sound of the Bronco revving in the yard. That's when I realized that the Bronco wouldn't be able to get out of the driveway with my car parked where it was.

However, the driver wasn't going to take "no" for an answer, and started down the shoulder of the driveway, picking up speed. Impulsively, I ran toward my car but could only watch as the Bronco sideswiped it, throwing my car off the driveway and into a tree. Then the Bronco's driver learned that for every action there is an equal and opposite reaction as the Bronco swung off of its trajectory and into another tree.

Cursing, I jogged toward the Bronco. The driver was cussing as colorfully as I was and trying to get his door open.

"Stop!" I yelled, grabbing my star and holding it up. "I'm with the sheriff's office. Keep your hands in sight."

The man hesitated, so I pulled out my Glock and held it at the ready.

"Hands up and in sight," I repeated.

I caught sight of Padilla approaching in my peripheral vision.

"Glad that wasn't my car he hit," she said.

"Thanks a lot," I told her as I moved to the side of the Bronco. The driver's door was jammed, so he had to scoot across the bench seat and exit through the passenger door. I escorted him over to what was left of my car, wrenched the driver's door open and dug for some handcuffs.

His driver's license revealed that his name was Derick Bauer. I called it in to dispatch and was not surprised to learn that his license was suspended and he had an outstanding warrant for failure to appear.

"Did you really think we would send the FBI to arrest you for a failure to appear on a misdemeanor charge?" I asked.

"I was half asleep, man." His words were slurred as he spoke to the ground.

"My dad's a dumbass," Waylon Bauer offered. He'd come out of the house to watch the show.

"Love you too, asshole," his father grumbled.

We were soon joined by Deputy Andy Martel. Feeling weak and nauseated, I turned the elder Bauer over to Martel, then took a closer look at my car. Seeing the damage didn't make me feel any better.

"And I liked this car," I grumbled.

"You want to interview the son?" Padilla asked.

"I'll come over in a minute," I said, reaching into the car for the bottle of Pepto Bismol and taking another dose.

I walked over to where Padilla was standing with Waylon Bauer. The twenty-year-old was frowning at the sight of his dad sitting in the back of Martel's patrol car as it drove away.

"He's an idiot." Bauer shook his head, causing his shoulder-length brown hair to flip in front of his face. The man looked a bit like Shaggy from *Scooby-Doo*, right down to the unshaved chin. "I need to find another place to live."

"I supposed you've heard about Davis Briggs?" I asked.

"Sure. I got a text about an hour ago. If my dad hadn't been asleep, I would have told him why y'all were here."

"How well did you know Davis?"

"I don't know. I worked with him sometimes. Super nice guy. I still owe him about fifty dollars from all the times he bought me lunch or loaned me a fiver. It's crazy that he's dead. What happened?"

"That's what we're trying to figure out," I told him.

"When you worked with him, did he ever go off on his own?" Padilla asked.

"Like leave the worksite? No. He was super strict about what we could and couldn't do while we were working. Some of the other guys will, like, take a break on the job, go get coffee or food. You know, nothing bad, just taking a break. Not Davis. We got a lunch break and bathroom breaks, that's it. Not saying he was wrong or that the other guys are right. It's just different ways of looking at things."

"Do you ever remember him acting odd?"

"Odd?"

"Like he didn't want you touching something, or he didn't want to talk about certain things. Stuff like that," Padilla explained.

"No. He seemed pretty normal."

"Did you like him?"

"Sure. What was not to like?"

"Did he have any enemies?" I had to ask the question, even though I could predict what Bauer would say.

"No."

"Did you ever hear him complain about anyone?"

"No. Look, I don't know how many ways I can say this, but he was just a good guy. He was the exact opposite of my father, who pisses off everyone and hates everyone. Like that Chinese thing, you know, yin and yang. If you want to know the truth, I was thinking about asking Davis if I could rent a room in his house."

"If you think of anything—" I said, then was interrupted by a loud *woof* from behind me. With a heavy sigh, I finished, "—give me a call."

I handed Bauer my card, then turned to see Dad and his enormous Great Dane, Mauser, marching up the driveway from where they'd left their van parked by the road.

"You're in trouble now," Padilla said with an evil grin as we walked back toward the cars.

CHAPTER FOUR

Dad had Mauser on a leash since the behemoth was only marginally trained. As soon as his dopey brown eyes locked on me, he started pulling Dad toward me, and I was forced to give the monster mutt some pats and ear massages.

"You should have stayed in bed," Dad said dryly, looking at the car. "I'm glad you weren't driving it at the time. Someone might question what type of drugs you've been taking."

"Pepto Bismol doesn't have any warnings on the bottle."

"Insurance is going to total it."

"I'd say Derick Bauer's insurance would cover it—except he doesn't have any."

"Of course he doesn't." Dad sighed. "And now we're going to have to give him a bed and feed him for who knows how long."

"I need to get my laptop and equipment out of the car."

"You can put it in the van. I hate to reward you for letting your car get destroyed, but one of the new SUVs we got with that federal grant is almost done being customized. I guess it'll be yours."

I thought of a few things I could have said, but I kept my mouth shut so I wouldn't stick my foot in it.

"I read up on the murders the FBI wants to blame on our victim," Dad said. "Gruesome stuff. I'm glad none of them were in our county."

"I know that there are serial killers who fly under the radar and everyone thinks they're good people. Still, the glowing reports I'm getting on Briggs are hard to reconcile with the crimes."

"Follow the evidence," Dad reminded me. "Don't get ahead of it."

"I won't let the fact that he's connected to two of our deputies get in the way either," I assured him.

"If you see it becoming a problem, tell me."

While we had been talking and ignoring Mauser, he'd been sniffing my damaged car. Dad didn't even correct him when Mauser pronounced his opinion by lifting his leg on the front wheel. I had to agree that was all the car was good for now.

"You want to give me a hand putting my stuff in your van?" I asked Dad.

Fifteen minutes later, we'd transferred my laptop, shotgun, rifle, spare clothes, med kit, ammunition, Kevlar vest, PPE bag, evidence bag and other miscellaneous items to the back of the van. While we were waiting for the wreckers, Padilla got a call that she was needed back at Briggs's house. Dad took pictures of the cars, then we managed to nudge my wrecked vehicle far enough out of the way so that Padilla could leave. After she was gone, I started writing my reports while sipping on Coke and nibbling on crackers.

"I've got a safety talk at the middle school," Dad told me, looking at his watch. Early in every school year, we held age-appropriate safety talks at the various schools.

"What about Garza? Isn't he the resource officer?"

"The principal has called me five times wanting Mauser to come and put in an appearance."

"Ah, yes, my famous furry brother."

"Hey, he gets the students' attention."

"Go on," I said. "I'll wait for them to tow the cars and catch a ride with one of the drivers."

"I hope you didn't spread your germs around to anyone else."

"Thanks for your concern."

"Keep me up to date on the investigation. If it looks like Briggs killed himself, then I'm good with turning it over to the FBI. Padilla assured me they're trying to keep the connection with the serial murders under wraps until they have some concrete evidence that he was the perpetrator." He gave me a wave and headed back up the driveway with Mauser.

The tow trucks finally arrived, and I caught a ride on one of them to the county garage, where I could pick up whatever loaner they had available while I waited for the new SUV. By the time I got out of the tow truck, I was exhausted. Working while I was still sick had really taken its toll on me.

"We got a couple choices. The best of the lot is that K9 Suburban over there," said Truett Walker, the garage manager. Truett reminded me of Morgan Freeman if Freeman carried an extra twenty pounds around his waist. He was renowned for giving county employees parental talks about how they should treat their vehicles and stern lectures when they didn't follow his advice.

Our K9 officers had been given the first of the new SUVs, so the garage had already sorted through the older ones, taking off equipment and sending them to auction, and adding the best of them to our loaner collection.

I took the key that Truett offered me and thanked him.

"It's got a few issues, but it runs good," he said to my back as I walked out of the shop toward the Suburban.

It had last belonged to Sergeant Mack Burrows and his German Shepard partner, Tornado, and it still bore Tornado's name on its sides. The smell of its former passenger lingered inside the vehicle, but after frequent trips in Mauser's van, I was used to *eau de wet dog*. Competing with the dog odor was the universal scent of a law-enforcement vehicle, which was heavy with old sweat and fast food.

The driver's seat was worn out and any lumbar support was long gone. The good news was that the engine roared to life and the gas gauge went all the way to the F. I drove to the sheriff's office and parked by Dad's van. I had my own key to the van, so I didn't have to hunt him down to open it up and retrieve all of my gear.

"You getting a dog?"

I turned around and saw my old partner, Pete Henley, walking toward me.

"No, I—"

"You don't need to tell me. I've already heard that you and Agent Padilla were on a date and the locals got rough."

I rolled my eyes. "Mind helping me with this stuff?"

"You don't look good," Pete said, his voice full of concern.

"I'm heading home as soon as I'm done with this."

He helped me load the last of my equipment into the Suburban, then stood back and looked at the side of the vehicle.

"You should keep this and have Mauser's name put on it," Pete suggested.

"Not on your life!"

Pete waved and headed into the office.

I climbed back into the Suburban and opened my laptop to check emails and reports before I left. I should have gone into my office, but I didn't have the strength. I didn't even have the energy to go back out to the Briggs house or to talk with Padilla about the evidence collection. Seeing that Julio had sent me his preliminary report on the crime scene, I decided to call him.

"I heard all about it," he said in greeting.

"Padilla and I never did make it out to talk with the three Sunshine employees who were working today."

"Don't worry about it. I'll talk to them tomorrow. The autopsy hasn't been scheduled yet, but the toxicology report is going to be the heart of it anyway, and we'll have to wait for that."

I filled him in on what Padilla and I had learned from everyone we'd talked to.

"Just more descriptions of Briggs being a wonderful person," Julio said. "Sandy and Dill say the same thing. But is he also a serial killer? I don't know."

I could hear the uncertainty in his voice, which was a good thing this early into an investigation. An investigator should never think that he knew all the answers before he'd gathered all the facts.

"Sometimes a good guy is just a good guy, and sometimes he's not," I said. "Are there any leads on his work van?"

"Nothing yet. I've got the information out to all the local agencies within a hundred miles."

"If he abandoned the van somewhere, then he'd need transportation to get home."

"There was a dirt bike in the garage. Funny thing was that it was stashed behind some boxes and old furniture, but when the FBI's evidence team got it out, you could tell that it had been cleaned up recently. Started right up."

"Dirt bike, huh? So it was small enough he could probably have put it in the back of the van."

"That's what the suits were thinking."

"I'm sure the FBI thinks he destroyed the van to get rid of any evidence inside of it. Which makes sense if he committed suicide but wanted to keep his reputation as a nice guy." I hated to admit that the FBI's viewpoint was reasonable. "With luck, we'll find the van, and with it, some answers."

There was a long pause from Julio's end of the line.

"Was there something else?" I asked.

"I saw Greer talking to one of the highway patrolmen outside Briggs's property today."

I cursed inwardly. Karter Greer had been a deputy with the department until Dad had fired him after he fell asleep on duty while a murder was taking place under his nose. Since then, he'd been knifing us in the back by egging on Tina Knightly in her vendetta against Dad and me.

"Nothing we can do about that now," I said. "Still, let me know if you see him again."

I went home and straight into the shower. Then I dosed myself with electrolytes and vegetable soup. By the time Cara called to see if I had made it home and if I needed anything, I was able to report that I was feeling better.

I sat on the couch with my laptop and scrolled through more reports. Even in a rural county like ours, crime never took a break. However, *I* needed breaks, so I shut my laptop and close my eyes for a minute. The next thing I knew, Alvin was jumping onto my stomach.

"Good to see you resting," Cara said. "Mom's package came."

"I'm perfectly fine now," I protested.

Cara ignored me and set the box on the kitchen table. "We'll see if any of it is safe for human consumption."

"Did she give *you* her backwoods remedies when you were a kid?"

"Are you kidding? Of course she did. First off, it was my fault if I got sick. She assumed I must have been eating candy or processed food when she wasn't looking, 'cause no one could possibly get sick eating all the healthy food and herbs she fed us. And once she decided I was really sick, she'd start brewing every medicinal weed she could think of into teas for me to drink."

"Sounds exciting… and repulsive," I joked.

"I'd pour most of them onto her potted plants. She never understood why some of them would be overwatered whenever I was sick. Usually, Dad would take pity on me and slip me a Coke when she was out of the house."

I got up and walked over to the table where Cara was separating the items from the box into two categories:

"probably safe" and "nope."

"To be fair, she was on the right track with most of her herbal remedies. There were only a few that were more likely to make me worse rather than better."

The odor from the open box caused my stomach to lurch.

"I'm better already," I said, backing away from the table.

"There are a few things," she said, pointing to the smaller pile of mason jars, "that would be good for you."

"We'll see," I said cautiously.

"Be brave." She turned toward me and gave me a kiss.

After we shared a dinner of chicken and dumplings, Cara looked at me appraisingly. "I think you *do* seem a little better now."

"I need to be."

"What's going on?"

I gave her the CliffsNotes version of Briggs's death as we cleared the table.

"Hard to think that someone could fool both Dill and Matti Sanderson," Cara said as we settled down on the couch.

"Yes and no. If you're in law enforcement, you can't go around looking at everyone like they could be a criminal. If you're going to live a normal life off the job, then you have to take some of what people tell you at face value."

"But you said that Dill lived with him while he was getting sober."

"Yes. But people, even savvy people, can be fooled. Remember that we were eating in the restaurant of a serial killer for years."

"Don't remind me."

"Even his daughter didn't see through him," I said.

"Point taken."

"If the FBI is right, it's going to be rough on Dill and Sandy's brother."

Thinking of Doug Sanderson, I hoped I could get to him before Padilla did. I texted Sandy to see if she'd arrange for her brother to come into the office in the morning. Almost immediately, she replied back that he'd be in at ten.

"I hadn't even heard about a serial killer in North Florida," Cara said.

"The murders have been spread out over five years, and the only thing that links them is victimology and the disposal of the bodies. It's possible that some, if not all, of the murders were committed by different people. The bodies have been so badly damaged by the fires that it's been hard to tell what they died of. Because of the lack of obvious physical trauma, the FBI has assumed suffocation."

"Why haven't the newspapers played it up?"

"Too many maybes. Most of the victims were picked up at night in parks or other wooded areas. Some of the victims weren't from around here, so the local reporters have a harder time making a good story out of it."

"Were they sex workers?"

"Maybe. Maybe just homeless or hitchhikers. Since the crimes didn't happen in Adams County, I only know what I've seen on bulletins that have come in asking for information on the victims. Only two of them had any connections to our office. One had been picked up for public intoxication, and the other was simply a contact when a deputy found her hitchhiking and did a welfare check."

I shrugged. "Let's not talk about it anymore. My brain is mush anyway."

We spent the rest of the evening curled up together on the couch with Alvin and the cats, watching a documentary about the search for Amelia Earhart's plane. Cara convinced me to try a cup of her mom's lavender tea before bed, then I was asleep before my head hit the pillow.

CHAPTER FIVE

I woke up on Thursday feeling more rested than I had in four days. I wasn't ready to give full credit to the lavender tea, but it certainly hadn't hurt. After a long, hot shower, I felt like I'd washed all of the sickness from my body. Clean and dressed, I found Cara in the kitchen.

"You look almost human this morning." She kissed me on the cheek. "Told you Mom's tea couldn't hurt."

"Yeah, yeah." I smiled, glad to feel healthy again.

"Everyone's been fed, so you can ignore the pitiful looks from Ghost and Ivy." She headed for the door with Alvin trotting along behind her.

I made some oatmeal and was sitting down with it when my phone started buzzing. I picked it up idly, wondering who was texting me. The answer was everyone. Or at least it looked like everyone. At least five texts had come in at almost the same time, followed by several more. Dad, Pete and Julio topped the list. Most of the messages just said: "Call me."

Wondering what sort of hell was breaking loose now, I called Dad.

"Your friend has been at it again," he growled. And it wasn't his normal, early-morning growl. This snarl sounded menacing.

"What are you talking about?"

"Another hit piece by your favorite journalist."

"How could she have anything left to attack us with? I thought she exhausted her yearly quota of innuendo the last time."

"Now she's using Davis Briggs's death and his possible career as a serial killer to club us over the head." Dad was clearly furious, and I could tell that he still considered me responsible for placing both of us in Tina Knightly's crosshairs.

"Julio saw Greer talking to a highway patrolman at the scene yesterday," I remembered.

"I can't blame the trooper for talking. Not everyone knows that Greer is working hand in hand with Knightly to smear us."

"I'll look at it and get back to you," I said.

"Are you feeling better?" Dad asked before I could hang up. It was out of character, especially considering how mad he was. He must have been mellowing with age.

"Much. I'll be at the office first thing."

"Good. There's work to be done," he said and hung up, sounding more like his usual self.

I opened my laptop and found the video of Tina Knightly's latest commentary. She'd hacked away at us like Michael Myers, wondering how we could have let a serial killer reside peacefully in our county. She stopped just short of suggesting that we knew he was a killer and had a deal with him that he would do all his killing elsewhere. Of course, she couldn't help mentioning that both our desk sergeant and one of our deputies had personal connections with the suspect.

After seething for five minutes, I took several deep breaths to get my emotions under control, and flipped through a dozen more texts that had appeared on my phone. Most of them were attempts to be supportive and I vowed to answer those later.

I responded to a text from Julio, asking him to meet me in my office at eight-thirty. Then a text popped up from Padilla that read: *Zing! You're in the crosshairs. I can meet you any time today.* I told her I'd get back with her, then suited up with my gun and badge and headed for the office.

My inbox was a mass of emails ranging from vital to spam. I dealt with the vital and semi-vital and left the rest for later. I had moved on to reading reports when Julio knocked on my door.

"Tina Knightly has been calling me all morning," he said.

I waved him to a chair on the opposite side of my desk.

"Ignore her. Nothing can be gained by engaging with her," I said, thinking about how we'd wound up in this mess with her in the first place, when I'd ignored the very same warning from Dad.

"What about Greer?"

"If he crosses the line onto a crime scene, or anywhere that we can charge him with trespassing or interference, give him one warning. If he doesn't leave, arrest him."

"It would be a pleasure."

"Do it gently. He's already got one lawsuit pending against the department. We don't need to give him ammunition."

"I haven't found anything that points definitively to suicide or murder for Davis Briggs," Julio said, settling back in the chair.

"Neither did the interviews we conducted yesterday. Everyone said that he was a great guy with a great attitude who never had issues with anyone. That doesn't help at all. Who kills someone like that? And who commits suicide when they're always in a great frame of mind?"

"I canvassed the neighbors and got the same glowing descriptions," Julio said.

"Anyone spot a stranger or a strange car in the neighborhood?"

Julio pulled out his phone and scrolled through his notes.

"An older lady who lives two houses to the east reported

that she saw a strange white van with some sort of writing on the side when she went out for her doctor's appointment on Tuesday. However, another neighbor told me she'd had problems with her well and had called Adams Well Drilling. They confirmed that their vans are white and that one of their technicians was in the neighborhood at that time.

"Two witnesses reported strangers. The first is from the same lady who reported the van. She saw a tall young man with black hair, carrying a knapsack. The other is from a farmer a quarter mile to the west, who saw a woman with green hair, skinny, wearing clothes that made him think that she was homeless. He thought it was odd since the area is rural with the nearest main road a mile away. But no one else saw the woman."

"Great," I said with no enthusiasm. "What about cameras?"

"Out in the country like that, it's not like everyone has a Ring camera that covers the road. I did go ahead and ask Sandy to pull footage from the feeder roads. There are four main roads that someone might have taken to get to Briggs's house."

"Chances are, that footage will only help us when we have a good suspect."

"That's what I was thinking. We need suspects," Julio agreed.

"I want to talk to the employees of Sunshine that we didn't get to yesterday. Which reminds me, I need to make sure—"

I was interrupted by a knock on the door, then Lieutenant Phil Eccles let himself inside.

"Good, you're both here," he said, inviting himself to sit in the other chair beside Julio. "How are you feeling?"

"Better," I told him.

"I'm glad you weren't in your car when it was destroyed."

"I'm guessing by your tone of voice that you aren't just thinking of my personal welfare."

"You're damn right. When you're sick, you're sick. Stay

home. If that had been an accident where you were driving, there'd be questions," Phil said.

I bit my tongue to keep from saying the first thing that came to mind. Phil had been known for taking chances himself, and had done some crazy stunts that could have gotten him in trouble if he hadn't managed to stay just inside the line. But I'd noticed a subtle shift in his attitude since he'd become a lieutenant.

"I know you're right," I said carefully.

"And I know it's hard not to push the line. Consider yourself warned. I'll tell Captain Grant that in the future, when you're sick, you'll stay at home eating your chicken soup like a good boy," he said, acknowledging the things I hadn't said. "Now, with that out of the way, let's talk about Tina. I'll state the obvious. That was ugly and doesn't help us get the job done. We need to avoid her at all costs."

Julio told him about seeing Karter Greer.

"I agree with Larry. If he does it again, warn him. If he doesn't comply, make sure that you or another deputy have your body cam on and arrest him. Use kid gloves, no verbal abuse or arguments. Let him spout whatever he wants and dig his own hole as deep as he can."

We both nodded. Greer had betrayed our trust, and it wasn't just about the thin blue line. He'd failed in his duty and someone had died. When we had called him on it, he retaliated by spreading dirt to the press. Now we had to suck it up and be professionals, regardless of his actions.

Julio and I brought Phil up to date on the Briggs investigation.

"Considering Tina's latest tirade, let's keep Deputy Sanderson away from it. It'll be for her own good as well as the department's. It's bad enough that she's collected camera footage. If any of it were to go missing, someone could point a finger at her and claim she was covering up for her brother."

"You're right," Julio said. "I should have thought of that."

"If the FBI is right, then we don't need to drag this out. Let the evidence lead you."

"We will. But we're going to need time before we're sure," I said.

Phil stood up. "I'm not going to look over your shoulders. Just keep me informed."

Once he'd left, I put my phone on speaker for Julio's benefit and called Agent Padilla.

"I got called into a meeting yesterday and wasn't able to finish interviewing the Sunshine employees," she told me.

"One of them, Doug Sanderson, is coming in to the station this morning. Julio and I are planning to talk to the others when we're done with that interview. You're welcome to come over here for it."

"I've got a conference call with Jacksonville." She didn't sound excited by the thought of talking to her bosses in the Jacksonville field office.

"Sounds like fun," I commiserated.

"They want reassurance that we have our man." She was quiet for a moment. "I won't give it to them until we finish our investigation into Briggs's death and possible crimes."

"I appreciate that."

"I'm not doing it for you. It's a question of whether the FBI is more interested in investigations or public relations. Opinion appears to be divided at the moment." She sighed. "I'd appreciate seeing your reports on the interviews. It might be tomorrow before I can talk to any of them myself. I want to hear immediately if there's any word on the work van. We've issued an alert for the vehicle."

"So have we. Any word from Darzi's office on when the autopsy will be?"

"Last I heard was it'll be this afternoon. Let me know if you hear anything different," Padilla said and hung up.

I looked at my watch and saw it was after ten. I was getting ready to text Sandy to check on her brother when Dill buzzed me from the front desk with the news that Doug Sanderson was waiting in the foyer.

I went to meet him while Julio headed for one of our small conference rooms. It was more formal than meeting in my office, but less intimidating than one of the interview rooms.

Doug was of average height, with the same fine nose and facial features as his sister. As I opened the door and waved him through, I could see his eyes darting around nervously.

"I hope you don't mind Deputy Ortiz sitting in on the interview," I said, leading him to the conference room. "He's the lead investigator on the case."

"Interview?" Doug asked nervously. "My sister just said you wanted to talk to me."

For a minute, I thought he was going to bolt for the front door.

"That's right. We just want to ask a few questions. Why don't you have a seat," I suggested, pointing him into the conference room and wondering why he was so nervous. With his sister being a deputy, I would have thought he'd be more comfortable around law enforcement. I kicked myself for not running a background check on him.

Doug sat down hesitantly, looking back and forth between me and Julio.

"There's no reason to be nervous," I tried to reassure him.

"That's what you *would* say, isn't it?" He giggled awkwardly.

"Do you have a reason to be nervous?" Julio asked.

"Look, I know Matti is a deputy, and I get that you guys have to ask questions. I... What did Matti tell you about me?"

"Nothing much. She said that Davis got you your job with Sunshine Industrial Paint," Julio answered.

"Did she tell you I was an addict?"

"No, but we know that Davis has helped people who've had... issues," Julio said diplomatically.

"I've been arrested a couple of times. Lost my license. Not good experiences. One reason I'm so nervous is that

I'm scared all of this is going to cause me to relapse. I worked damn hard to dig myself out of that hole. I don't want to go back."

I saw tears forming at the corners of his eyes.

"Relax. We're just going to ask you a few questions. And we can connect you with resources that can help you. If you don't want us to tell your sister, we won't," I promised.

"I'm okay." Doug wiped at his eyes.

"How would you describe your relationship with Davis?" I asked.

"I guess sort of a mentee/mentor situation. I've got a sponsor with NA, and he's been a great help, but since Davis got me the job, I've sort of considered him a sponsor too. I've called him a couple times when… you know, I might have felt like I was in danger of getting back into my old habits."

"Do you know if he's helped other people with addiction issues?"

"A few. Hey, I'm not going to give out names. You know, that's kind of a thing," he said defensively.

"We're just trying to find out what happened. The more of his inner circle we can talk to, the sooner we'll have answers," I explained.

"He didn't kill himself," Doug blurted.

"Why do you say that?" Julio asked.

"He just wasn't that kind of guy. I mean, I know people that get down, way down, and I can see that. Bipolar or whatever. I crash sometimes. That wasn't Davis. Like the counselors I've talked with, Davis was a rock. Every day same as the day before. Never super high or low. Do you get me?"

"So who would hurt him?"

Doug looked puzzled, then slowly shook his head.

"No idea, man. Maybe he trusted someone with bad intentions. Like he let them into his house and they killed and robbed him."

"Can you think of anyone who might do that?" Julio

pressed.

"No… Wait, there was a woman a couple of months ago. Davis let her stay at his house, then she used his credit card and stole some money out of his wallet."

"What's her name?"

"I'm not sure. Kaley or Kelly, something like that."

"Any last name?"

"No idea. She was scraping the bottom, man. Not a lot of last names on the street, you know what I mean?"

"What did she look like?"

"I only saw her a few times. Tall for a girl. Eyes were mean."

"Hair color?" Julio asked.

"Cut short, dirty. Brown, I guess. She'd been using for a while. You could see that."

"Was she fat or skinny?"

"Skinny. Addict kind of skinny. Her clothes were all right, but I think Davis had bought her clean clothes before I met her."

"Any tattoos or piercings?"

"Not like some people. You know, the ones who've been down for a while, or in prison, will have them all over their face, neck, back, real amateur stuff. She just had a rope of leaves, I think, going up her neck. Whoever inked her had some talent. The tat was the classiest thing about the woman."

"Who else met her?" I asked.

"She came to an NA meeting, but she sat in the back and didn't say anything. I wouldn't have even noticed her except that Davis introduced her to me."

"You met her at a meeting. Where else did you see her?"

"At his house. I came over and she was there. As soon as I got there, she went in a back room and didn't come back out."

"What did Davis say about her?" Julio asked.

"Didn't say much. I mean, he didn't have to tell me she was a drug addict. It was obvious. But he liked helping people. If a guy rescues cats and you see a cat at his house, you don't have to ask what it's doing there."

We talked for a few more minutes, but Doug couldn't provide any more insights into Davis Briggs. I walked him to the front door.

"You need a ride?" I asked, remembering what he'd said about his license.

"Nah, Col dropped me off and said he'd pick me up if I texted him."

"Colson Holloway?"

"Yeah, he's pretty cool to work with."

I gave Doug an encouraging pat on the shoulder. "Thanks for coming in. I know how hard it was. Let us know if you need anything."

CHAPTER SIX

Before heading out to interview the rest of the Sunshine employees, Julio and I both spent some time with emails and paperwork. Most of mine was spent on filling out various forms for our human resources department about my totaled car. Dealing with the amount of paperwork involved in law enforcement often left me feeling liked I'd walked through a river of molasses, and the feeling had only increased with the bureaucracy associated with being a sergeant.

By eleven-thirty, we were in Tornado's old SUV, heading for the address that Joey Zavala had given us. The crew was working on a construction site for new student housing in Tallahassee. We soon found the company van parked near a unit that looked almost ready for occupancy. Zavala had warned me not to delay his crew any longer than necessary, as the owner was having a fit that the apartments weren't already available for the fall semester.

From the van, Julio and I followed various hoses and the sound of a radio playing country music to the open door of an apartment. Inside were two people wearing PPE suits and masks, painting the walls. The sound of the compressor and the radio drowned out our approach. I had to tug on one of the hoses to get their attention.

Both men were only a few inches above five feet tall. With similar dark eyes, black hair and wide smiles, they looked like they were related.

The older of the two said, "Mr. Zavala told us that someone would be coming to talk to us about Davis. It's very sad."

I introduced myself and learned that the older man was Luis Juarez and the younger one was Guillermo Esquival. He went by "Mo" for the sake of non-Spanish speakers. Luis spoke adequate English, but Mo could only speak a few words and phrases and understood little that was spoken at normal speed. Glad to have Julio with me, I turned the questioning over to him and he translated it all for me later.

"How well did you know Davis?" Julio asked Luis.

"Not so well. He worked nights most of the time while we mostly work days."

"He didn't speak Spanish, and my English is not good," Mo added.

"When was the last time you saw him?"

"I don't know. Maybe a week ago. The boss wanted to tell us about some problems, so we all met at the warehouse in the morning," Luis said.

"What was the problem?"

"Messy sinks, drop cloths not taken to the dumpster, other little stuff." Luis shrugged.

"Did Davis seem normal?"

"Sure, sure, same as always," Luis said, and Mo nodded.

Since both of the men had barely known Davis, we soon let them get back to work and followed the hoses to find the third member of the crew.

We found Brooke Dunham in an adjacent apartment. This time I didn't have to tug on the hose. The young brunette had turned off her sprayer and pushed back her googles and mask to take a Red Bull break. As soon as she saw us, she put down the drink and walked over.

"You must be the cops."

After I told her who we were, she said, "I'm still in shock

about Davis. What a super guy. Was it an accident?"

"We're looking into it," I said. "How well did you know him?"

"I heard he might have killed himself," she continued, ignoring my question.

"We don't know anything yet. But you can help us by answering a few questions. Did you know him well?"

She looked down at the concrete floor of the unfinished apartment. "We went out a couple of times," she finally said. It was clear that she hadn't wanted to tell us they'd dated.

"When was this?" I asked.

"Maybe a year ago. Right after I started working for Sunshine."

"How long did you all date?"

"A month, maybe two." She wasn't volunteering anything.

"What did you do on your dates?"

"Went to movies and bars. You know, the usual."

"Listen, I can pull the story out of you question by question, or you can just tell me what you know about Davis and what your relationship was like." I wasn't in the mood to dance.

She sighed. "Nothing, it was nothing. When I went to work at Sunshine, he helped me learn the ropes. He was nice. I was in the mood for a nice guy. One day he asked me out, maybe a month after I started, and I said yes. It was refreshing being with an older man. He showed up on time, didn't talk about video games and never acted like I should pay for stuff."

"Did it become an intimate relationship?"

She rolled her eyes. "Yes, we had sex. Very vanilla. Are you happy?"

"Why did you break up?"

"We didn't 'break up,'" she said, making air quotes. "We were never a real couple or anything. We just went out, had some fun, had a little sex. All of it as friends." She shrugged.

"But you stopped being friends with benefits," Julio

pointed out.

"Sure. I wasn't having that much fun. He was nice, but nice only goes so far."

"You were the one who broke it off?" I asked.

"It's funny, but I'd say it was mutual."

"What's funny?"

"There was no real ending to it. I told him I was busy once or twice when he asked me out, and then he just stopped asking. Kinda like he was glad he didn't have to ask anymore." She looked a little surprised at this revelation.

"How did you all get along afterward?" I asked.

"It was fine. We were friendly. Looking at it now, I guess we both were tired of dating, so it was no big deal when it was done."

"How was he acting over the last couple of weeks?"

"Same as always. That was Davis. Steady as a rock and just as boring." Her eyes widened at her own comment. "I didn't mean anything by that. He wasn't exciting, that's all."

"Did he have any problems with anyone?"

"Davis? Never."

"Not a customer or someone he tried to help?"

She started to shake her head, then froze. "There *was* someone. A woman. She stole some money. He was… irritated. It was the only time I ever saw him… well, angry isn't the right word… just irritated."

"Who was she?" I asked.

"I don't know. He said she was staying at his house. I didn't ask a bunch of questions 'cause we had already stopped dating and it wasn't any of my business."

"When was this?"

"A couple of months ago."

"Did you ever see her?"

"No."

"Did he ever tell you her name?"

Brooke shrugged. "If he did, I don't remember."

We finished up with Brooke and headed back to the Suburban. I looked at my phone and saw a text from Dr.

Darzi's office, confirming that the autopsy on Briggs would take place at three. I called Padilla.

"I can make it there," she told me.

"We'd like to be briefed on the murders that you think our victim committed, and if you have any other suspects," I said.

"I'll think about it when I have some time. With the autopsy this afternoon, it won't be today."

"We could ride over to together," I suggested.

"Why?" It was clear that she wasn't receptive to the idea. To be fair, law enforcement officers never liked to be without their own cars.

"You could brief us on the drive over."

"I can't share much information."

"We're part of the same investigation," I reminded her.

"No, we aren't. You're investigating the death of Davis Briggs. We're investigating multiple homicides, none of which occurred in your jurisdiction."

"You have a point. However, your suspects could be suspects in Briggs's death."

"You would need to show a link between them and the deceased."

"The box of trophies left at Briggs's house is certainly a link," I pointed out.

"Touche."

"Are you convinced that Briggs is the serial killer?" I asked.

"No."

"If he wasn't, then it would be very helpful for both investigations to know how those souvenirs got into his house."

"Where are you going with this?"

"If he isn't the serial killer, then the box of souvenirs is a link to whoever the *real* killer is. Which puts the bullseye on your suspects."

"All right, all right." She made it sound like I had tortured her into agreement. "Fine, I'll share what I can about the murders and our suspects."

"That's all we're asking."

"No files. Just names and a few details. You'll have to take it from there."

"Meet us at the sheriff's office at two," I told her.

Julio and I grabbed lunch and headed back to the office. Adams County didn't have the resources to maintain our own morgue, so we contracted with Dr. Darzi to act as our coroner out of his office at the hospital in Tallahassee. Two trips into town in one day was a lot, but it would be worth it to have Padilla trapped in a car with us.

She showed up right on time.

"That's what you're driving?" she asked, frowning at the K9 Suburban.

"You know what happened to my other car. This is my loaner."

"Then we'll take my car."

I called shotgun while Julio climbed into the backseat with boxes of case files and notes.

"Okay, give us the background on the murders," I said as she pulled out of the parking lot.

"They started five years ago and have been spread out across North Florida and South Georgia. There are ten that we're confident are related, and three more that might be."

"What are the common denominators?"

"All of the victims were women between the ages of twenty and thirty-five. They all were engaged in some form of sex work. None of them weighed more than a hundred and ten pounds. They were found in rural areas and their bodies were burned. We know when six of them were abducted, and in each of those cases it was between midnight and two in the morning. Four were in public parks and two along wooded sections of road."

"What about your missing witness?"

"She was in a city park after hours. The park is known to be a pickup spot, and she admitted that she used the area to troll for customers. Unfortunately for us, he didn't try to pick her up. Instead, he came up behind her and grabbed her around the throat. But he underestimated her. She'd had martial arts training when she was a teenager and was able to break loose. She ran and he chased her for a few minutes but must have given up."

"You're lucky she reported the crime," I observed.

"She didn't at first. Another sex worker told us about the incident. Kat, our victim, told this third party, who reported it to us. We've been posting warnings and canvassing sex workers."

"What are the odds that he came back for her?"

"It's hard to say. Kat was extremely paranoid. Didn't trust us. It was freaking her out that we were watching her, so it's possible that she left on her own. It's also possible that someone else didn't like that we were keeping track of her. We took a deep look into her activities and learned that she was involved with a nasty crowd of drug dealers and sex traffickers."

"Would you walk us through each of the murders?" I asked.

For the next half hour, Padilla told us everything she was willing to reveal. Two facts impressed me. One was Padilla's ability to remember the details of ten murders, and the other was how similar the murders were.

"He's methodical," I said.

"Exactly. These were not murders of opportunity. He stalked his victims and had a plan for the disposal of their bodies. With other serial killers who have stalked sex workers, we've been able to get a description of his car, and sometimes even the killer, from other women or men working the same area. This guy has been extremely careful not to be seen by anyone except the victim."

"I'm beginning to see why you like Briggs for the killings. Everyone we've talked to has said that he was always in a good mood and never got angry. Who's like that?"

"A person who keeps a tight control on his emotions," Julio said from the backseat.

"Even his death seems well orchestrated," Padilla pointed out.

"So where's his work van?" I asked.

"He destroyed it to maintain the illusion that he's a good guy," Padilla said.

"I hate to admit it, but that all makes sense. He would have had to use the van to commit the murders, since he was supposed to be working when they happened."

"And they were usually an hour or more from his house."

"So the van would have been filled with forensic evidence," I agreed.

"In this day and age, he couldn't have gotten it clean enough to get rid of all the hair, skin cells, blood and DNA. We'd be sure to find something."

Padilla pulled into the hospital's lot and parked in one of the spaces reserved for law enforcement. "That's it, boys. Let's go see if the autopsy helps answer any of our questions."

CHAPTER SEVEN

As we were walking down the hall to the morgue, a text came in from Cara that read: *Call me when you can.* Knowing that she would have made it clear if it had been an emergency, I responded that it'd be an hour or two, and she sent back a thumbs-up. I was curious what she wanted to talk about, but tried to put it out of my mind as we entered the exam room.

"See, I told you the next autopsy was important." Darzi nudged his assistant, a new addition to the team named Avery who towered over him… and everyone else in the room. "We are honored to have local *and* federal law enforcement. I'm surprised FDLE didn't send someone."

"Your victim is on that table."

Avery pointed to a table five feet away from the one where they were currently working on the body of an older man whose girth took up the entire stainless-steel surface. Darzi had told me that they'd upgraded their exam tables to hold cadavers that weighed over three hundred pounds. "It's a sign of our times," he'd said.

"You can finish up with this one," Darzi told Avery, then he stepped back to look at the monitors hanging overhead. He pressed a few keys on a laptop, then said, "Technology.

Making our lives wonderful except when it doesn't. Our recording system was down all day yesterday. We had to get the hospital's IT department to rig us up something so we could get our work done. Today, everything is working as it should. Hurrah!"

He walked over to the table where Davis Briggs's body was displayed without any regard for the dead man's dignity.

"I don't have to tell you that we will probably not find out anything too exciting today if this was an overdose. We'll take samples and the labs will test them. It will be weeks."

"We're looking for anything out of the ordinary," Padilla told him.

"Why is he so important?" As the pathologist, Darzi had the right to know any information that might help him determine the cause of death.

Padilla hesitated for just a moment, then said, "There is a strong possibility that he's a serial killer."

"Ahhh, that does make him interesting."

"There are differing opinions on his culpability in the murders," I clarified.

"Good!" Darzi said. "We always have a better chance of seeing justice done under an adversarial system. Special Agent in Charge says we have a serial killer, and Mr. Investigator says not so fast. Let's see what the body of Mr. Davis Briggs has to say."

Darzi started at the top of Briggs's head, using his eyes, hands and nose as he moved all along the body. This was always his first step. He stopped when he came to a discoloration on Briggs's shoulder. Darzi looked up and tapped on a keyboard, making crime scene photos of the body appear on the monitors. For the recording of the autopsy, he described the location of the discoloration, then took out a solid ruler and put it next to the mark and pressed a key, which snapped a picture.

"This bruising is possibly from him collapsing to the floor," Darzi explained for our benefit, then continued the exploration of the body. He found other marks and described them in detail, taking pictures of each. After inspecting the soles of the feet, he looked up.

"Avery, please help me turn the body."

Once both sides of the body had been thoroughly inspected, Darzi selected a scalpel and hovered for just a moment above the chest before he began to cut. Then, with quick and sure motions, he made a Y incision across the torso.

Normally, I could hold my own when things got gory. Today my stomach churned, reminding me that I had just gotten over a virus. I swallowed hard and breathed deeply.

Julio, on the other hand, moved closer to the table and watched intently. He'd come a long way in his efforts to become a seasoned investigator. Still, I saw him look away as Darzi collected Briggs's stomach contents.

"Curious," Darzi said as he studied the bile and undigested food.

"What?" Padilla asked, beating me to the question.

"You said that there were pills? An overdose? See, there are no undigested pills in the stomach. With most overdoses, you'll see some remnants. I'll need to consider the fatal dosage of the pills in question and compare it to the lab reports. Of course, there can be explanations. The victim might have crushed the pills before taking them or dissolved them in a drink."

"There was a glass and a bottle of Jack Daniels on the table," Julio said.

"The glass, bottle and any utensils present should be examined for residue. I would like to see those reports before I make a determination on the cause of death," Darzi said.

"I'll make sure that our lab conducts all the required tests and sends you copies of the reports." Padilla looked concerned, like a golfer facing a difficult putt on the eighteenth hole.

The rest of the autopsy revealed nothing unusual. We were still stuck waiting for the results of multiple lab reports.

"The lack of pills in the stomach is interesting," I said as we walked to Padilla's car.

"Doesn't prove anything," she said.

"I just said it was interesting."

"Which it is," Julio added, smiling a little at the irritated look on Padilla's face.

Once we were headed out of town, I picked up the conversation where we'd left off earlier. "Give us the lowdown on your suspects."

"They *were* our suspects," Padilla said, emphasizing the past tense.

"Okay, tell us about the suspects you had before Briggs died with a box of murder memorabilia in his house." I figured it was best to humor her.

"Number one on our list was Garcia Montrose, a real piece of work. But you can remove him from consideration."

"Why?"

"He's been in the Leon County Jail for the last two weeks. He was picked up for stealing a car and can't make bail. We made sure the judge knew his history, so the bail was set at a million dollars to help keep him locked up until other charges can be brought."

"Other charges?" Julio asked.

"We suspect him of several rapes and are waiting on the DNA results. The point is, he couldn't have killed Briggs."

"Who's your next suspect?" I asked.

"Joe Fisher. He's thirty-eight, a plumber with a history of violence toward women. He works the areas where the murders took place, and we can place him within twenty miles of most of them. We haven't been able to get a warrant for his phone records, though, so we don't have a good map of his movements."

"Other than his worksites, what evidence do you have?" Julio asked.

"Not much. That's why we can't get the warrant for the phone data. There is his history of violence, plus he's been suspected in two arsons."

"I guess you can't directly tie him to any of the victims?"

"We'd have a chance at a warrant if we could."

"I'd like to find out where he was when Briggs died," Julio said.

"Good luck. He lawyered up and won't talk to law enforcement," Padilla answered. "I'll send you his information. No harm in you trying."

"Third suspect?" I asked.

"He's interesting. Smartest of the three, and he doesn't tick off many boxes on the profile we developed for our killer. Ricky Hubbard is married with two kids. He's the sole proprietor of a pool cleaning and repair business in Gadsden County. He also drives the perfect van for transporting bodies. It's big and always smells of chlorine."

"Yeah. Who would know if he just washed it out with bleach?" I said thoughtfully.

"Exactly."

"What put him on your suspect list?"

"We did a search for burglaries and rapes within five miles of where our victims lived. His name came up twice. First was a woman who claimed he attacked her. It was next door to a pool he was cleaning. There was no evidence, and the woman has a history of being bipolar, and has an arrest for attacking a man she claims touched her at a Dollar General. Needless to say, the prosecutor took one look and refused to even consider charges."

"What about the second one?" Julio asked, leaning forward from the backseat.

"The sheriff's office down in Eaton County responded to a suspicious activity call. A deputy found him driving around in a wooded area of the county. When he stopped him, Ricky said that he was just looking for an address. The deputy asked where it was and gave him directions on how to get there. Ricky thanked him and the deputy drove off. However, he reported that he thought Ricky had been acting oddly."

"You have to pay attention when the hairs on the back of

your neck bristle," I said.

"This deputy certainly went with his intuition. He waited for Ricky to drive back to the main road and followed him. He didn't follow the directions that the deputy had given him. When Ricky stopped at a gas station, the deputy confronted him and asked if he could look in the back of the van. Ricky refused. The deputy didn't have probable cause, so he had to let Ricky get the gas and drive off. He followed him to the county line and filed a detailed report."

"And?"

"Two weeks later, one of our victims was found in a wooded area not five miles from where Ricky was originally confronted by the deputy. The coroner couldn't give us an exact date, but Ricky was in the area within the window for the woman's approximate time of death."

"Do you think the body was in the back of the van?" I asked.

"It makes you wonder. He was definitely up to something nefarious." She shrugged. "That's been this case from start to finish. One odd coincidence after another without any probable cause that would let us take a closer look at any of our suspects."

"I'd like his information too," Julio said.

"Again, good luck. He hasn't lawyered up, but he says no, repeatedly. 'Can we talk to you?' 'No.' 'Can we look around your property?' 'No.' 'Can we look inside your van?' 'No.' We did do surveillance on him for a week and managed to get a sample of his DNA from a cup he tossed away at a Whataburger."

"Did Davis Briggs ever show up on your radar?" I asked.

"Never. Since discovering the box of souvenirs, we've combed back through all of our notes. His name doesn't appear at all." Her frustration was obvious. "We're still working on his phone and other electronic devices.

"One of my agents talked to Joey Zavala, and he agreed to go over his records for the last five years to try and reconstruct Davis's work schedule, including when and where he was on a job. So far, all of the evidence points toward Briggs as the killer, but if there is evidence that eliminates him, I'll accept it." She looked over at me and all I could do was nod.

Five minutes later, we pulled into the parking lot of the sheriff's office. I still had paperwork to catch up on and planned to spend the rest of the afternoon sitting at my desk. Once I was in my office, I took my phone out of its case and set it on my desk. That's when I remembered that I was supposed to call Cara. Feeling guilty that I'd forgotten, I tapped her number.

She was oddly evasive. "I'll tell you when you get home."

"I have time to talk now," I assured her.

"It's nothing that can't wait," she said, then added, "I love you," before hanging up.

Feeling uneasy, but knowing it wouldn't help to brood on it, I put all my focus back on my work. I asked Julio to work up a presentation on the Briggs investigation for our next roundtable discussion. The roundtables were a new method we were using to share ideas and information on each other's investigations that I'd started once I took over CID.

By the time I got home, I was exhausted. I hadn't realized just how much being sick had taken out of me. As much as I wanted to simply grab a bite to eat and pass out, I was more focused on finding out what Cara had to tell me.

"So what's up?"

"Would you rather have the Band-Aid yanked off or pulled off slowly?" she asked, biting her lip.

"Pull it off fast."

"Mom and Dad are coming to stay for a few days."

"No," I said and put my hand up to my forehead. "I must still be sick. I'm having a fever nightmare."

"They're kind of in a mood."

"What do you mean by 'in a mood?'" I didn't like the way she'd said it.

"They heard about Tina Knightly and have watched all of her video commentaries. They're not happy and want to come up and… I don't really know what they want to do."

"There's nothing they *can* do. Knightly's not an amateur. She knows how to stay just on the non-libel side of the line. I don't see what they think they can do." I realized my voice had gotten louder as I spoke, and I took a deep breath. "There's nothing they can do, so there's no reason for them to come up here."

"I already called them back and tried to talk them out of it. Now they won't take my calls. I got a text saying they'll be here by noon tomorrow." Cara was staring at me as she spoke. I knew she was trying to evaluate just how upset I was.

"What do you think they'll do when they get here?" I asked as calmly as I could. I loved her parents, but they were a little unpredictable and unorthodox. They were both a bit on the hippie side, and her father was a lot on the Viking side.

"You know how they are. All I can tell you is that they're mad," Cara said.

"I can't have them flying off the handle about this."

"They aren't acting like that. It's more kind of a cold anger."

"Have you seen them like this before?"

"Only once." She looked down at the floor.

"When?"

"I was sixteen. We were living in Tennessee at a commune with a one-room schoolhouse sort of deal. There was a boy who was a year older then me. His name was Robby. He seemed nice enough and asked me out to the movies. He drove us in his dad's van. He got handsy during the movie, so I told him to knock it off. Coming home, he stopped the van at an overlook. When he touched me again, I slapped him, so he dumped me out of the van and drove off."

I was speechless. Angry and speechless.

"I'd walked half of the five miles back home by the time Dad picked me up. When I'd been late, they'd gone to Robby's cabin and found out that he'd left me on the side of the road."

"What did your dad do to him?" I asked, imagining all sorts of possible tortures.

"I never found out. Dad told me that Robby would learn that he couldn't treat a woman like that and for me to not worry. A week later, he came to school with his feet all bandaged up. He never spoke to me or looked me in the eyes again. Rumor was that Dad had made him walk the five miles from the overlook to the commune barefoot."

"I guess I'm not surprised that he didn't call the police."

"The commune had a 'no police' rule. Everything was handled by the council."

"And you think they might try something like that on Tina?" I had to admit that I found the idea of Tina being forced to walk five miles barefoot intriguing, but I shook the idea out of my head. "I don't want them to break the law. I'd be embarrassed to arrest my own in-laws."

"I can't promise anything. You know who we're talking about." Cara's cheeks were flushed. I knew that she was as worried as I was.

I pulled her into a hug. "I know you can't control your parents. When they get here, I'll have a talk with them. Tina isn't anyone they want to mess with."

"And I'm not sure Tina wants to mess with my parents."

"That either."

"I'm sorry for all of this. You're still recovering from being sick and don't need the baggage they bring with them."

"I'm okay."

"I picked up a loaf of fresh bread from the bakery and there's leftover vegetable soup," she said, gently pushing me toward the bedroom. "Go get cleaned up and I'll have it ready when you come out."

After a shower and dinner, I felt better and could think

more clearly about the impending visit from the in-laws. I assured myself that I could talk them down from the ledge they were on. It turned out that I was seriously overestimating my ability to handle certain situations.

CHAPTER EIGHT

The next morning, I was shaving and thinking about how I would convince Henry and Anna to leave Tina Knightly to me when my phone buzzed. I walked out of the bathroom and picked the phone up off the nightstand.

"They found Briggs's work van," Julio said. "It's down south, out in the woods and burned."

"Our county?"

"Nope, Eaton County, down by the coast."

"Send me the location, and I'll meet you there."

An hour later, I pulled off the side of the road about five miles north of Pelican Island. An Eaton County deputy sat in his patrol car, blocking a sandy path that led into the woods. As I got out of the Suburban, my nose picked up the distinctive smell of burned rubber and plastic that signaled a torched vehicle.

The deputy walked over and greeted me. He was half a head shorter than my six feet and looked about five years younger than me.

"The van is back down that trail. After I ran the VIN number and the BOLO popped up, I walked back here and decided to sit on it until y'all arrived."

"That's perfect," I said, holding out a hand and

introducing myself.

"I know you," he said, and I had a moment's concern about what was coming next. Two years ago, Dad and I had had a run-in with the local sheriff that had ended with his arrest and resignation. For all I knew, this guy could have been his cousin.

"You and your dad helped get rid of that asshole Sheriff Duncan. He wouldn't hire me. Told me I was too short. I'm Roy Russo." He shook my offered hand, and I tried to hide my sigh of relief.

"You can go on if you want," I told him. "We're going to have to wait for the FBI before we can look at the scene."

He shook his head. "My supervisor thought I ought to stay and watch. We don't get much in the way of serious crimes down here, and we don't have a bunch of money to send our deputies out for training."

"Makes sense," I said, then turned as Julio's car pulled up behind my SUV.

"Padilla is on her way with the crime scene techs," he said as he got out of the car.

I made the introductions, then explained to Russo why everyone was so interested in this particular van.

"It's a mess," he said. "I've seen a lot of burned vehicles, but the only one worse than this was an electric car on the beach after the lithium batteries caught fire."

"We're hoping to get some forensic evidence from it," Julio said.

"Good luck with that." Russo shook his head. "I had to compare two VIN number plates to get the whole thing."

I looked down the sandy lane to where the back of the scorched van was just visible.

"No chance of collecting vehicle tracks from that sand," I lamented.

"Hey, if you want to get a look at the van while we wait, I've got a drone in my trunk," Russo offered.

"Sure," I said, figuring it couldn't hurt to get a bird's-eye view.

"I'm on our search-and-rescue team." Russo opened his trunk to reveal a two-foot-by-two-foot drone sitting on top of all his other patrol gear. "Always keep it charged, just in case. Since we don't have a helicopter, we've used it to follow suspects too."

Soon he had it up and buzzing overhead. He attached a shade to his laptop so that we could see the video images despite the glare of the sun.

Russo flew the drone over the van, though it was hard to recognize the flattened rectangle as anything that had ever been drivable. Other than the hood and the front of the cab, it was just a hunk of melted metal.

"Did the burning paint do that?" Julio was leaning in, looking at the screen.

"Probably paint thinner too," I said. "Were there any reports of the fire?"

"I'll get our dispatch to check, but I doubt it," Russo answered. "If there had been, one of us would have come out and eyeballed it.

"We've had a fair bit of rain lately, so some people have been burning yard debris. Plus, a quarter mile east, they're clearing land for a condo. My guess is that anyone who might have seen the smoke just assumed that it was being done by a landowner."

"Who owns this land?" I asked.

"A lumber company. They have a couple thousand acres in the county."

Russo brought the drone down to within five feet of what was left of the van. I could just make out a few letters and part of Sunshine Industrial Paint's logo on part of a door. The steel wheels, the axles and the engine were the only parts that had survived the intense heat intact.

"What a mess." I couldn't imagine getting any forensic evidence from the van except maybe a chemical analysis of the accelerants that had been used.

We heard more vehicles pull up behind us. Padilla hopped out of her car, looking out of place in her dark suit and dress shoes as she walked awkwardly in the sand toward us.

"What shape is the van in?" she asked.

I waved her in so she could see the video screen.

"Our friend sure knows how to throw a barbeque," she grumbled. "Get the drone out of there so we can get to work." She turned and gracelessly walked back to her crime scene crew.

Once they went to work, the rest of us retreated to our cars. The sun reflecting off of the sand had made it feel like we were standing in an oven.

Even though we were in the middle of nowhere, there was a surprisingly strong cell signal, so I was able to work on reports and monitor what my other investigators were dealing with. Most of them were the usual burglaries and assaults. The only other major case we were working was a shootout at a party the weekend before, which had left several people dead and another half dozen wounded. Mick Klein was the lead investigator, so I called him up to see where he was on the case.

"Do we have ourselves a drug war?" I asked him.

"This is going to take teamwork. These guys are bad, and they have everyone in the area scared to talk, even the older generation," Mick said.

"Who are they?"

"They aren't locals. I've been talking to the DEA, and it looks like we've got two cartels looking to expand into Adams County. The shooting was one group trying to put pressure on the other."

"Is there any good news?"

"The DEA is excited about the shooting," Mick said sardonically.

"Bully for them."

"They're seeing it as an opportunity to snag some of the mid-level players in both groups. The good news is that they're willing to give us some resources, including a full-time liaison. His name is Agent Briers, and he's already given me a rundown of the major players, as well as the lower-level ones that they know are operating in Calhoun. Now for the bad news."

I winced. "What?"

"Briers said that their informants are telling them that this could all boil over on Labor Day Weekend."

"Wonderful. All right, go ahead and brief Lieutenant Eccles, and prepare a report for our Monday roundtable. Invite Agent Briers to be there too. Anything else going on?"

"We found some connections between a series of Peeping Tom reports and a pair of break-ins that Lynn is working. We've moved it up to a priority so we can catch him before we have a rape on our hands," Mick reported.

"Let me know if you need any additional resources from patrol."

"For the moment, we're good. I did let the night watch commander know the area that the reports have come out of so that he can channel a few more ride-bys. What would help is to get your dad to call FDLE and make the fingerprints and DNA a priority."

"Fingerprints shouldn't be a problem. DNA could be. Last I heard, the lab was backed up for months with priority being given to homicides and rapes only."

"I guess a private lab is out of the question?" Mick asked.

"Wouldn't be if we had the money."

"Maybe the sheriff's office should start buying lottery tickets."

I laughed. "I'll run that by Captain Grant and tell him it was your idea."

"I've heard all the rumors about Dill's cousin," Mick said, changing the subject. "Latest is that a van has been found."

"That's where I am now, down north of Pelican Island. There's not much left of the van. I'll be surprised if any evidence we find moves the needle."

"Someone thought it was important enough to burn the van."

"But *who* is the question. Did Briggs do it? Or whoever

killed him? Or was this a random act by a car thief?"

"Could be. Car thieves have a habit of burning the vehicles or dumping them into bodies of water."

"Few of them do this good a job. Though, with all the paint and chemicals inside the van, someone might have just thrown a match through the window and ran."

"Sounds like we need to experiment."

"Maybe. Still, I don't see it adding up to any answers."

"When Dill was my training officer, he told me that policework is the same as boxing. It's all in the footwork."

"This is going to take some luck too."

"Like he said, it's just like boxing."

After I hung up with Mick, I went through and assigned the cases that had come in overnight to the other investigators. The burden would be heavier on them while Julio and I were out of the mix, though we couldn't continue to give the Briggs case all of our attention. At some point, we'd have to sideline it until the lab reports came back.

I looked at my watch and wondered if Cara's parents had shown up yet. The drive from their co-op near Gainesville to our place was only about three hours, and both of them were early risers. I could already envision their yurt set up in my yard. I sighed and got out of the Suburban.

The three FBI crime scene techs were talking with Padilla. As I walked toward them, I could read the frustration on all of their faces. All three techs were continually wiping sweat from their brows.

"We photographed and took video of the scene, and dusted surfaces for prints. I don't know what else we can do with what's left of the van," one of the men said.

"We did collect some items, about fifty of them from around the van and along the path. Those will be your best chance at a DNA or fingerprint hit," the heavyset woman on the team told Padilla.

"Send me a list of the items and where they were found, and I'll let you know what we want tested. Fingerprint all of it," Padilla told them.

The sad truth was that most of what they'd picked up would prove to be junk that had been thrown out of cars for years and had ended up here. The odds that any of it came from the person who had torched the van were not in our favor.

All three techs nodded. Looking like a defeated football team, they walked back to their van with their bags and equipment.

"I don't know whether to hate or admire this asshole," Padilla said, though her face made it obvious that hate was winning out.

"Are you going to take the van to an evidence yard?" I asked.

"I called FDLE and they agreed to keep it. There's a tow truck on the way."

I debated whether or not I should stay until the truck arrived. I couldn't see how my being there would make a difference. Convinced I'd just be wasting my time, I walked over to the FBI's crime scene van, where Julio was talking to the techs.

"They're going to tow the van to an FDLE lot," I told him.

"I heard. I can stay here if you want to leave," he offered.

"I guess one of us should, just to keep an eye on the operation. See if you can pick Padilla's brain. I think those other murders hold the clues we need to solve Briggs's case. The FBI might be right. If they are, then Dill and Doug Sanderson will have to get over it and move on."

"The burned-out van fits with the theory that Briggs was the killer. He wants to get rid of any evidence of the fact, so he burns the van because of the possible forensic evidence that could tie him to the murders."

"But if that's the case, then why did he leave the box of souvenirs in his house?" I asked.

Julio shrugged. "What Dr. Darzi found in the stomach… Do you think that means anything?"

"You saw Darzi's reaction. He was surprised that there

wasn't any sign of the pills. I trust Dazi's knowledge and experience, which means Briggs got those pills into his system some other way than just popping them into his mouth. If he took them at all."

"I'll talk to Padilla and make sure that her techs are following up. Darzi *did* say that Briggs might have crushed the pills or dissolved them."

"She's probably on top of that, but it doesn't hurt to make sure. I can tell how badly she wants to wrap up this series of murders and Briggs offers her that opportunity."

"You don't think she'd purposefully overlook evidence?" Julio asked.

"It's not in her nature. Then again, people can act a little screwy when they're put under pressure."

Half an hour later, I was headed back to Adams County and still thinking about the van. On the one hand, it made sense that if Briggs was the killer he might have destroyed the van before committing suicide. On the other hand, if he was being framed then it made sense for the real killer to destroy the van in order to make it *look* like Briggs did it to cover up evidence. I was wrapping my mind into knots trying to puzzle it out, and for no good purpose. What was left of the van wasn't going to offer any new clues.

As I pulled into the parking lot of the sheriff's office, focused on finishing out my day and heading home to deal with my in-laws, my phone buzzed. I hadn't yet connected my phone's Bluetooth to the loaner SUV, so I couldn't answer it right away. By the time I parked, the phone stopped ringing. I picked it up and saw a missed call from Julio, which was followed almost immediately by a text.

911 There was a body under the van.

I swore enough to make a sailor blush and called Julio.

"They almost had the van on the back of the tow truck before Padilla started screaming for them to stop. It's a mess," Julio said.

"I'll be back down there as soon as I can."

As I hung up, I saw Dad walking out to his truck and decided he deserved an update. I got out and hustled over to him.

"What's up?" he asked when he saw my expression.

Once I'd filled him in, he frowned and said, "I would be glad to turn this whole thing over to Padilla and her crew. Thoughts?"

Whenever Dad asked me for my thoughts, I knew he was conflicted.

"I think there's something hinky about Briggs's death and his connection to the murders. If he burned the van to eliminate forensic evidence, then why did he keep the box? It's more incriminating or, I should say, more *obviously* incriminating than the van."

"Good point. Is there any other reason to destroy the van?"

"Maybe just to mess with us and to destroy the body that was under it," I suggested.

"Let's get out of the sun," Dad said, moving toward the shade of one of the live oaks that lined the edge of the parking lot. Sweat was soaking through his shirt. "Do we have any idea whose body it is under the van?"

"A woman who had been staying with Briggs hasn't been seen since he died. According to witnesses, he was angry at her for stealing some money."

"So he kills her and destroys both her body and the van, then goes home and commits suicide, leaving a box of incriminating evidence scattered on the floor of his bedroom," Dad said, one eyebrow raised.

"Maybe he was planning on… No, that doesn't make sense." I was running several scenarios through my mind, and none of them were logical. Of course, murders don't have to be logical.

"How about this?" Dad said. "Could the van have gotten stuck in the sand, leaving him with no choice but to destroy it and the body? Then he goes home, realizes he's messed up 'cause when the van is found with the body under it the jig'll be up, so he kills himself without worrying about the box of evidence. Maybe, at that point, he even hoped the connection would be made and that he'd get credit for a string of murders."

I thought about it. "Makes more sense than anything I've come up with."

"If that's the answer, then we can let go of the case. Hand it all over to the Feds."

"Maybe." I didn't like not having a solution that I believed in one hundred percent.

"Go forth, my son," he said and shook his head. "Do whatever you think is best. Just remember that you have more responsibilities than the Briggs investigation."

"I'm going back down there and see how big of a mess we have, give Julio any help he needs and then come back here. Then it will just be waiting on the lab work. Having seen the van, I'm guessing it's going to take DNA to identify the body."

"Keep me updated," he said.

Dad was heading back toward his truck when I realized that I needed to update him on another situation.

"Anna and Henry are coming to town."

He stopped and turned back to me.

"For the Labor Day weekend?"

"Not exactly," I said, then gave him the details.

"They're good people and love their daughter. I'm not surprised they're pissed," Dad said, remarkably calm.

"I'm just worried they'll do something that will cause more trouble with Tina Knightly."

"Henry's got a level head on his shoulders. I'm not concerned." He gave me a wave and walked off.

Dad and Henry got along well, but I thought Dad was giving him more credit for common sense than he deserved. I loved Henry, but he could be a very large loose cannon when he got upset.

I called Cara and told her how my day was going.

"I just got a text from Mom. They're on their way. If you aren't home by the time I get there, I'll sound them out on whatever crazy plan they've come up with. I know it's hard, but try not to worry about it." Cara knew her parents better than my dad did.

CHAPTER NINE

I tried to push my concerns about Cara's parents and Tina Knightly out of my mind and focus on the job at hand as I drove back to Eaton County. As a first responder, it could be a struggle to separate home life from work life. I'd always been amazed at how well Pete was capable of juggling calls and texts from his wife and daughters while working on cases. Of course, with my father also being my boss, it hadn't made it any easier for me to keep the two parts of my life separate.

When I arrived back at the scene, it was crowded with FBI agents, local deputies, crime scene techs and a worried-looking tow truck driver. The tow truck was down at the end of the sandy path with the remains of the van pulled halfway onto its bed.

Julio greeted me as I got out of my SUV.

"I would have handled it, but with the Feds and another county involved…" He looked frustrated.

"You were right to call. This situation is going to take some teamwork."

"The tow truck driver threw up a couple of times. I don't blame him."

"Did you see the body?"

"Padilla saw it before I did, but I was right there. There's not much left. Some of the van melted onto it, the sand… All that was left of the head was the skull. This is the worst I've ever seen."

"I don't think it can compete with the body I found in a hot tub," I assured him.

"I heard about the smell." Julio shook his head. "Luckily the smell of the burned van and all the chemicals inside it covered up most of the odor from this body."

"Have you talked to Lieutenant Eccles or Captain Grant?"

"Both. They want a report as soon as I can get it to them. I guess I should go to my car and start on it if you'll handle all the politics." He waved his hand toward Padilla and the dozen other people milling around her.

"Go," I told him, and he seemed relieved to retreat to his car.

I watched Padilla arguing with a man in a sheriff's office polo shirt and khakis. Sweat made his bald, ebony scalp glisten in the sun as he shook his head. I decided to walk over and find out what the argument was about, though I assumed it was over jurisdiction.

"The body is in our county." His angry tone made it clear he wasn't in the mood to compromise.

"This is a multi-jurisdictional investigation, covering seven counties across two states. Eaton County is welcome to participate in the investigation, but there's no way in hell your department is going to be the lead on this one," Padilla said forcefully.

The man glared at her and wiped his hand over the back of his head. I figured he was remembering his father's admonition against hitting a woman.

"This is Sergeant Macklin from Adams County. I know he wants to be front and center on this investigation too." Padilla nodded to me. I wasn't sure I appreciated her deflecting his anger on to me.

"I know about the Macklins. They stir up trouble every

time they come down here." He glared at me.

"I don't think I know you," I said, sticking out my had at the risk of having it slapped away.

"Lieutenant Hendry." Grudgingly, he took my hand.

"My point is that this death is part of a far-reaching investigation," Padilla said.

"You don't think our little ol' sheriff's office can handle a great big important murder case." Hendry smirked.

"That's not what I'm saying." I could tell that Padilla was exasperated. "I'm saying that you can be a part of the investigation, but an umbrella organization like the FBI is better able to coordinate resources."

"Lieutenant, it pisses me off when I have to deal with the Feds. They are notorious for stepping on the feet of other organizations," I said, and saw Padilla glaring at me as if trying to decide which side I was on. As a peace offering, I added, "Whether they mean to or not."

"That's what I'm saying, man." Hendry gave me a short nod.

"I'll work with you to make sure Special Agent in Charge Padilla here and her pals don't forget whose jurisdiction they're in," I told him.

Padilla's face turned red, but she held her tongue.

"I can work with that," Hendry said with a slight smile.

"So we're agreed. We'll all cooperate so long as the FBI doesn't get too bossy." I smiled at Padilla, who took a deep breath.

"Whatever." She dropped her professional façade, looking like a mother with a couple of misbehaving children. "Can we get to work now?"

"Who's stopping you?" Hendry asked.

Padilla started to respond, then clamped her mouth shut and did her best to stomp off through the deep sand. I was beginning to like Hendry.

We all walked down to where pieces of the body were lying in the sand behind the tow truck. Between the fire and the damage done when the tow truck moved the van, the body was a wreck. What was left of it was broken and scattered on the ground.

I found it hard to make sense of what I was seeing. There were bones, but very little tissue left. Several of the bones, including the skull, had melted metal or plastic stuck to them. Piecing the body back together and determining a cause of death would be a nightmare.

"Will Dr. Darzi's office be handling the autopsy?" I asked Hendry.

"I assume so. Boss lady over there vetoed the idea of having the local doctor who normally handles our, shall we say, less complicated deaths get his hands on it. Between you and me, she's right. He couldn't make heads nor tails of this mess."

"The big question is who this was." I looked closely for any piece of evidence on the corpse. A ring, a necklace, a piece of a purse or even some hair, but the fire had done its job too well. "According to Padilla, the murderer is very skilled at using fire to destroy evidence."

"Is? Agent Padilla told me that the murderer committed suicide." Hendry's brows furrowed. "She been lying to me?"

"Maybe, maybe not. Opinions vary."

"Do tell."

I filled him in about the discovery of Davis Briggs's body and the reported character of the man the FBI thought was a serial killer.

"You're stuck between a rock and a hard place." Hendry shook his head. "You say this was his work van?"

"That's right."

"So he comes down here to get rid of the body, which is part of this serial killer's MO. But for some reason he decides to burn his company van too? Then goes home… How'd he get home?"

"There was a motorcycle, a dirt bike, in his garage, which appeared to have been used recently."

"I see. In a big van like this, it would have been easy enough to cram a motorbike in the back. So then he rides the bike home and kills himself, leaving an incriminating box of souvenirs behind." He looked thoughtful. "Seems crazy. But bad guys do crazy things every day. You'd have to be off your leash to do the horrible things this perp is accused of doing. Guess the big question is, was your goody two-shoes actually a homicidal manic?"

"That's a question we still have to answer. As I said, opinions are divided."

"What's your opinion?" Hendry asked.

"I don't like it. I don't like this." I nodded toward the remains of the body. "I'm curious to know who this poor person is."

"Woman," Hendry said.

I turned and looked at him. The corner of his mouth turned up a little, and he pointed to a black object near the body.

"That's what's left of a shoe. Looks small for a man. Guess it could be a kid's shoe. However, the skull looks like it belongs to full-grown person."

I peered at the blackened piece of leather. He was right. It was the sole of a shoe. If it had been rubber instead of leather, it would have been just a black blob.

"Could have been here before the body and van," I said, a little embarrassed that I hadn't noticed it myself.

"Could have." He nodded. "Y'all have any idea who the victim could be, assuming it is a woman?"

"There are two women missing. One narrowly escaped being a victim of the serial killer, and the other stayed with Briggs and stole money from his wallet. She's the only person that anyone will admit ever seeing Briggs get mad at."

"Guess you hope it's not the second one," Hendry said.

I heard laughter behind us and was surprised to see Dr. Darzi, dressed in white PPE, headed toward us.

"What are you doing here?" he asked, smiling at me.

"This van belonged to the man you autopsied yesterday."

"Ahhh, I see. You have your hand in every murder in North Florida." Darzi looked down at the victim's remains.

"Agent Padilla told me it was bad, so that's why I decided to come myself. Trust her to understate the poor condition of the body."

Darzi raised his head and looked south toward the Gulf. I followed his gaze and saw dark clouds building on the horizon.

"You need to get a tent set up," he said. "I'm going to be here for a while."

"I'll take care of it," Hendry told me before turning and heading back toward the cars.

I watched as Darzi walked carefully around the area where the remains of the body were strewn. His eyes scanned the area as he surveyed what was left of the victim. Then he stepped back and took out his phone.

"Linda's at the van," he told me. "I wanted to see what the situation was before I told her what to carry out here."

He called his assistant and recited a long list of supplies. Before she arrived, Hendry returned with a pop-up tent that we erected over the body. A loud roll of thunder assured us that we weren't wasting our time. Afternoon thunderstorms were the norm in Florida during the summer.

Julio joined us as we watched Darzi and Linda pick up and sort through the body parts. Mostly they found bone, charred and otherwise. Padilla's crime scene techs were standing by. Occasionally, Linda or Darzi would point out a piece of evidence that wasn't organic and the techs would photograph and bag it.

The rain came, and everyone but Darzi and Linda got wet. It was late afternoon by the time Padilla gave permission to the tow truck operator to finish putting the van up on the bed of the truck. Then she turned to one of her crime scene techs.

"Yates, you follow the tow truck. When he takes the van off, look over the bed of his truck and make sure nothing is left behind. At some point we'll have to examine the undercarriage for evidence. That can wait." She sounded as tired as I felt.

It was six o'clock by the time we all headed home. When I pulled in my driveway, the sun was disappearing behind the tree line. The gate was open, which I'd expected. Cara would have left it open for her parents.

Halfway up the drive, I heard a loud crack and turned to see a thirty-foot pine tree come crashing down not ten feet from the Suburban. Out of the woods came a Viking wearing ear and eye protection. He looked like some mad scientist had mixed the DNA of Robbie Coltrane with that of Hafþór Björnsson. It was Henry Laursen, my father-in-law.

I rolled down the windows as he stomped his way over to me, struggling to get his earmuffs off and grinning widely.

"The center pole for our yurt is broken so I figured I'd just make a new one."

"Of course you did," I said, knowing he wouldn't catch the sarcasm.

"I know you've had a long day, so don't feel like you have to help me. I can handle it. Do you have a peeling spud?"

"I don't even know what a peeling spud is."

"You use it to take the bark off a log. Never mind, I can use an axe. Won't be easy or pretty, but it will get the job done."

Knowing that I'd regret it, I told Henry that they could stay in our house.

"No. Anna thinks that mobile homes have too much plastic and artificial wood and the like. Gives off toxins." He must have seen my face. "You know her. I think she gets carried away with some of that. Stubborn, though."

I knew he was right about that. Suddenly, I had a brilliant idea.

"Hold that thought." I took out my phone and called Dad. Ten minutes later, I put the phone down. "Get in and we'll drive up to the house," I said to Henry.

"What was that about a cabin?" he asked as he climbed into the passenger seat. "Hey, when did you join the K9 squad?"

"This is just a loaner. I'll tell you about it later. Dad and Genie bought a cabin. The property is next to theirs, and Dad said he'd be glad to have you and Anna as guests."

"Well… Would he let Mauser stay with us?"

Henry had a real affinity for the canine Godzilla.

"I don't see why not."

"Sounds great to me. Still, I'll have to talk to Anna."

"Sure." I parked by the house but didn't get out. "Now tell me what you came up here for." Even though I was tired, I wanted to find out what kooky plan they'd come up with to get revenge on Tina.

"Nothing. Don't you worry about a thing." Henry started to open the door.

I put my hand on his arm.

"What Tina has done to us is shitty. But if you strike back at her and it boomerangs on us, you'll feel bad, we'll feel bad and we'll all be in a worse position than before you came up here."

He reached over and patted my hand, then lifted it off of his arm. "Don't worry," he said and clambered out of the SUV.

I was more worried than ever.

Inside, I was greeted by a nervous Cara, who was trying to ride herd over her mother. It looked like Anna was using every pot and pan we owned to make dinner. But I had to give her credit: it smelled good. I'd barely eaten anything all day.

Henry explained about Dad's cabin, and Anna reluctantly agreed to stay there. Well, at first she was reluctant, but then she seemed suddenly eager to stay there. I was too tired to think about why she might have changed her mind.

"We'll have dinner first," Anna insisted. "I fixed chicken and yellow rice, and garbanzo bean soup. I also brought some Cuban bread that a friend of ours makes in his stone oven."

The food was filling and comforting. I only half listened as Henry and Anna told a long story about a new type of wine that they were developing on the co-op. The tale had a full measure of drama and gossip about their neighbors. Some of the details were scandalous enough to make Cara blush and roll her eyes.

"I didn't mean to chase your parents away," I said after seeing them off to Dad's place. Though I leaned against the front door to make sure they couldn't get back in.

"You handle them better than I do." Cara leaned in and kissed me.

"Where are the cats?" Alvin had been following Henry around, getting treats every time the big man thought we weren't looking.

"Mom gave Ghost a slice of chicken and I think he's crashed on our bed. Hopefully he didn't throw it up. Ivy took one look at who was coming through the door and disappeared. I imagine she's under our bed or behind the washer."

"Did you get a chance to ask your mom what they're going to do to Tina?"

"No. If we're lucky, she's just going to try and hex her."

"Come on! Your mother's not a witch."

"She's not above trying some herbal hoodoo. Especially when she's really pissed off."

"Is she really pissed off?"

"Oh yeah. When I said Tina's name, her eyes turned red. I'm not kidding."

"Maybe they'll cool off in a few days," I said hopefully.

Cara shook her head. "I doubt it."

I pushed thoughts of Anna and Henry getting arrested for stalking Tina out of my head and sat down with my laptop to catch up on all of my work. Soon, I was going to have to turn the Briggs case over to Julio. I couldn't keep spending time on it when I needed to supervise all the other cases we were handling. I texted Julio and told him to prepare a presentation for our roundtable meeting on Monday. Maybe some of the other investigators could come up with a new angle.

I had emails from both Phil Eccles and Captain Grant asking for my thoughts on the Briggs investigation. There were two unspoken questions in their emails. One was if Julio could handle the case, and the other was if the case was going to blow up in our faces politically. I responded to both of them that I'd brief them in person on Monday. In this day and age, there were things that I just didn't want to put in emails, which could later be seen by prying eyes. In person, all I had to worry about was the other person going rogue and stabbing me in the back.

With my eyes burning, I closed the laptop and took a shower before bed. The hot water helped to clean out my head as well as wash my body. I decided that I'd turn the Briggs case over to Julio on Monday. I knew he would do a thorough job investigating the case, and my time would be better spent on other things. Captain Grant had admonished me for not seeing the bigger picture only a week earlier.

When I came out of the bathroom, Cara looked lovely, lounging on her side of the bed with a book.

"I'd take you where you are if I wasn't exhausted," I told her.

"And I still have a chapter to go before I find out who did it." She smiled.

I made it to bed and crawled under the sheets. The dreams came quickly, sending me into a world where I was chasing Anna and Henry, who were chasing Tina. I had almost caught up to them when Mauser came charging out of nowhere to tackle me.

"He'd be a great detective," Dad's voice said from the darkness, which irritated me because I didn't know if he meant Mauser or me.

The weekend passed by without any surprises. Cara and I saw her parents a couple of times, but still couldn't get any answers out of them. When we weren't over at the cabin, we lazed around the house or did a little work in the yard. The slow pace helped to rejuvenate me, and I went to bed Sunday night planning to make the next week especially productive.

CHAPTER TEN

For two minutes after I opened my eyes, I felt great. Then I remembered that Cara's parents were still in town, and our office was neck-deep in a death investigation that looked like it was going to be a study in frustration. I tried to conjure up the optimism and enthusiasm I'd felt when I'd gone to bed the night before, but the light of a Monday morning had stolen it all away. I rolled out of bed and hoped that a shower might perk me up. Instead, I spent the entire time reviewing all the possible nightmare scenarios that I might be facing in the coming days.

I came into the kitchen as Cara was getting up from the table.

"You looked so peaceful that I decided to let you sleep in for a few minutes." She gave me a kiss on the cheek. "I'm taking the day off to take Mom to Stone Age in Tallahassee, and some other stores she wants to visit. A friend of hers gave her a list of crystals she'd like her to pick up. And I'll continue to try getting her to talk about their plans."

"Thank you. I know asking you to keep tabs on them is putting the burden on your shoulders."

"They *are* my parents. Maybe later I'll drive them around and show them some of the sights. Try to keep them busy."

"You can remind them that Tina is doing this to me, not them." I sat down at the table with my bowl of cereal and was quickly joined by Ivy. She was always interested in my breakfast.

Cara gave me another kiss on the top of the head, then headed out the door with Alvin.

I looked at the messages on my phone and shook my head at the amount. I was just old enough to remember having a job and not needing a cell phone. When you left work, you left work. Now, electronic connectivity often felt like a physical bond. I responded to most of the messages as I finished my cereal, then headed out the door.

Our roundtable review of cases was scheduled for nine o'clock in the large conference room. Before the meeting, I assigned the weekend's reports to various investigators and managed to answer a few of the emails in my inbox. The ones requiring longer replies would have to wait.

When I walked out of my office, I was surprised to see Agent Padilla in the hall.

"Did you need to see me?"

"Never." She gave me a crooked grin. "Julio invited me to your meeting."

Julio is learning how to lead an investigation and *to play politics. Good for him*, I thought.

"Any word from Dr. Darzi?"

"He was so fascinated with the puzzle pieces that he spent part of the weekend putting the body together. He's going to do the official autopsy tomorrow, but there's already some good news. He found a piece of bridgework that could be identifiable."

"That would be better than waiting three months for the DNA," I agreed.

Shortly after nine, we were all gathered in the conference room. In addition to Padilla and our investigators, we were joined by Phil Eccles, Agent Briers from the DEA and Matti Sanderson, who was our liaison with patrol. We were scheduled to discuss multiple cases, and I'd decided to save the Briggs one for last.

Lynn Lewis, who was our chief investigator for sex crimes, presented first with a disturbing case involving several kids who had reported a man approaching them. Nothing had happened, but the suspect had acted oddly and was using the same ruse of asking the kids to help him count lampposts.

"You said he was disheveled. Could be homeless and possibly suffering from mental health or addiction issues," Julio suggested.

"Trouble is, we can't find him," Lynn said. "Most of the homeless population in the county can't stay hidden for more time than it takes to sleep off a bottle of MadDog 20/20, but this guy is like The Shadow. Three times, dispatch has sent deputies to the area he was seen in and… nothing."

"Could it be a guy pretending to be homeless?" Mick asked.

"Possibly."

"I guess you've checked Ring cameras and surveillance cameras in the area," he said.

"Of course. Nothing there either," Lynn said.

"These days, every first grader has a phone. You'd think one of the kids could have taken a picture of him." Mick wasn't very fond of the younger generation.

"How old are the victims?" Padilla asked.

"Two are ten years old, one's eleven and the oldest just turned twelve. Three are girls, while one of the ten-year-olds is a boy."

"Any chance that they're imagining the encounters?" Padilla suggested.

"Like the clown scares? I've thought of that. But we have to respond to every call with the same urgency, so I've been reluctant to label them as hoaxes."

"You'll have to play it out," I told Lynn. "Prepare a press release that says there have been reports of a man approaching children, and that the sheriff's office is asking everyone to be vigilant. Send it up the chain of command and let's see if we can get it distributed to schools and bus drivers, plus on our social media."

"Should I include the description of the man?"

"What you have is pretty weak. It could just wind up generating a bunch of false alarms targeting the homeless population," Phil said. "When you've finished with the press release, you can skip me and send it straight to Captain Grant."

I pointed to Mick, who stood up. "As most of you know, there was a shooting… well, more of a shoot*out* at a party last weekend. When deputies got to the scene, the only folks left were the victims and grieving family members. Along with the four dead were half a dozen wounded. No one will talk. They all act like bullets mysteriously came out of thin air. To be fair, these people are scared. There are two drug cartels who are eyeing Adams County. They want to expand, and they see an opportunity here since we busted up the Thompson clan.

"But this shooting gives us an opportunity. If we can arrest a number of players from both groups, it would go a long way toward stopping their expansion here. And we aren't going at this alone. The DEA has offered us a number of resources, including a liaison who's working with us full time right now."

Mick introduced Agent Biers, who walked us through a PowerPoint presentation about the two drug cartels, including the major players and the mid-level drug dealers they thought were responsible for the party shootout.

We discussed a few smaller cases, then Julio reviewed what we currently knew about the death of Davis Briggs. I saw Matti Sanderson look down at the table when he got to the part about the box of serial killer souvenirs we'd found in his home.

"So there are two investigations?" Mick asked at that point. "One into Briggs's death and an another into all the other murders?"

Julio nodded. "Right. We're handling the Briggs death investigation while the FBI is in charge of the serial murders."

"Is there anything other than the box, not that that's insignificant, that ties Briggs to the murders?" Lynn asked.

"That brings us to what happened Friday. They found Briggs's work van down in Eaton County. Underneath the van, we found a body." Julio went on to explain the condition of the corpse.

"Do you have any idea whose body it is?" Lynn asked.

Julio detailed what we knew about the FBI's missing witness and the woman who had been living with Briggs.

"I saw Davis talking to a woman a couple of weeks ago. They were having a pretty heated conversation at the Supersave. I stood by to see if it was going to go beyond a verbal altercation," Mick said.

"You knew him?" I asked.

"Sure. He helped me with a couple of hardcore addicts, got them going to rehab and AA. They were petty crooks who were stealing to feed their habits."

"What did the woman look like?"

"I can do better than that. Her name is Kelly Airlie; her street name is Airhead. She's got some of that meth-face thing going on these days. She's in her early thirties, but it's hard to tell with her living rough. Most people would look at her and think she was in her late forties."

"How'd you get to know her so well?" Julio asked.

"She's been around a while. My last run-in with her was on an auto burglary. She reached into a car parked near the courthouse and took a phone and some change. She hasn't been nailed for any other criminal activity since then."

"She was staying with Briggs for a couple of months," I said.

"That would explain that. You said she was missing?" Mick said, looking like he was holding back a grin.

"We been looking for her," Julio said.

"Apparently not too hard. She was at the Fast Mart north

of town this morning."

"Are you sure?" Julio said without thinking. Mick just rolled his eyes in response.

"Would you mind cruising around the area and seeing if you can spot her?" I asked Mick. He gave me a thumbs-up.

"So that leaves the FBI's potential witness, or possibly a person unknown, as our corpse," I said.

"I'd like to hear more about the serial murders." Phil looked at Padilla. "Might be good for all of us to learn what kind of man you think Briggs was."

Again, Sanderson looked down at the table.

"I can give you the broad strokes," Padilla offered, then went on to give the group essentially the same details that she'd already given me and Julio.

"What have you done to pinpoint the first interactions between the killer and his victims?" Lynn asked.

"Good question." Padilla sounded like a professor recognizing a bright student. "With most serial murders and rapes, there is a point when the killer must interact with his victim for the first time. This may be a quick snatch-and-grab, a con or a seduction. Snatch-and-grabs usually happen when the abduction or murder is a crime of opportunity. Signs of this could be an eyewitness or an earwitness hearing the victim scream, or marks on the body that show a struggle. Unfortunately, in our cases the bodies have been too badly burned to tell much about how they were handled before being murdered, and there aren't any witnesses. What we do have is a woman we *think* was a potential victim of our killer. She claims he grabbed her from behind at night in a park."

"But if you don't know the murderer's MO, then how do you know he was the one that attacked the witness?" Sanderson asked.

"We don't." This time, Padilla looked at her like a professor looking at a student who asked too many annoying questions. "We're going on victimology. Our witness is similar to our other victims. Sex workers or women who work alone at night. Very petite, less than a hundred and ten pounds. The other attacks probably took place in secluded areas near small towns. We think all the attacks took place at night." She shrugged.

"Either you haven't done a very good job with the investigation, or the killer is clever," Mick said.

"Clever or lucky," Padilla admitted. "I think he's clever."

"Then why kill himself? Assuming it's Briggs," Phil asked, leaning forward.

"Our assumption is that he felt like we were on his trail. We had let the media know that we had a witness. The plan was to force his hand." Padilla frowned.

"So you probably set your witness up to be killed." Mick shook his head.

"I'm not going to defend what happened. We spooked the witness. She had a checkered past that made her leery of working with law enforcement. What she didn't want was any impediment to her lifestyle, which involved sex work and regular drug use, not necessarily in that order. One of our agents thought she was getting out of line and told her we'd arrest her for all the criminal activity we'd witnessed her participating in. Naturally, she took off."

"Did you punish the agent?" Mick was on her like a tick on a hound.

"I'm not at liberty to discuss personnel decisions." She gave him a cold look that challenged him to make one more impertinent comment.

Mick just leaned back in his chair looking satisfied.

"Do you have your witness's dental history?" I asked, thinking about the bridgework that Darzi had found.

"No. I've got an agent trying to track it down now. I doubt she's seen a dentist in ten years."

"How old is she?"

"About the same age and description as the homeless woman who was staying with Briggs."

We wrapped up the meeting and everyone headed back to their own cases.

Phil walked with me to my office. "If they hadn't found the body under the van, I'd tell you to just let Julio handle the case. Unfortunately, with the body and van found in another jurisdiction, it's more complicated, even without the serial-murder angle."

"He can handle most of the details. I'll just keep an eye on the political issues and keep tabs on things when there are other agencies involved."

"Fine. Go with him if he's going out of the county."

"Julio is a good investigator," I assured him.

"I know that. I'm not worried about his work. I want to make sure he can mature in the job. It's easy to step in the manure when you're in someone else's feed lot."

"Now you sound like a farmer."

"I spent summers on my uncle's farm. Gave me a downhome perspective on people."

As Phil was walking away, I wondered if I should have warned him about my in-laws, just in case any of my worst-case scenarios played out. Instead, I decided to wait and see what happened. *How bad could it be?* I thought naively.

I was digging into my backlog of work when Julio leaned into my office.

"I got the contact information on Padilla's two suspects. I'm ignoring the third one that was in prison when Briggs died," he told me.

"She made it sound like they won't talk to you. Still, you can't get a break if you don't try."

"Are you going to the autopsy tomorrow?"

"No. I can't imagine that Darzi will be able to pull any rabbits out of his hat with this corpse. It'll be almost impossible to tell what damage was done by the killer, the fire or by moving the van. Who knew that we should have tipped over that pile of rubbish to see if anyone was underneath it?" I shook my head. "You can go if you want to. The dental work is what I'm pinning my hopes on."

"What do you think the chances are that the body we found is Padilla's witness?"

"I think the chances are good. But with this case, who knows?" I was about to turn back to my computer when I had a thought. "Come in and sit down."

"What?" Julio looked worried.

"I want to think about this. If that *is* the body of the witness, then what does it mean for the case?"

"I guess Padilla is right. Why else would Briggs kill her?" Then Julio looked thoughtful. "Now if Briggs *didn't* do it, then this whole deal was planned by the killer."

"Clever. Isn't that what Padilla said about the killer? Maybe he killed Briggs to mislead us. Figures he can do a twofer by getting rid of the witness at the same time."

"That makes as much sense as Briggs killing the witness and burning the body and the van before killing himself."

"I think if we can figure out the motive for all of this, we'll learn who the murderer is," I told him. "And a part of me doesn't think Briggs is the who."

I spent the rest of day at my desk catching up on paperwork. I was feeling good about my progress when Cara called at three.

"We've been invited to dinner." I could tell by the sound of her voice that she expected me to be less than thrilled. "Dad and Mom are making dinner for us, your dad and Genie down at the cabin."

"Ah…" I said. What I really wanted to do was go home and relax, maybe read a book or watch a movie. But I surrendered to the inevitable. "What time?"

"Seven. Do you want me to tell them that you're working late?" she asked, giving me an out.

"Nah, I'm good. I'm caught up and, barring any of the usual problems that might come up, I should be able to get home and get a shower in time so we can go together."

"That would be nice."

"Have you found out anything about their plans?" I asked.

"They're continuing to be cagey. I've only seen them like this a couple of times. When dad was a kid, his favorite TV show was *Mission Impossible*. We almost never had a TV when I was growing up, but whenever we did, he'd always manage to find a station playing reruns of the show."

"You're telling me that he's going to hang from the ceiling and dodge lasers in his efforts to seek revenge against Tina Knightly?"

"It's possible. One time, he was helping to build a commune in Arizona and the county commission tried to ban it. Dad got about five of his friends from all across the country to help him shut the commission down. The building's electricity failed, the plumbing backed up, and even the streetlights in front of the building went screwy. There was an awful stench in the building for weeks, and people couldn't even work. The commissioners made the cops try everything they could think of to catch him and his friends, but in the end, they met and agreed to a mutual ceasefire. The commune is still there, and he's treated to a hero's welcome whenever he goes to visit." Cara told the story as if reciting the legend of a Norse god. Knowing Henry, maybe in a way she was.

"We need to figure out how to call off whatever screwball plan he has," I said.

"What's scary is that Mom seems more angry than Dad. They like your dad and love you, and that's why they're so pissed. They can't stand the thought that a crazy lady with a megaphone is hurting y'all's reputation. That's an almost direct quote from Mom."

"And she can recognize a crazy lady when she sees one," I mumbled. I knew Cara heard me, but she made no effort to correct me.

We were on our way to dinner by six-thirty. We pulled up in front of the cabin where I saw Dad's van parked next to the Laursens' ancient Volvo station wagon.

The cabin looked great. Genie and Dad had painted it and landscaped around the porch. I could smell something grilling in the backyard and my stomach told me it was ready for food.

We knocked on the door and received a loud bark from inside in return. I could hear the monster dog jumping up and down on the rough-hewn cypress floor. As soon as Dad opened the door, Mauser pushed past him and threw himself against Cara and me.

"If you weren't the size of a freight train, your antics might be cute," I told him as Cara ruffled his ears.

Inside, we found Anna at the stove stirring a boiling pot of green beans. The cabin had two small bedrooms and a living/kitchen area with large windows that looked out on a deck and beyond to a sparkling pond. The sun was still bright, and we could see Henry standing out on the deck, watching over large slabs of meat on the grill.

"We'll eat inside," Genie said and gave me a hug.

"Jimmy couldn't come?" Cara asked. Jimmy was Genie's son. He lived in a group home in Tallahassee with other roommates with Down Syndrome and worked at a Publix supermarket.

Genie smiled proudly. "He's joined a softball team. They play once a week and practice twice a week. He's become a fanatic. I'm surprised he hasn't been demanding your presence at his games."

"Jimmy told me that he wasn't going to invite his brother until he felt he was good enough," Dad said, smiling. Dad loved Jimmy as a son. While I was sometimes jealous of his obsession with my four-legged brother, I was never jealous of his feelings for Jimmy. The young man was the kindest human being I'd ever met.

"I may sneak up and watch a game with or without his invitation," I said.

"They're playing a game in Gadsden County on Friday," Genie told me.

"Text me the details."

"Dinner will be ready as soon as the ribs are done," Anna said.

I went outside on the pretense of helping, though I had no real skills with a grill. My ulterior motive was to see if I could shake any information out of Henry concerning their revenge plans.

"Smells fantastic," I said, noticing that there were several husks of corn grilling alongside the ribs.

"The ribs are from the co-op's grass-fed, free-range cattle, and the corn is a hybrid that a friend in Albany developed." Henry poked at a slab. "If I'm right, these came from Paint."

"Paint?"

"That was his name. Looked like someone took a brush and slapped a stroke of white on both sides of him."

"You name the steers you're going to slaughter?" I asked, surprised.

"Name them, love them and respect them. No reason for them not to know love just because they're going to end up feeding us." Henry made it sound reasonable.

"Makes sense." I wasn't so sure, but I wanted to move on to the revenge thing. "You know, I'm surprised that you're so angry about Tina Knightly."

"Are you?" Henry gave me a skeptical look. "Then why didn't you tell us about the first attack in July?"

"Didn't come up in conversation." I shrugged, knowing he wouldn't believe it.

"If what she said was fair, then I wouldn't be mad. And if I could get our lawyer to go after her, I'd let him sue her. Unfortunately, she's lying while staying just inside the law. Makes her conniving as well as nasty." He turned the meat over and spread the slabs with barbecue sauce. "Made with our own tomatoes and honey."

If the food wasn't so darn good, I might have been annoyed at the way that he and Anna always pointed out the superiority of the co-op's food production.

"I'm not going to say that she hasn't pissed me off. What I will tell you is that anything you do will make it worse," I said.

"No."

"Tell me what you have in mind." I was trying not to beg.

"No," Henry said again. "Ribs are done. Corn should be too."

"Wait. You have to give me a chance to talk you out of whatever it is you two have cooked up."

"No." I thought he was going to leave it at that, but then he sighed and said, "If I tell you, you'd become an accessory, right?"

"Technically," I admitted.

"You're too young to remember Nixon, but he was a great one for plausible deniability." He pointed the tongs at me.

"And just how did that work out for Tricky Dick?" I asked, showing him that I remembered my history.

"He never went to jail while others did. Let's eat." He picked up a platter and loaded it with ribs and corn.

During dinner, Dad and Henry made jokes while Cara and her mom talked about mutual friends. I spent most of my time fending off Mauser, who was barely controlling his urge to leap onto the table and eat everything in sight.

"You need to get Henry to tell you what they're planning," Dad said later as I was helping him dump the coals from the grill into his fire pit.

"Tell me something I don't know. But Henry and Anna aren't going to tell anyone anything until they're ready. Trust me, Cara and I have both tried. And I've warned both of them not to do anything illegal. I don't know what we can do short of place them under house arrest in this cabin."

"When I pressed him, Henry assured me that it was like Tina's commentaries, on the edge but not over the edge," Dad said doubtfully.

"I guess that's a little relief," I said, though it wasn't much comfort. Henry and Anna regularly crossed the line of legality when it came to drugs, local ordinances and any other rule they thought was stupid. I certainly didn't trust them to know when to step back.

"Maybe they're going to lay a hex on her, or some sort of weird hoodoo spell." Dad leaned in and half whispered, "From Anna, that wouldn't surprise me."

"Just make sure that whatever they're planning doesn't involve Mauser," I said, looking at the cabin window where the Dane stood with his nose pressed to the glass, waiting for us to return.

"Heh, I had the same thought. I'll warn Henry, but he loves Mauser. He'd never put him in any danger."

I nodded, knowing that was true.

Later, Cara and I drove home, both lost in thought as the radio played Nineties music. A half moon was shining above us as we got out of the car and headed for the house. Before we got to the porch, I pulled Cara into my arms and hugged her.

"I love you, even if your parents are crazy."

"Your dad has his moments too," she said, giving me a playful kiss.

"I can't argue with that."

CHAPTER ELEVEN

The next morning, I'd been in my office less than ten minutes when I got a text from Mick Klein. *I'm at the Fast Mart north of town; got an eye your witness.*

Is she on the move? I responded.

Sleeping.

On my way.

I called Julio and filled him in. He was assisting a deputy with a domestic dispute, so I told him I'd let him know how it went with our homeless person of interest.

When I rolled up at the Fast Mart, I saw Mick leaning against the building with a coffee cup in hand. As I walked toward him, he put a finger to his lips and pointed to the side of the building. Behind the dumpster and under a hedge, a woman was curled up, fast asleep. Even over the morning traffic, you could hear her snoring.

"Good job," I whispered.

"This is my kind of wanted person. Even I can catch 'em," Mick said, grinning.

I approached her carefully. Even in the humid Florida heat, she was wearing lounge pants and a sweatshirt over another shirt. She smelled of alcohol, sweat and urine. I was tempted to pick up a stick and poke her. Instead, I knelt down beside her and shook her shoulder. With a start, she leaned up on her elbow, poking her own head on a branch of the bush she was sleeping under.

"Shit," she cursed, stumbling to her feet. I was surprised she could move that well. Then I took another look at her and realized that Mick was right. She was much younger than she looked. Her face told me that life, and all the drugs and alcohol, hadn't been kind to her.

I showed her my ID.

"Whacha want?" she mumbled through the few teeth she had left.

"What's your name?"

"Why ya pickin' on me?" She spat at the ground.

"I want to ask you a few questions about Davis Briggs."

"Never heard of him," she answered, pronouncing the words carefully and loudly.

"We've heard otherwise." I gave her my best LEO stare that was meant to convey a rejection of all bullshit.

"So what?" She looked everywhere but at my eyes.

"Did you take his wallet?" This was a calculated question to see if she knew that he was dead.

"What's he telling you? The man's a liar!"

"We want to hear your side of the story."

"Betcha do," she growled.

"What's your name?"

"Me to know, you to find out." She smiled with lips covered in sores, then looked over at Mick. "*He* knows my name."

"But I'm the one who's asking," I pointed out. "What's your name?"

"Mary Mary Quite Contrary."

"Are you always such a ray of sunshine in the morning?" Mick asked.

"Screw you!" she snarled.

"Mind if we look in your bags?"

Mick pointed to a black garbage bag and a cloth shopping bag from Walmart that where stuffed under the bush where she'd been sleeping.

"Keep your hands off of my things," she shouted, stepping between Mick and the bags.

"Do you have stolen goods in there?" he asked, leaning a little bit toward her but still leaving room in between. I had a good idea what he was trying to do.

Sure enough, he got the reaction he wanted when she reached out and started slapping at him. Gently, Mick took her arm and brought it around behind her back. By the time she realized what was happening, her hands were cuffed together. She started to howl and struggle, but to no avail.

"Too little too late," Mick said. "Drugs and alcohol don't improve your reaction times. Now let's try again. What's your name?"

Profanity flew like confetti on New Year's Eve.

"Fine, we'll do it the hard way. Jane Doe, I'm arresting you for assaulting an officer. We'll see what other charges we can toss at you if you don't start cooperating."

Mick read her rights to her while she continued to cuss him out.

"She may have been a sailor at some point in her life," he said cheerfully. "Let me guess: you don't want me to put her in your car."

I shrugged. "Go ahead. It's a loaner anyway."

Mick half dragged her over to the SUV. Normally, we wouldn't have baited her like that and then arrested her when she took the hook, but I didn't want a possible murder suspect, or at the least a witness, to get away. She might not have had a car to get out of town, but without a phone and no qualms about sleeping rough, a homeless person could be very hard to find when they wanted to be.

We took her down to the jail, which was located across the street from the sheriff's office. A search of her person and bags revealed a state ID that confirmed her identity as Kelly Airlie, age thirty-four. Fingerprinting her was like wrestling with a grumpy octopus. I could have told her that Davis Briggs was dead and the person who killed him might come looking for her, but I wanted to save that information for when she was more receptive to having a genuine conversation that didn't include quite so much foul language.

"Has cussing ever gotten anyone out of jail?" Marge Jones asked her sweetly.

A large and intimidating woman, she was the nicest guard in our department and had a special knack for getting inmates to cooperate. "Guess you'd like to see if we can get her cleaned up and out of those nasty rags," she asked me.

"That would be nice. If you can feed her and simmer her down a bit, that wouldn't hurt either."

"I'll say a prayer for her." Marge smiled at me. "You'd be surprised how often that makes a difference."

I thanked her, then Mick and I headed back across the street to the office.

I put in a couple of hours at my desk, then headed to the taco stand for lunch. As I was getting out of the SUV, I was happy to see my favorite chief of police drive up. Darlene Marks had been my partner at the sheriff's office before she quit to take the job of Calhoun's top cop. She managed less than a dozen officers, but she managed to do a lot of the work inside the city limits. When she needed extra badges, she had us to fall back on.

"Hasn't your doctor told you to cut back on the tacos?" I joked. Darlene was lean and tough.

"Listen here, wrangler, you need to watch who you're tossing a rope at. I haven't had a sunshiny morning and I'm hangry."

"Then I'll buy you lunch, and you can tell me all about it."

"That's more like it. Keep it up and I might not poke you in the eye with a sharp stick."

We went up to the van and ordered. I got a barbeque chicken taco and a side of waffle fries. The owner liked to change things up every couple of months and seldom had a misfire.

"So what has you in a bad mood?" I asked after we'd sat

down at a bench and taken the edge off our hunger.

"Politics with a side of corruption, and I am sure it's going to turn ugly."

"What's it about?"

"It looks like a certain city commissioner has been mishandling funds *and* mishandling the ladies on his staff. One of them came to me and spilled the beans. She was scared to go to HR 'cause the commissioner has ties to that office—close ties." Darlene rolled her eyes. "Of course, this is the same office that sends me my paycheck. The guy's a dick, so I'm not going to mind putting him in cuffs. Still, it's like reaching into a jar full of rattlesnakes. Odds are, it's not going to end well."

"You can reach out to the state. Let them handle it. Or even Dad," I suggested.

Darlene shook her head. "That's chickenshit. It's in my henhouse; I'll deal with it. Just don't ask me to be happy about messing up my easy life."

"We're here to help if you need us."

"Thanks, Sunshine. Are you going to eat all those fries?" Darlene proceeded to pick at my food, then asked, "What's this I hear about you dating that sexy FBI agent?"

"Now who's cruising for a bruising?" I responded, frowning. "I'm in my own pot of hot water."

"I saw the latest Tina Knightly scorcher. That woman hates your guts. By the way, why *have* you all been letting a serial killer live peacefully in our community?"

I discreetly gave her the bird and said, "You and the horse you rode in on." Then I explained about how Davis Briggs was Dill Kirby's cousin as well as friends with Matti Sanderson's brother.

"Now that you mention how this guy helped people out, I think I remember him. Older guy, medium height, bulky, brown hair?"

"Sounds like him."

"So what do you think?" she asked as she took another fry.

"There's facts that don't sit right with me. I know bad guys aren't logical most of the time, but this just seems… wrong."

"You've always been one for the feelings. Mr. Intuition, they call you."

"And they call you Iron Pants behind your back," I joked.

"I hope so." Darlene stood up and patted her butt before picking up her trash from the picnic table and heading back to her car.

At three, I got a call from Marge that Kelly Airlie was doing better and had agreed to talk to me. Julio had gone to Tallahassee to meet with Dr. Darzi, and I considered waiting for him, but settled on doing the interview alone. When I stepped back outside and got hit with a wave of hot, wet air, I decided to drive across the street rather than walk.

"She's still feisty but swears she'll be nice," Marge told me as she opened the door to the interview room at the jail. "I'll be watching on the monitor, so if she gets crazy, I'll come save you." She smiled and left me alone with Kelly.

"I don't want to talk to you," was the first thing out of her mouth as I sat down at the table.

"That's funny, because the nice guard said you wanted to talk to me."

"No." She clamped her lips tight.

I took a deep breath and wished I'd saved her for Julio.

"Why don't you want to talk to me?" I asked, trying to keep my happy face in place.

"You're a cop, and I don't trust cops."

"Fair enough. But I'm not trying to get you arrested or in trouble. If you answer a few questions, I'll see that you're released as soon as possible."

"No."

She continued to say variations on the same theme for the next five minutes. Exasperated but not surprised, I stood up. "Have a good night," I told her.

"I don't want to stay in here all night," Kelly whined.

"Then you have to answer my questions."

"No. I want Albert."

"Who's Albert?" I asked, figuring she was referring to a pet or even an imaginary friend.

"Albert, the book guy."

That got my attention.

"Do you mean Albert Griffin?" I asked, unable to imagine a link between the two.

"Mr. Albert." She nodded her head.

"How do you know Albert?"

"He's a friend, you idiot." She slammed her fist down on the table.

I thought for a minute, then said, "Okay, I'll be back soon." Reluctantly, I added, "Would you like coffee or a Coke?"

"I'd take a bottle of water and some potato chips."

I thought about telling her that my offer didn't include snacks, but there was a vending machine in the deputies' lounge. In the interest of bonhomie, I would get her the chips.

Outside the room, I took out my phone and called Albert Griffin. I wasn't surprised that I had to leave a voicemail. Mr. Griffin was in his seventies and, unlike most younger people, he wasn't attached at the ear to his phone. I followed up my message with a text, then headed down the hall to fetch the food for Kelly.

I was halfway back to the interview room when my phone rang.

"Sure, I know Kelly. Is she in jail?" Mr. Griffin asked, proving that we were talking about the same person.

"Yep. Not because we want her there. We arrested her because we need to talk to her. She's a witness and I was afraid she'd be hard to catch again."

"Like a feral cat. I understand."

"If you have time, would you be able to come down to

the jail and talk to her?"

"Of course. I'll be there in fifteen minutes."

I gave Kelly her water and chips, which seemed to put her in a better mood.

"How do you know Mr. Griffin?" I asked again.

"He's a friend of my dad. But my dad's dead."

"I'm sorry to hear that."

"Yeah." She shrugged. "Mr. Griffin's helped me out sometimes."

"He's a good guy."

"Yep."

"Did Davis Briggs help you out too?" I asked, trying to sneak a pertinent question into the conversation.

"I'm not talking to you," she said, shutting down again.

We sat in silence until Marge came to the door to let me know that Mr. Griffin had arrived. I went out to the reception area to meet him.

CHAPTER TWELVE

Mr. Griffin was tall and lanky. He was Adams County's unofficial historian and a fountain of knowledge about many things. He was usually chipper and chatty, but I could tell that a trip to the jail had affected his usual good mood.

"Sorry to bring you down here," I apologized.

"Glad to do it if it gives me a chance to see Kelly. These days, if she sees me first, she runs off."

"She said you were friends with her dad?"

Mr. Griffin nodded. "He was the maintenance man at the high school for years. A gentle, nice man, but there wasn't a single four-leaf clover in his life. His wife left him with Kelly, who had emotional and developmental issues as a child. She made it to high school, just barely, and rebelled against being labeled 'special.' Got into alcohol, drugs and boys early. Right after she turned sixteen and quit school, her father was diagnosed with cancer. He went quick. One of the last times I saw him, he asked me to do what I could to help Kelly. I'm afraid that hasn't been much. I got her into rehab years ago, which didn't take. I used to take her to the doctor and tried to get her treated for her bipolar issues. She'd be good for a few months, and then fall back into her old habits."

"Did you also know Davis Briggs?" I asked.

"Sure. And I don't believe the rumors that are going around. Can you tell me anything?"

I shook my head. "I would if I could. Hopefully, we'll know more once the toxicology results come back. Did you know that Kelly was staying with him a few weeks ago?"

"No. But I'm not too surprised. Kelly has an internal radar for nice people that she can take advantage of."

"She stole some money from him."

"You don't think she had anything to do with his death?" Mr. Griffin asked.

"I thought it was possible. But now that I've met her, I can't see it. Davis's work van was found in Eaton County, torched and with a body underneath. I think whoever was responsible for his death left the van down there."

"I'm not sure Kelly could drive a van. She's never had a driver's license."

We entered the interview room, and as soon as Kelly saw Mr. Griffin, her face blossomed into a smile that improved her looks.

"Mr. Albert! I'm glad you're here. Get me out of jail…" She paused and tried to look innocent. "Please."

"Let's talk to my friend, Sergeant Macklin, and see if he'll let you go," Mr. Griffin suggested.

"He's a cop."

"He's my friend. A good guy, you can trust him."

"Whatever." She crossed her arms over her chest and pouted.

"I don't care that you stole money from Davis Briggs," I told her.

"I didn't steal nothin'"

"Maybe you didn't. I just want you to know that the sheriff's office isn't concerned with that. When did you meet him?"

"A while ago," she said reluctantly.

"Are you talking about a year ago, or maybe a couple of months?" I prompted.

"I guess it was a couple months ago."

"Where did you meet him?"

"He hit me with his car." She looked at us defiantly, as if she expected me to challenge this statement.

"Where was this?"

"Fast Mart."

"How badly were you hurt?"

"Bad, real bad!"

"What part of your body. Arm, leg, where?"

"Yeah."

I decided to let that line of questioning drop. I didn't believe she'd been hurt at all. "What happened after he hit you?"

"He offered to help me. I just wanted some money, but he wouldn't do that. He said he could help me get sober. Not that I wanted to get sober. I could do that on my own if I wanted to."

"But you did let him help you?"

"Sure, I did. He said I could stay at his house while I got better."

Mr. Griffin leaned forward and said, "Why don't you tell my friend all about Mr. Briggs and what happened when you stayed at his house?"

"Davis was mean. He made me go to AA meetings and told me I had to stay sober if I was in his house. I told him he hit me with his car and he shouldn't have all those dumb rules. But it didn't help. He even tried to get me to see a doctor."

"I did too," Mr. Griffin reminded her.

"I'm not goin' to a doctor," she insisted.

"When was the last time you saw Davis?" I asked.

She gave me a dirty look. I knew she was thinking I was still concerned about the money.

"Davis Briggs is dead," I said, wanting to shake her up to see if that improved her attitude any.

"Dead?" she said as if hearing a foreign word.

"We're trying to figure out what happened to him," I said kindly.

"He was okay. I'm sorry he's dead." She looked contrite. "I saw him, like, maybe two weeks ago."

"Where?"

"At his house. He came back from work, and I left while he was asleep."

I could picture her walking out of the house and seeing his wallet sitting on the table, unable to resist the temptation to open it.

"How long did you stay at his house?"

She sighed dramatically. "Toooooo long. All those rules."

"Think about it. Did you stay at his house for a couple of days? A week? Two weeks?" Mr. Griffin asked.

"More than a week. Not two weeks. I could never stay that long with all the things he wouldn't let me do."

"Did you see any other people visit Davis while you were living there?" I asked.

"I guess, you know, guys from his job. Oh yeah, a couple other people. I think they were neighbors or, like, friends." She made "friends" sound like an alien concept, which it probably was to her.

"Can you remember any of their names?" I asked, and she rolled her eyes. "Think. You must have heard him call some of them by name."

"I didn't care," she said honestly.

"Did any of them argue with him?"

"He never argued with anyone but me."

"What did he argue with you about?"

"Can't drink. Can't invite anyone over. Can't have a party. The TV is too loud. Blah, blah, blah."

"Did you ever see *him* drink alcohol?"

"Ha! I wish."

I would have asked if she'd ever seen a bottle like the one that had been left on the table, but if she had known about a bottle of alcohol, she would have taken it.

"Did anyone ever ask you questions about Davis?"

"You."

"I mean before now."

"I don't like talking to people." I believed her.

"We might need to ask you some more questions. If we let you out of jail, will we be able to find you again?" I knew it was a stupid question.

"I'll be around."

I thought about suggesting that she stay with Mr. Griffin, but even if I hadn't liked the man, I wouldn't have done that to him. I doubted she was in any danger. Even if she helped us find a suspect, she'd never be able to testify.

"Okay, Kelly, we'll get you out of here," I said. "Get a good meal and rest."

"I'm ready to go now."

I knew what she really meant was that she wanted a fix or a drink… anything that would help her self-medicate.

I walked Mr. Griffin out to his car.

"How's Eddie?" I asked.

"Good. Not that I ever see him anymore. He's either working at the library or running around with Jessie."

"She should be done with the academy in a couple of months."

"Top of her class," he said with obvious pride in the young woman who'd come to mean a lot to all of us. Jessie Gilmore had had her share of problems, but she'd become laser-focused on a career in law enforcement, and she was proving all of her original doubters wrong.

"Are they, like, serious?" I asked.

Mr. Griffin just grinned and shrugged as he got into his car.

Eddie Thompson had once been my confidential informant. He'd never been as strung out as Kelly Airlie, but he'd been a serious addict who'd spent some time on the street. After he'd helped put the criminal half of his family behind bars, he'd cleaned himself up and was now living in a garage apartment above Mr. Griffin's house.

Partly as a way to deal with his tumultuous upbringing

and largely due to natural inclination, Eddie was also a crossdresser. I wondered if Jessie knew about that part of his life and, if she did, how she was handling it. But it wasn't a question I felt comfortable bringing up, and I wasn't sure I really wanted to know the answer.

I went back to the office where there were more reports to be read and to be written. I also got into a long back-and-forth between Mick and Captain Grant. Mick wanted help from patrol to track suspects from the gang shooting. However, patrol was already feeling like they were shorthanded, and they'd be running double-time because of the upcoming Labor Day weekend. We eventually reached a compromise where Mick would get the help he needed, but not until after the holiday.

Julio texted me shortly after four. *Heading back to the office. Do you want to review autopsy and your interview with homeless woman?*

Sure. I'll be in my office, I responded, then called Cara to let her know that I might be running late.

"Dad and Mom have been entertaining themselves all day," she said.

"Is this good or bad?"

"Normally I'd say it was great. Now, I'm not so sure. They're acting like the cat that swallowed the canary."

"Unless you can think of a way to draw it out of them, we'll just have to wait them out."

"You're the investigator. Can't you take Dad into a back room and slap him around with a rubber hose?" I wasn't sure if she was kidding.

"Your dad's huge. He'd probably take it away and slap *me* with it," I joked.

"Yeah. And if you ask me, I think Mom's the one who's pushing whatever crazy scheme they've dreamt up."

I was surprised to hear real concern in her voice.

"You don't think they'd do anything too crazy, do you?"

"They're acting screwier than normal."

"Do you have any idea what they've done today?"

"Dad sent me pictures of a couple of fish he caught in the pond. Nothing from Mom. Normally, they'd be all over me. I expected them to pop into the clinic, but I never saw them. When I texted and asked if they wanted to meet for lunch, I didn't hear anything back for almost an hour, and when I did, it just said: *Thanks, we have plans.*"

I was starting to feel a little nervous.

"I feel like I should call and warn Tina," I said, half seriously. "Not really. Still, if they end up in jail…"

"Sorry to pass my worries on to you," Cara said.

"That's what marriage is all about."

Julio came into my office just before five and plopped down in a chair across from my desk.

"The autopsy wasn't too bad. It was more like an archeological dig with mostly just bones. By the way, Darzi is pretty confident the body is female, but don't quote him on that."

"Could he tell anything about the cause of death?"

"Maybe this, maybe that. Between the fire and the tow truck pulling the van over the body, there was too much damage." Julio shook his head. "He did show me the pictures of the dental work. With luck, that might give us a positive ID, or at least probable ID, one good enough to run with."

"Any word from the FBI?"

"No. Padilla didn't even bother to show up. I emailed them before I went to the autopsy asking for an update, but I haven't heard anything."

"Keep on them. They'll forget we're here if you don't pester them. To be fair, they *are* working with about a dozen different jurisdictions."

"What did you find out from Briggs's houseguest?"

"That I should have let you handle her. She's a piece of work." I went on to tell him what little I'd learned from the interview.

"I've got a cousin who's like that. Sad, not right in the head and into drugs. You just wish people like that could be housed in Chattahoochee or somewhere where they might get the help they need. My cousin is good when he's on his meds, but they make him feel numb. He quits taking the pills and soon he's back on the streets."

"Any luck with Padilla's two suspects?" I asked.

"First, I followed up and made sure the third one was actually in jail when Briggs was killed."

I gave him a thumbs-up. "Trust no one."

"I've left messages with one of the others. The second one referred me to his lawyer, so now I'm playing phone tag with him."

"Let me know if you need me for anything. I know this is your case and I've been sticking my nose in it more than I should."

"With the personal connections to Dill and Sandy, and the FBI being involved, I don't mind having you looking over my shoulder. When my wife heard about the FBI, she was afraid I'd goof it up and get in trouble. She doesn't always have faith in my skills."

"I do," I assured him. "However, if I were in your place, I'd want to be able to spread the liability around."

Julio just grinned.

CHAPTER THIRTEEN

Wednesday was uneventful until about midday when Pete showed up with a big smile on his face.

"You got to see this video," he announced, holding up his phone as he barged into my office.

"Don't you have a building to rappel down or something?" These days, Pete was seldom in the office, spending a lot of his time running drills with the tactical team.

"Seriously, watch this." He pulled a chair around to my side of the desk and sat uncomfortably close to me. He hit the play button on a YouTube video and made sure I could see his phone screen. "Watch."

It took me a minute to recognize Tina Knightly coming out of an office building in downtown Tallahassee. I got a queasy feeling in my stomach.

As she started up the sidewalk, an older woman approached her and asked her for an autograph. Tina reached out and shoved the woman to the ground. For a moment, it looked like she might have regretted her actions and was considering helping the woman to her feet, but then Tina snarled and hurried away.

"She's toast," Pete chuckled. "This is already going viral."

"Do you really think she pushed an old lady down?"

"You saw the video."

"Let me see it again."

I watched carefully. The video had been shot from an angle behind the old woman. I peered closely at the screen and assured myself that the woman wasn't Anna.

"Look at Tina's hand as she reaches out. You can't really see it because of the filming angle. You never see her hand make contact with the older woman," I pointed out.

"Come on! You see how the old lady reacts. She's been pushed. I think Tina was having a bad day and didn't want to give out autographs." Pete was clearly enjoying this.

"Couldn't have happened to a better person. Still, it looks like a setup to me."

"Do you care? No one else is going to give a damn what Tina says about the incident. The video is going to speak for itself."

"It's karma," I said. *Just the type of karma that two old hippies might cook up.* Like a headache coming on, I felt a moral dilemma approaching like a runaway train.

We heard laughter from outside my office.

"Wanna bet they've found the video?" Pete asked.

"Close the door," I told him.

Once Pete was seated again, I told him about my in-laws being in town and my suspicions that they had cooked up a crazy revenge plot against Tina.

"Good for them." Pete looked me straight in the eye as he said it.

"Don't you think this smacks of vigilante justice?"

"Ahhh, but vigilante justice is still justice!" he said smugly. "Besides, you don't *know* that Cara's parents are behind this."

"If Tina didn't push this woman, then she's being tarnished by a fake video."

"Right. So?"

"Come on, fair is fair."

"My thoughts are that Tina brought this on herself. Henry and Anna don't have a mean bone between the two of them. Tina, on the other hand, is a vicious climber who will step and stomp on anyone. This time she picked on you and, through no fault of your own, you happen to have a couple of crazy hippie in-laws. You were right the first time. This video is karma. Well- deserved karma."

"I wonder who they talked into playing the fall woman. I can't believe this isn't going to come back and bite them in the ass." I wished I could have enjoyed Tina's bloody nose.

My phone rang and I saw that it was Cara. Pete got up.

"I, for one, am going to enjoy the Tina Knightly fall-from-grace show." He waggled his phone at me.

As he left my office, I answered Cara's call.

"Have you seen the video?" she asked.

"I saw it."

"Mom and Dad are behind this." There wasn't a hint of doubt in her voice.

"I figured. Have they said anything to you about it?"

"I haven't heard from them. Dr. Barnhill just showed me the video."

"We need to talk to them."

"And say what?"

"I don't know. Can't we send them to bed without dinner or something?"

"I've watched the video five times and can't stop smiling, thinking of Tina being run out of town," Cara admitted guiltily.

I felt frustrated, partly because I wanted to enjoy this moment of revenge on Tina like everyone else. But because I knew that Anna and Henry were behind it, I couldn't just laugh and let Tina sink down into the mire of social media.

I worked until five-thirty, though my mind was focused on what to do about my in-laws. When I got home, Cara met me at the door and the smell of dinner was enticing.

"Mom brought a pot of stew by the clinic. I'm heating it up now."

"Did you ask her about the video of Tina?" I asked, losing most of my appetite.

"Every time I mentioned the video, she just gave me her irritating I-know-something-you-don't-know smile."

"She's not going to be smiling if Tina slaps her with a million-dollar lawsuit." I stretched, trying to relieve the tension in my back from all the anxiety.

"I know Mom and Dad. They aren't going to worry until there's a knock on the door."

Before I could respond, I got a text from Dad: *Tina has been put on paid leave.*

It was impossible to tell how he felt about the video. Dad wasn't stupid, so he had to know that Cara's parents were behind it. I wasn't even sure if I should talk to him about their involvement. What if we got subpoenaed? It might have been better if I gave Dad the opportunity to claim some plausible deniability. I took a few deep breaths and told myself that I was catastrophizing. There was a chance Tina's reputation would suffer and then recover, and she'd just let it go. *Right,* I thought, giving myself the full measure of sarcasm the idea deserved.

"Are your parents staying for Labor Day weekend?" I asked, helping myself to stew and a couple of homemade biscuits.

"The downside to you getting your dad to let them stay at the cabin is that they're having a great time. And *your* dad likes having *my* dad around so he can drop Mauser off with him whenever he wants. So, yeah, they'll be here over the holiday."

"You would think they'd want to get out of town before the posse catches up with them," I grumbled.

"Are you working this weekend?"

"Not *this* weekend. Rumor has it that we all might be working on Labor Day weekend. At least on Saturday for the big picnic at the lake. Mick and the DEA are worried that there could be some trouble. Retaliation for the shooting at that party earlier this month."

"That doesn't sound good." I saw the concern in Cara's eyes.

"They're being cautious. The more of us there are at the lake, the less chance there is of anyone causing trouble."

I took my bowl of stew and biscuits over to the table. Cara made her own bowl and joined me.

"Any luck with the death investigation?" she asked.

"Short answer is no. For someone who was very popular, there just aren't many witnesses to what went on in Briggs's life. He had a homeless woman with multiple mental issues staying with him just before his death. I interviewed her yesterday and got nothing. All I want is to get a lead for Julio to follow. I feel bad for throwing this one on him."

"How are you getting along with Agent Padilla this time?"

"She's as frustrated as we are, so she's not putting on the usual FBI airs. There's just no hook for this case. Our best hope is if the body under the van presents us with some surprising information. If it's not the witness that Padilla thinks it is, then that would throw a minor wrench into their theory."

The rest of the evening was quiet, as I read over some reports while Cara worked on her side business, ordering supplies for local veterinary clinics and large animal vets. I was proud of how successful she'd become at saving them time, and helping them minimize the hassle of keeping up with their own inventory. She also saved them money by combining orders while managing to carve out a nice percentage for herself.

Julio called me first thing on Thursday morning. "I got Joe Fisher's attorney to agree to let us interview him."

"Great. When?"

"He's coming in at ten."

"I wonder why the attorney agreed."

"According to him, his client is innocent of the murders

and is tired of dealing with the FBI. Now that we have a dead suspect, Fisher wants to clear his name."

"I'll be there."

Bad guys and gals could fool you. Often, they thought that if they came in willingly, we'd just assume that they were innocent and believe whatever they said. Other times, they'd be guilty as sin, walk in and talk themselves right into jail, even with a lawyer present. I was looking forward to meeting Mr. Fisher.

At nine-thirty, I was preparing for the meeting when I realized that I couldn't find the file with my notes on the case. Figuring that I'd probably left it in the loaner Suburban, I walked out of the building toward the parking lot. I'd gone only a few feet when I saw Karter Greer walking toward me. I should have ignored him.

Instead, I asked, "What are you doing here?"

"None of your damn business."

"Did you forget that you don't work here anymore?"

He clenched his teeth and looked like he was thinking of taking a swing at me. A second later, his muscles relaxed and a smile creased his face.

"I know you pulled that stunt on Tina. That was a stupid move."

"You don't know anything." I almost added "you big moron" but wisely bit my tongue.

"We'll see about that."

"You and Tina are close. Word around the office is that you're working for her, so I guess it's going to eat into your spending money if she's out of a job."

"I'm a private detective now." His face lost any sign of amusement.

"Sure you are," I said in the most patronizing tone I could muster.

"You and your dad think you own the sheriff's office. I've got news for you. Both of you could wind up without a job. Guess that would eat into *your* spending money," he snarled.

"You sure are full of talk for someone who let a man get killed on their watch."

"We'll see how the lawsuit comes out," he said, furious now. He'd sued the department for terminating him. According to Dad, our lawyer was waving it off as frivolous.

Greer and I were standing on the sidewalk in front of the building, facing each other. I think we both wanted to cut the confrontation off, but that would have meant that one of us would need to yield the sidewalk to the other.

"Step aside," he told me.

"Not likely."

Just as I was beginning to wonder how long we would be standing there like the Zax in Dr. Seuss, I saw my salvation coming up behind Greer. Henry, with Mauser at the end of his leash, came striding around the building.

Greer heard them coming and I saw his face twitch. He wanted to turn and see who was behind him, but he didn't want to break the stare-down with me. A moment later, Mauser bounded into his backside, causing Greer to stumble off the sidewalk.

"Sorry!" Henry said cheerfully as Greer cursed at Mauser. "Hey, it's not his fault." Henry wouldn't have minded being cussed out himself, but he wasn't going to let Mauser get verbally abused.

I watched as Greer turned toward Henry, who straightened his back and rose to his full height. Though Greer wasn't a small man, Henry still had several inches on him. Greer seemed to consider his options for a second, then he turned, stepped off of the sidewalk and stomped on past me and into the building.

"Thanks," I told Henry.

"What's that guy's problem?"

I explained the situation with Greer, then asked Henry what he was doing there.

"Your dad is giving a safety talk at the elementary school, and Mauser is going along."

"What about you?"

"I wouldn't miss it. I love to see peoples' reactions when they see this guy," he said, rubbing Mauser's ears.

"I want to talk to you about that business with Tina Knightly."

"Sorry, I need to get Mauser inside. Your dad said we'd need to leave before ten," Henry said hurriedly, heading for the front door. I wanted to waylay him and get some answers, but then I saw a man in a polo shirt and shorts coming toward the building accompanied by a lawyer I knew.

"Later," I told Henry ominously. He gave me a backward wave over his shoulder and kept walking.

Once I'd retrieved my file, I joined Julio, Joe Fisher and his attorney in our small conference room. It was wired to record, same as our two interview rooms, and we sometimes used it when we wanted the witness or suspect to feel more at ease… or relaxed enough to make a mistake.

Once Julio explained that the interview was being recorded, we all gave our names. Fisher's lawyer was Enrico Valencia. I'd had a few experiences with him in the past and felt that he was as reasonable as any defense lawyer could be when dealing with law enforcement.

"For the record, my client has voluntarily come in to talk with you. I will add that this was against my advice. However, he is anxious to clear his name of these heinous allegations."

"You understand that we are only investigating the death of Davis Briggs and the suspected murder of an unknown person whose body was found in Eaton County," Julio explained.

"If the body was discovered in Eaton County, then why are you investigating the murder?" Valencia asked.

"We have reason to believe that the murder could have been committed in Adams County, giving us jurisdiction to investigate," Juilo said.

"In order to properly protect my client's rights, I'd like a better explanation."

Juilo looked at me.

"The body was found close to an abandoned vehicle that we know came from this county," I said. "There was an obvious connection between the body and the vehicle, and there were no signs that the murder was committed in that location."

"I see. For the record, is there any connection between the vehicle and my client?"

"No," I admitted.

"For the record, the address my client gave at the beginning of the interview has been his legal residence for over a year and remains his home. That address is not in Adams County."

"Noted," I said. I wanted to add that we were there to interview Joe Fisher, not his lawyer, but I let it go.

"Can you tell us where you were last Monday and Tuesday?" Julio asked.

Fisher leaned forward and gave us a condescending smile. "At work."

"All day, both days?"

"I work my own hours. Let me think." He leaned back in his chair, put his hand up to his chin and gazed up at the ceiling as if he were thinking hard about his answer. "I worked until ten o'clock Monday night. I'm a plumber and work emergency calls. I got another call around five in the morning. Some dickhead had broken off his shower nozzle and couldn't wait until daybreak to get it fixed. After that, I went on calls for the rest of the day."

The thought of a man with a history of violence against women and arson going around to peoples' houses in the middle of the night to fix their plumbing was disturbing. I suppressed a shudder.

"Can you provide names and contact information for the clients you saw?" Julio asked.

"I don't use a computer to do my billing." He tapped his head. "It's all up here. Guess I can come up with most of them."

"Have you ever met Davis Briggs?"

"Not that I know of."

"Have you ever heard of Davis Briggs?" Julio continued.

"Who knows? I might have worked on his plumbing. I don't keep records of everyone I work for. I've been in business for ten years. I've fixed a bunch of peoples' plumbing in that time."

"For the record," I said, "Joe Fisher's home is only fifty minutes from the home of Davis Briggs."

Valencia looked like he wanted to object, then remembered that he wasn't in court.

I took out my phone and pulled up a picture of Davis Briggs that Dill had sent to me. I turned my phone so that Fisher and his lawyer could see the screen.

"For the record, I am showing Joe Fisher and his lawyer a photo of Davis Briggs taken two months ago and given to me by Seargeant Dill Kirby. Do either of you recognize this man?"

"No," they said in unison.

"When was the last time you were in Adams County?" Julio asked.

"Two weeks ago. I had a sexy MILF that needed her drain cleaned out," Fisher said with a leering grin.

Julio ignored the innuendo. "What type of vehicles do you own?"

"Man, don't play stupid. You know what cars I got." Fisher shook his head.

"Humor us," Julio insisted.

"Waste of time, but okay. I got a car, a truck and a van. My truck is a jacked-up Chevy Silverado, and my work van is a Ford Econoline that I've fixed up for my tools. My car... Now, my car is special. A 1974 Camero. I bought it when I was in high school and restored it. Hell, I did more than restore it. I rebuilt that machine from the ground up to be the hottest chick-magnet in North Florida. Woooeee! She's sweet." His smile was predatory.

"We'd like photos of all three of your vehicles," Julio

said, keeping his voice calm and controlled.

"I'd like to know exactly what you think my client might have done," Valencia said. "From the sound of this interview, you're on a fishing expedition."

"We're looking for anyone who had contact with Davis Briggs within a week of his death. We're also looking for anyone that might have been involved in the dumping of a body and the ditching of a vehicle in Eaton County." Julio was leaning forward with his hands flat on the table. I could tell that Fisher's insolent and vulgar attitude was irritating him.

"I'm sure the FBI already has photos of all my vehicles. They've been on my ass for a year now."

"I was hoping you'd come here to cooperate," I said.

"Give them the pictures," Valencia instructed. "Like you said, the FBI already has them."

"Yeah, sure, okay. I'll email them to you when I get home," Fisher grumbled.

The rest of the interview proved beyond any doubt that Joe Fisher was an ass. Julio and I were both left wishing that we could find a reason to lock him up. Regrettably, my gut reaction was that he hadn't had anything to do with Briggs's death and that he was being honest when he said he hadn't met him.

At one o'clock, Dad called me into his office. I found him at his desk looking pensive. The big dog was nowhere in sight, so I assumed that Henry had taken him home after the school rally.

"Sit," Dad told me in a more commanding tone then he ever used with Mauser.

Unlike Mauser, I obeyed.

"I got a call from Tina Knightly's lawyer. Do you want to guess who she's hired?"

"No."

"David Thorne."

"Of course she has. That just puts a cherry on the top." I'd had several run-ins with Thorne lately, including one where his teenage son had made fools of both me and Phil Eccles. "I thought he was a criminal defense lawyer, not an ambulance chaser."

"He's apparently making an exception for Tina. He told me that she's asked the Tallahassee Police Department to look into the incident. Thorne also said that he's going to hire a private investigator to get to the bottom of the affair."

I felt a chill, wondering who that private investigator might be. "Karter Greer was here earlier. He's playing private detective these days."

"I know. I've got my eyes and ears out. And I know he has a history with Tina, so I wouldn't be surprised if he gets hired. The only reason he might not is that Thorne is too smart to buy the bullshit that Greer is likely to spout."

"You have a point."

"How sure are you that Henry and Anna are behind the video?" Dad asked.

"One hundred percent."

"I talked to the department's attorney, and we agreed that, as long as no one tries to blackmail Tina or use the video to coerce her, no laws have been broken. In a way, it's very similar to the commentaries she's been putting out about us. They smear us without being slanderous, always walking that thin line of truth."

"As much as I don't like the guy, Thorne won't do anything illegal. It's Greer and Tina I'm not so sure about."

"We need to keep our eyes out for their next attack," Dad said as if he were defending a fortress.

"Have you tried to impress upon Anna and Henry that if Tina and crew suss out who's behind the video, then they might be in danger? At least in danger of being smeared by Tina's next video."

"I'll have a sit-down with Henry. See if Cara can talk to her mom."

"Have they said how much longer they plan to stay in

town?" I asked, hoping it wouldn't be much longer.

"Just through the holiday weekend," Dad told me.

I left his office trying to piece together all the moving parts of my life. I felt responsible for the whole Tina Knightly mess. I'd picked that fight and had regretted it ever since. Greer was a different matter. He'd brought all of his troubles on himself by his dereliction of duty. The problem was that I wasn't sure Greer hadn't been pushed over the edge. He'd always been an arrogant jerk who could talk a good game, but having been shown up in front of everyone as an incompetent fool might cause him to do something stupid in a misguided effort to redeem himself.

Later, Julio called and asked if I wanted to ride over to Gadsden County and interview Ricky Hubbard, the last person on Padilla's list of suspects for the serial murders. At least he'd been the last of her suspects until Briggs came into the picture.

I looked at my calendar and realized I could do a twofer. "Would you be willing to wait until tomorrow afternoon? Then I can hang around for Jimmy's softball game."

"Sure. I've got work to do now and, according to Padilla, we don't stand much of a chance of Hubbard talking to us anyway."

I made a note to check with Genie about the time and place of the game. It would be nice to get away from work for a while and watch Jimmy play softball.

Still obsessing a bit on Tina Knightly, I did an Internet search for her name. It was immediately apparent that she was getting hammered by social media. If she hadn't played dirty with us, I'd have felt sorry for her. Even if she succeeded in proving that the video had been faked, it would take forever for her reputation to recover. If Cara's parents were behind the video, and I was sure they were, they'd done an excellent job paying Tina back for the vicious attacks she'd launched against me and Dad.

When I got home, I ran the plan for the next day past Cara. She was excited at the idea of going to Jimmy's game, so I spent the next half hour texting with Dad, Cara's parents and Julio to coordinate everything.

With that out of the way, Cara and I settled into a comfortable evening that didn't involve work for either of us. We curled up on the couch, with the cats at our heads and Alvin in between us, and watched a documentary about ghosts that had Cara spouting ideas for Halloween decorations. We drank adult beverages which led to adult behavior in the bedroom. After all of that, I slept better than I had in days. If I'd known what was coming, I wouldn't have been so relaxed.

CHAPTER FOURTEEN

It rained early Friday morning but stopped soon after the sun rose, leaving the air insufferably heavy and moist. Steam rose off the pavement as I walked into the sheriff's office.

We held another roundtable discussion that morning to review some new cases. They were all familiar, everyday crimes that everyone at the table felt like they could wrap their minds around.

The first case was a series of auto burglaries that had been committed, depending on the witnesses, either by kids, homeless people, addicts or a combination of all three. Stolen items had included spare change, electronics and other odds and ends. The reason the case was brought to the table concerned the fact that a Sig Sauer handgun had been stolen from one of the cars, giving the junior crime spree a sense of urgency. Guns stolen out of cars one day often showed up at crime scenes the next.

The second case involved a serial abuser. The man had a number of arrests for physically assaulting various other men he'd been dating or living with. Unfortunately, as was common in many domestic abuse cases, the current significant other didn't want to file charges or testify against the abuser. These days, it wasn't necessary for the victim to file charges, but we almost always needed them to testify. Lynn was seeking suggestions from the group about how to lock the man up for longer than the couple of months he'd previously served.

The last case involved a dozen hit-and-run accidents that had happened Wednesday night. All of them had likely occurred during the same two-hour span, though the damage to some of the cars hadn't been discovered until the next morning. Scrapes of paint left on the damaged vehicles indicated that the perpetrator had been driving a robin's-egg-blue car. From the extent of the damage, the driver's car was probably banged up on both sides. Mick was the lead investigator and had checked all reported stolen cars, thinking it could have been kids on a joy ride, but he'd had no luck. He'd also put out word to all of the body shops in the area, but so far no one had reported seeing a car that matched the description. Mick wanted to make sure that all patrol deputies kept an eye out. Sooner or later, the car would show up with enough evidence to point a finger at the culprit.

The rest of the morning was quiet. The only annoying thing was an email from Captain Grant letting me know that all supervisors would be required to take evaluation training in early September. I dreaded doing evaluations. Sitting across from the great investigators that I worked with and having to grade them was going to feel awkward and pretentious. I'd always felt uncomfortable being evaluated, and I was sure it wasn't going to be any better being on the other side.

Around lunchtime, Pete walked into my office dressed in full tactical gear. I was impressed again with the weight he'd lost and how strong he looked after recovering from his accident back in March. He was still a big guy, but there was less fat and a lot more muscle.

"Are we at war?" I asked as he sat down across from me.

"Feels like a war getting some of these knuckleheads to follow instructions. I've been running drills with different patrol shifts. Great guys and gals, but there are a few of them that… I worry about. Not mentioning any names, but a certain freckled-face kid has a bad habit of jamming his finger inside the trigger guard when he gets excited. He's going to shoot himself or someone else if he doesn't break himself of the habit. He isn't a gun guy, and he has a couple of kids, so he doesn't like to do dry-fire drills at the house. I told him to take all the ammo out of the gun, go out to his garage and practice drawing and moving with his finger outside the trigger guard. And I told his sergeant that I wanted him back next month and, if he hasn't improved, I'll send a note to the watch commander." Pete rattled all of this off in record time. It was obvious how seriously he was taking his new job.

"So the short answer is, you hate training deputies," I teased him.

"Are you kidding? I love it." His grin was huge. "I feel like R. Lee Ermey in *Full Metal Jacket*. I need to get myself a drill sergeant hat."

"If I recall, Gunnery Sergeant Hartman's career didn't end well."

"Don't worry. I quit before I make anyone crazy," Pete said with a wink.

"Don't you ever miss the more cerebral exercises of CID?"

"I'm not scared to go to the doctor anymore." He patted his flatter, though not completely flat, stomach. "Sarah lets me have a second piece of cake without giving me the look. The range is my home, and I have a virtually unlimited amount of ammo. Life is good."

"Glad you're happy, Rambo."

"Speaking of joy, have you heard anything from Tina Knightly?"

"Lawyers have been talking to lawyers, but Dad's confident that we're in the clear as long as no crimes have been committed."

"Does anyone know who the old lady in the video is?" he

asked.

"My guess is that she's a friend of Cara's parents. The person who uploaded the video is an environmental activist who's very wily in ways of media and the law. He claims that he was just passing by and captured the moment. That's the last I've heard."

"Sounds like you're golden. Can you enjoy Tina's comeuppance now?"

"I'm getting there," I said cautiously. "But I'm still worried about her relationship with Greer."

"Funny you should mention him. I saw him over at the jail this morning."

"What's he doing hanging around there?" I grumbled.

"According to my confidential sources, it was work for his own detective agency, which is a joke. He was one of the laziest deputies we had when he worked here. Running your own business is for type-A personalities, or least type-B. He's a D-minus on his best day."

"With an A-plus-plus mean streak," I pointed out.

"Lazy and mean," Pete said, standing up.

"I feel like he's stalking me."

"Now you're being paranoid."

"He's been giving information to Tina since he got fired, and I wouldn't doubt he's helping her now."

"I'll admit that those two working together doesn't give me the warm fuzzies. I'll keep my eyes and ears open and see if I can get a handle on what he's up to these days." Pete had one of the best grapevine networks in the county that had helped him solve many of his cases when he worked in CID. "I'm heading out to an afternoon training session for our emergency dispatch personnel."

"Are we arming *them* now?"

"I want to make sure they know what's happening on the ground when we've been called out," he responded, ignoring my joking tone. Pete was one of the most laidback guys I knew, and when he'd been in CID, he'd always seemed to take things lightly. But when it came to his new responsibilities as the trainer and sergeant over the tactical team, his attitude had become more focused and serious. Which wasn't a bad thing, considering the level of threats his team could be called out to handle in these days of mass shootings and other horrors.

"I appreciate what you do," I assured him.

"Which brings up the matter of training for CID. I talked to Phil about rotating all your investigators through the tactical team to get them up to speed."

"Up to speed for what?" I wasn't sure about anything that might infringe on my team's already large workload.

"They need to understand how the tactical team works." Pete gave me a look. "It's not like you guys don't call us out every time someone doesn't hold their hands out to be cuffed."

"Now wait a minute—" I started, feeling my face flush.

He held out his hand to stop me. "All I want is a week from each person in CID. It isn't going to kill them. If you want, I'll come in and work some cases to help manage the load."

Once I thought about it, I knew he was right. "It probably *would* be good to keep everyone's hands on the tactical side of the business. Besides, I want to see Lynn and Mick in tactical gear." I smiled at the thought.

"Hey, now, Lynn's a good shot." Pete looked at his watch. "Want to go to lunch?"

"I'm going to watch one of Jimmy's softball games in Quincy tonight, then Dad's taking us out to dinner. I think I'll just grab a snack somewhere."

"Where are you eating tonight?"

"Don't know."

"There's a place in downtown Quincy. Big Papa's Chophouse. Amazing steaks. Sarah always has seafood and says it's good too."

"I'll check with Dad and give him your recommendation," I said, though I was sure Dad would go for it. If Pete said a restaurant was good, then it was *good*.

On my way to the Fast Mart to grab a drink and a bag of chips, I kept looking over my shoulder. Maybe Pete had been right that all the buzz about Tina and Greer was making me paranoid. Just when I was ready to laugh it off, I saw Greer parked by the taco truck where I often had lunch. I couldn't convince myself that it was a coincidence.

Julio came to my office shortly before two to pick me up for our interview with Ricky Hubbard.

"I have news," he told me as I gathered my things to leave.

"What?"

"We got a preliminary ID on our body. It *is* Padilla's witness."

"Remind me of her name?"

Julio flipped open his notebook.

"Kat Fergusson, thirty years old. She had a couple of convictions for petty theft, solicitation and possession."

We left my office and headed out to his car.

"I don't know if Hubbard will be home," Julio admitted. "When I talked to Padilla, she said he's lazy when it comes to his pool-cleaning business. He has about forty regular clients and does a couple every day. Still has a lot of free time. According to Padilla, he brings women home whenever he wants, even with if his wife and kids are there."

"Sounds like an awesome guy. He and Joe Fisher ought to form a club."

It took us an hour to get to his address. It was on the north side of Gadsden County in a subdivision that looked like the developer had had big plans that never went very far. Hubbard lived in a small, ranch-style home on an acre of land. The yard was a week overdue to be mowed and filled with toys, half of them broken. In the driveway was a minivan that looked like it hadn't moved in at least a year, and a light green panel van with "Hubbard's Pool Cleaning" printed on the side.

Julio parked in the driveway, blocking both vehicles. We got out and headed for the front door. *The house could use a paint job*, I thought as I stepped around a plastic toy lying on its side. We could hear a TV playing inside.

I gave Julio the honor of knocking on the door, but there was no answer. He tried the doorbell, which didn't seem to work, then knocked louder. Finally, the TV's volume decreased, and we could hear footsteps from the other side of the door.

"What?" called a man's voice.

"Sheriff's office. We'd like to have a word with you," Julio said. I approved of the ambiguous use of the term "sheriff's office," leaving Hubbard to assume that it was the local sheriff's office.

"What do you want to talk about?" he asked, still keeping the door closed. I couldn't hear any concern in his voice.

"Open the door and we can talk," Julio said.

"Go away and we can *not* talk."

"We can talk to your wife." Julio gambled that this might worry him and apparently it did. The lock turned and the door creaked open.

The man looking out at us was in his late thirties or early forties, with a scruffy, unshaven face and blond, shoulder-length hair. He looked like a beach bum. I also noticed that his nose and the whites of his eyes were red. The smell of beer sweat confirmed that he'd already gone through his share of alcohol.

"Bringing the wife into it is low," he said. "Let me guess: some bitch is accusing me of taking advantage of her. Bet she's forty pounds overweight and dresses like a slut."

Julio ignored the comment and asked, "Are you Ricky Hubbard?"

"You bring up a good point. Let me see some ID," he shot back.

Julio and I took out our badge holders and held them up.

"Adams County?" he asked, puzzled.

"Are you Ricky Hubbard?" Julio asked again.

"What's this about?" Julio and I just stared at him. Finally, he said, "Yeah, I'm Ricky Hubbard. What's this about? I haven't been to Adams County in months."

"Do you know a man named Davis Briggs?" Julio asked.

"Ohhh, so that's what this is about." He pretended to peer around past us. "Where are the damn FBI suits? Why are you coming to me now that you have the killer?"

"Have you ever met Davis Briggs?"

"How the hell would I know?" He took a breath and appeared to get control of himself. "If I did, I don't remember. Did he have a pool? Like I said, the last time I was in Adams County was for a client I had over there. An old guy and his wife had a pool. I think the wife liked to watch me clean it 'cause as soon as she died, he canceled the account."

"Where were you on Monday and Tuesday of last week?" Julio asked.

"Here or working. First, you all think I killed a bunch of women, and now you think I killed the guy that killed a bunch of women. Who do you think I am?" He shook his head and gave a short laugh. "I shouldn't be talking to you except that I can't see how even you could pin this on me."

"Do you have any witnesses to where you were on those days?"

"Sure. Some. I guess you can do all your electronic GPS stuff on my car and phone. I'll give you a clue. You are absolutely barking up the wrong tree on this one. I never heard of this Briggs guy until I saw he was dead on the local news and that the FBI thought he was some kind of serial killer."

His phone rang and he yanked it out of his shorts. He listened for a minute before disconnecting the call.

"Sorry. That was the school letting me know that there's a problem with my kid's bus and I'll need to pick him up. Third time it's happened, and they've only been in school for two weeks."

Julio took out his card and handed it to Hubbard.

"Email me a list of where you were and contact information for anyone who can give you an alibi. If you have any questions or think of anything that might help us in our investigation, please call me."

"I send you the list and then you get off my back, right?" He started to push the door closed and Julio stuck his foot in the way.

"We may need to ask you more questions."

"Sure, we'll make a date of it. Dinner, a movie and more questions. Call me any time." With that, Hubbard put more pressure on the door and Julio pulled his foot back. The door closed with a bang.

"Charmer," I said as we headed back to the car.

"I hate to say it, but he seemed honest about not knowing Briggs," Julio said.

"As much as I'd like to toss the guy in jail, I agree."

We headed over to the public park where the softball game was to be held.

"So we've pretty much eliminated Padilla's suspects regarding the death of Davis Briggs. And we've identified the body under the van. Where does that leave us?" I asked.

"Either Briggs killed himself, or someone in his inner circle did it and also killed the witness," Julio suggested.

"That's how I see it. The theory that he killed himself is quick, clean and ties up loose ends in a serial-murder case. But if someone close to Briggs is responsible, then that opens a can of worms. Who? Why?"

"They killed him to pin the murders on him and to get the heat off of themselves," Julio said as if it were obvious.

"That's possible. And they put that box of souvenirs in his bedroom knowing it would be found," I mused.

"I need to go back to the people in Briggs's inner circle."

"There is an even crazier theory," I suggested. "Someone wanted to kill Briggs, and somehow had access to that box of trophies and the body of Kat Fergusson. They threw all of that into the mix just to confuse the investigation into Briggs's death."

"But that theory would require someone to have a motive for killing him," Julio pointed out.

"Which seems unlikely from everything we've heard about him. You might want to do a check on his finances. Maybe he gambled and owed a mobster money. Or had a relative leave him a fortune and someone else wants to claim it."

"This all sounds farfetched."

"And that's why everyone is going with Briggs being the serial killer. It's the Occam's razor explanation." I didn't like it, but it was starting to look like the only explanation that made any sense.

Julio dropped me off at the park, where I found a bench in the shade to wait for Cara. Forty-five minutes later, she showed up with a kiss and a cold drink for me. Both were appreciated.

We moved to the bleachers by the ballfield. My face burst into a grin when I saw Jimmy, wearing his team uniform and with a sparkle in his eye. The joy he got out of life was refreshing.

Dad and Genie joined us as we watched the two teams warm up before the game. The teams were made up of men and women with developmental disabilities who lived in group homes in the area. They threw, hit and caught balls, reassuring and cheering each other until the coaches and umpire signaled that it was time to start the game.

"You don't see college or professional players put this much heart into the game," Dad said.

"Or practice sportsmanship like these players do," I said, watching as opposing players helped their opponents to their feet and even encouraged them as they rounded the bases.

The game was scheduled for five innings. As the last one started, I needed to use the restroom and excused myself to make my way down from the stands. The bathrooms were in a small, unpainted block building not far from the field.

When I came back out, my eye caught a quick flash of movement at the tree line on the edge of the field. I looked closer and saw a man moving into the woods. I was almost positive that it was Karter Greer. *Is he really stalking us?* I wondered.

Trying to convince myself that I hadn't really seen what I thought I saw, I found myself moving toward a point in the woods where I might have a chance of intercepting the man. My clothes were soaked with sweat by the time I reached the woods. I stopped, looked and listened, but saw and heard nothing.

I spent another fifteen minutes crisscrossing through the trees and underbrush. By the time I gave up and headed back toward the ballfield, I was a mess and my clothes were filthy.

"Did you have to go in the woods like a bear?" Dad asked. The game had ended, and they were coming out of the stands as I reached them.

I pulled him aside and whispered, "I thought I saw Greer."

He gave me his *Should-I-believe-you?* look. When I nodded, he asked, "Can he be that far off his rocker?"

"Who?" Cara asked as she and Genie came up behind us.

Dad sighed and looked at me. "If you're right, then it's best that they know about it. Karter Greer, the deputy I fired this summer, has been working with Tina Knightly and seems to be coming a bit unhinged. Larry thought he saw him over by the woods just now."

"He's watching us?" Genie asked, her voice uncertain.

"It might be nothing," Dad said, trying to be reassuring and then screwing it up with his next comment. "The man fancies himself as some kind of private detective. Trouble is, he has judgment and anger issues."

"Great." Cara frowned.

"Let's not get too worried about this," Dad said. "We'll grab Jimmy and head to the restaurant."

Big Papa's Chophouse was everything Pete had said it would be. I had a twelve-ounce skillet steak that was tender and perfectly seasoned. We grew quiet when the food arrived and ate steadily until all of our plates were clean. The owner of the restaurant, clearly taking pride in his food, walked around and talked to the diners. With food like that, he could be confident of receiving rave reviews. We didn't disappoint him.

Cara had to poke me once as I drove home through the darkness. Between the food and the hot weather, I had to work to keep my eyes open.

I was getting ready to hit the bed early, already anticipating the cool sheets and soft pillows, when my phone rang. It was Julio. With reluctance, I answered.

"I heard a call go out over the radio about a hit-and-run out by the interstate. When I got here, turns out the victim is one of the guys from Sunshine Industrial Painting."

"Dead?"

"Almost instantly, judging by the injuries."

"Anyone see the accident?" I asked.

"No. It's a dark corner of the side road behind the truck stop. We're pulling CCTV footage now. They may have caught the vehicle coming or going, but from the spot where the victim was hit, I can't see any cameras that could have caught it."

I sighed and looked longingly at my bed. "I'm on my way."

CHAPTER FIFTEEN

It had been raining near the interstate, and even though it had stopped by the time I got to the scene, a blur of flashing red and blue lights reflected off the wet concrete. There were two highway patrol cars, a fire engine, Julio's unmarked car and one of our patrol cars. The vehicles were angled so that they blocked the body from view. The accident had happened on a service road that ran parallel to the interstate and never got much traffic. I parked near Julio's car and quickly found him.

"Whoever hit him was going at a good clip. The car did a number on him," Julio told me. "The coroner's office is sending someone, and Shantel is on her way now."

"Have you called Padilla?"

"I wanted to check with you first."

"Do it. She needs to be kept in the loop, but I'm not letting her take over this case. We don't even know if it has any connection to Briggs's death, let alone the serial murders."

Julio pulled out his phone as we walked past the fire engine, which was there mainly to present a highly visible roadblock while we processed the crime scene. The firemen always liked to get their engines out of the garage and drive them around. At least that's what it looked like from the blue side of the line.

"She seemed interested, but not eager to stick her nose into this death," Julio reported after talking to Padilla.

"Do we know who the victim is?" I could see that the bloodied body was wearing Sunshine coveralls, so I assumed that's how they had known he worked for the company.

"Not yet. He's not one of the guys we interviewed. I was hoping you'd recognize him."

"Who reported the accident?"

"A truck driver. He was here when I got on scene. I got his contact information, took pictures of his truck and let him go. There wasn't any damage to the truck at all."

The body was approximately three feet off the road on the gravel shoulder. Twenty feet away, Julio had set out orange cones at the point of impact, which was clearly marked by pieces of plastic on the ground and a lot of blood. Even from a distance, the amount of damage that had been done to the body was clear, but I was still able to identify him. It was Colson Holloway.

"This wasn't done with a Smart car," I said.

Sergeant Will Toomey, the department's chief vehicular homicide expert, looked up from where he'd been measuring marks on the road.

"I'd say it was a truck, maybe even one that's been jacked up. The victim's stomach and chest took the brunt of the impact... not that I'm a pathologist."

"I trust your judgment when it comes to man versus machine." I turned to Julio. "Do you remember Joe Fisher saying he had a jacked-up truck?"

Julio nodded and pulled up a picture on his phone and held it out to me. "This is the photo he sent."

"Nice that he followed through on our request. I doubt we could be so lucky, but just to be sure..." I called dispatch and asked them to work on putting a deputy's eyeballs on Fisher's truck. The vehicle that had done this was going to have some damage.

"Accidents like this are never pretty," Toomey said, joining us on the edge of the road. "I can tell you that the driver didn't put his brakes on. There are no skid marks. Even with the wet surface, I'd have expected some evidence if he'd tried to stop. You can see that the impact point was a foot or two off the pavement, and the vehicle tossed gravel onto the road. I'm confident in saying that the victim was standing just off the road when he was hit."

"Could the driver have hydroplaned into the victim?" I asked.

"I'd check the weather for that time, but I don't think the rain was that heavy. It was more like a shower, and we've been having regular rain in the afternoon anyway, which would keep the roads clear of any oil buildup. Also, it's pretty clear that the victim was taken out by the front bumper of the vehicle and not the side."

All of the streetlights from the exit, the truck stop and the nearby industrial park cast a sulfurous glow over the landscape. I looked from the body to the cluster of businesses in the park that included Sunshine. The distance was about a hundred yards, and a rough gravel drive led from the body to the buildings in the distance. I could see a few cigarette butts and pieces of litter just off the road.

"Looks like people sometimes come down here to wait for a ride," I observed.

"I guess that would save the person picking them up from having to go through the industrial park," Julio said.

"According to what we know about Holloway's schedule, he'd have been going to work, not getting off," I pointed out.

"Plus, doesn't he have his own vehicle? Why would he have been waiting for a ride?" Julio asked.

"If you want to stay here, I'll go up to Sunshine and—" I started to say, but I was interrupted by voices coming toward us.

We looked up to see several people walking from the industrial park. They were using the flashlights on their phones to help them navigate the path. As they got closer, I recognized Joey Zavala, the owner of Sunshine, followed by Doug Sanderson, Kian Burch and Wayne Bauer.

"We saw the lights. What happened?" Zavala called out to us from about fifty feet away.

"Stop where you are!" Julio instructed.

Keeping our flashlights pointed closely at the ground, we walked carefully toward them, not wanting to disturb any potential evidence.

Doug Sanderson suddenly caught sight of the body, screamed and ran toward it. I was just able to intercept him. "You need to stand back," I told him.

"That's Col!" Doug's voice was high and near hysteria. "Where's the ambulance? You have to help him!"

"I'm afraid he's beyond help," I said, holding him in a bear hug as he struggled to break loose.

"I don't understand." Zavala sounded confused.

"Mr. Holloway was struck by a vehicle and killed," Julio told him.

"All of you, stop and listen to me!" I said loudly to get their attention, one hand still holding Doug's arm in a firm grip. "Don't text or call anybody. Colson's family deserves to hear about it in person and from law enforcement. If y'all start spreading the news, rumors will start flying. Is that clear?"

The group nodded their heads.

"What was he doing down here?" Zavala asked.

"We were hoping one of you could tell us that," I answered.

"He was up in the shop an hour ago," Zavala said. "His van is still behind the building where he was loading it for tonight's job."

I saw Shantel pull up in the crime scene van and park behind the firetruck. The firemen were starting to look a little bored. I let Julio continue the questioning while I did my best to comfort Doug, who was crying softly and clearly in shock.

"Did you notice anything odd about his behavior tonight?" Julio asked.

"He was just normal Col," Zavala said.

"Did you see him talking on the phone?"

"Everyone talks on their phones," Zavala snapped, then said more quietly, "I guess, yeah, maybe… I mean, what the hell is happening here? Two of my employees are dead in less than a week." He didn't sound as hysterical as Doug, but it was obvious that his nerves were near the breaking point.

"Would you like me to call your sister?" I asked Doug. Knowing he had a substance abuse problem, I wasn't going to leave him without someone to support him.

"Yeah, yeah, please." Doug wiped at his eyes. "I can't handle this. Davis was my best friend. Now Col. This is crazy." His voice was weak, and I could feel him trembling.

I took out my phone and called Sandy, who wasn't on duty that night. I briefly explained the situation, and she was hitting the door before we finished talking.

"She'll be here in fifteen minutes," I told Doug.

"I got to sit down."

He leaned into me as his legs gave out. I eased him down to the grass embankment.

"We're going to need any footage from security cameras inside and outside your business," Julio was telling Joey Zavala.

"Whatever you need. Was this an accident?" Zavala asked.

"We can't be sure of anything right now. That's why we're covering all the bases. What we *do* know is that the driver left the scene."

"Why would someone leave him on the ground all… bloody and broken?"

"Did he mention meeting anyone this evening?" Julio raised his voice so all four men could hear him. No one answered. "Did he ever get picked up or dropped off by anyone?"

"No." Wayne Bauer stood up. "But I did think he was

acting nervous this evening."

Julio stepped closer to him. "How so?"

Bauer looked thoughtful. "Normally, he's kind of in your face. Jokes around, that sort of stuff. Nothing crazy, just being a guy's guy, ya know? Tonight though, nothing. He was just doing his thing, getting his van ready. I didn't think anything about it 'cause he wasn't bothering me."

"Did you see him on his phone?" Julio asked.

"I don't know. Like Joey said, everyone's always on their phone. I guess he was looking at it." Bauer shrugged.

Shantel walked up with one of our interns following behind her and lugging all the gear. Julio led them to the body while I took over questioning the group.

"Do any of you ever come down the hill to meet people?"

"I have." Kian Birch half raised his hand. "My roommate used to drop me off and pick me up when I first started the job. Meeting him down here was quicker than him driving through the industrial park. Plus, I could come down here and vape and look at my phone. You know, without being at work."

"I've had other employees do that," Zavala said. "And I know that employees of some of the other businesses in the complex have too. At one time, there was talk of getting a bus stop out here."

Julio left Shantel and the intern to document the scene. Then Sergeant Toomey waved to both of us.

"I've got measurements of everything that I can see right now. I've talked to Shantel about what photos I'll want. I took some, but she's a lot better at it than I am, especially at night. I'll come back out in the morning and look at the scene by daylight."

We thanked him, and then he drove off in his patrol car. The exhaust from his engine had barely cleared the air when the coroner's van pulled up and Linda, Darzi's assistant, got out. I went to talk to her while Julio returned to the group of Sunshine employees.

"What have you got now?" Linda asked. She was perpetually in a good mood. I couldn't understand how she or Darzi could look on the tattered remains of human beings day in and day out and still keep a positive attitude about life. On the other hand, they might have had similar thoughts about me, having to deal with the living, breathing bad boys who made the messes that they had to document.

After I explained, she said, "You're making it easy for us on this one. You already have as good a time of death as we could ever give you. You even have a good idea of the cause of death, if not all the gory details. This is boring, not a bit of mystery."

"You want to try and figure out who committed the crime?" I asked.

"Sorry, that's your job. We clean up the bodies and you jail the bad guys. It's a fair division of labor."

"I don't think so. You never have to chase a corpse."

"And you don't spend time with your hands elbow-deep in someone's chest cavity."

I held up my hands. "You win. If we keep playing this game, I'm going to throw up."

"Softy." She punched at my stomach, causing me to flinch.

Julio came up to me and pointed back toward Joey Zavala and his employees. "I'm going to herd them back up the hill. Is there anything else we need from them except the security footage?"

"No. If we have more questions, we know where to find them. I'll stay with Sanderson until his sister shows up. Have you put out a BOLO for a vehicle with front-end damage?"

Julio nodded. "Including the fact that the vehicle is most likely a truck with at least one broken headlight."

Linda started assembling her gear so she'd be ready when Shantel and her intern finished taking their photos and videos. I left her and went to sit in the wet grass in front of Doug. He had his head between his knees.

"Were you good friends with Col?" I asked, keeping my

voice as soft and soothing as I could.

"Maybe. I… worked with him sometimes. He's a… was nice enough to me. I got the feeling some of the other guys were standoffish 'cause of my being a recovering addict. Not Col. He treated me just like he treated everyone else." He looked up at me. "What's happening? Who's doing this to us?"

"We're working hard to figure that out. Tell me about Col and Davis. How did they get along?"

"Okay. Davis was kind of quiet and Col was loud, so they weren't real compatible. They were friendly. Still, neither one would stay in the other one's space if they didn't have to."

I saw his sister pull up in her personal car, a blue RAV4 that looked washed-out under the sodium-vapor lights. Sandy got out and walked quickly in our direction.

"Your sister's here," I told Doug, who wiped at his eyes and looked up.

Sandy knelt beside him, and I got out of her way so she could tend to her brother. She took his hand and talked to him gently, reassuring him that he wasn't alone. Working for the sheriff's office, I'd seen the full spectrum of sibling relations. It was heartening to see a relationship that seemed genuinely caring and supportive.

For the next few minutes, I watched as Shantel and the intern finished with their work. Shantel had dropped several markers as she took pictures of the various spots on the road, the blood, the body and pieces of debris that might or might not be related to the incident.

When they were done, she walked over to me.

"I saw some evidence that might be important." She flipped through the pictures and pulled up the one she wanted, then turned the camera's screen toward me. The image showed several pieces of plastic on the ground. They were blue and shiny. "This looks like pieces of a phone to me."

"Did you find the phone?" I asked.

"I don't think it's there unless it's under the body, which

doesn't seem likely."

"Wow. If that's true, then whoever hit him stopped long enough to pick it up. Or someone else came along and picked it up, and that's just a disturbing thought."

Julio had come up beside us and heard the details.

"If it was the person who hit him, they might have wanted the phone to keep us from seeing who he was meeting," Julio suggested.

"This is beginning to sound premeditated. So who did it and why?"

"If Briggs was murdered, then did the same person kill Holloway?" Julio asked.

"Crazier and crazier," I mumbled, trying to see the hook.

Why had someone killed Davis Briggs? Had *he* been the serial killer, or was the person who killed him the killer? And had that same person killed Colson Holloway? But why kill either of them? If the killer had murdered Briggs in order to divert attention from themselves, then why add Holloway to the hitlist and risk exposure? None of it made any sense.

I looked at Julio, whose face reflected the same confusion that was clouding my thoughts.

"I think I want to go back on patrol," he said, shaking his head.

"We'll get to the bottom of this," I assured him.

"I need to look at this differently. In my mind, I keep wandering down different paths, but each one branches off into more paths. Nothing takes me to the answer."

"I think of murders as puzzles," I told him. "When the puzzle isn't making sense, it's because you don't have all the pieces."

"Footwork and talking to people," Julio said.

"Exactly! That's how you gather the pieces."

"The missing phone is a piece."

"We can pull his phone records," I said.

"The vehicles are pieces. First is the burned-out van. And now we have whatever vehicle was used to kill Holloway."

"I have a feeling we'll soon find a truck burning in the

woods somewhere," I said grimly.

"I can put out an alert for smoke in wooded areas, here and in the surrounding counties."

"Good idea. If the firefighters get there soon enough, there's a chance that we might be able to preserve valuable evidence."

Julio got on his phone to Marti in dispatch. Marti would prepare a bulletin and make sure it got into the hands of the right people in all of the different agencies that could be involved, including the state fish and wildlife commission and the U.S. Forest Service.

"You can tell them that we would expect the vehicle to be burned within the next twenty-four hours," I told Julio.

Once Shantel and the intern finished collecting whatever items on the ground might prove to be actual evidence versus roadside garbage, I waved to Linda.

"You can examine the body."

I followed her over to Holloway's remains. With gloves on, I went through his pockets. In one of them I found a brand-new iPhone. When I tilted it, the screen lit up, revealing a lock screen showing a band that I didn't recognize. We'd need our IT guy, Lionel, to break into this phone without the password.

My brain thought "this phone" because I was thinking about the pieces of the other phone Shantel had found. Had Holloway been holding that phone when he was struck, or were the bits of plastic simply pieces of some other phone that had met its end on the side of the road as punctuation to an argument in a passing car?

Everything else in his pockets was standard: keys, wallet with cash and ID, the remains of a joint. The examination of the body didn't take long, and it was soon in the back of Linda's van.

"The autopsy on this one is going to run more than a couple of pages, what with Dr. Darzi describing all the broken bones and internal injuries," Linda told me.

"What we want is anything that will help identify the

vehicle."

"We'll look for paint chips or any other cross-contamination. On top of that, we'll make you a nice 3D virtual model of the shape and size of the object that hit him, then all you'll have to do is match it to a particular make and model of vehicle. The modeling could go a long way in court when you find the driver." Linda took her job seriously and had aspirations of being one of the great forensic pathologists. I'd heard that she'd lobbied for her current job just so she could work with Dr. Darzi.

I walked back over to Julio and held up an evidence bag with the phone in it. "Guess what our victim had in his pocket."

"So are the pieces of plastic Shantel found from a phone or not?"

"Are they from his *other* phone?" I asked with raised eyebrows.

"Burner?"

"Maybe he was using a burner to arrange a meeting, but then the person he was supposed to meet comes here and slams him into next Tuesday." I shook my head. "Burner phones could mean drugs or sex trafficking."

"Whoever it was might have seen us and the FBI around Holloway's house or Sunshine Industrial Paint. Maybe they got worried he was going to get caught and might talk, so they ran him down," Julio suggested.

"Which means that this death might be completely unrelated to the Briggs case."

"Did I tell you that I'm putting in for a transfer? This case is making my head hurt."

"We're heavy on theories and light on evidence." I pointed up to the industrial park. "Zavala or one of the other employees might know something they're not telling us."

"I want to get to his house and take control of his electronics. There's probably a trail there."

"We also need to notify his ex and ask her a few questions."

"I'll take the employees if you want to seize his computer and seal off his house," Julio offered.

"You just don't want to write the request for the warrant," I chided him. When Julio had first come to the department, he'd been grilled over his poorly written reports. Finally, the watch commander had talked him into taking some classes at the local community college. Since then, his writing had improved, but not his enthusiasm.

"We can flip a coin," he said.

"If I really didn't want to do it, I'd just pull rank. I'll handle it, and I'll talk to the ex as well. Though I don't like doing notifications, and just 'cause it's his ex doesn't mean it's going to be any easier."

CHAPTER SIXTEEN

I drove over to Sunshine and got the home address of Colson Holloway's ex-wife from Joey Zavala.

"He and Mia have been divorced for a couple of years. He went through a tough time during the breakup. For a while, when he came into work, you never knew if he was going to be angry or withdrawn. Once they had all the paperwork done and had figured out how to share the kids, his mood improved. He got to where he could talk about her, and even be in the same room with her, and not get angry or depressed," Zavala told me.

The address he gave me matched a very nice house on the east side of the county. I was surprised and wondered what Mia Holloway did for a living that allowed her to afford a house at least three times larger than the one where her ex-husband lived. But when I got out of my car, I noticed that there were two mailboxes, and that the driveway led around the side of the large, Federal-style brick home. I followed the drive to a garage that someone had spent quite a bit of money converting into a nice apartment.

It was almost midnight, but the lights were on inside and I could hear the sound of a TV. Knowing that there were kids inside, I knocked softly, hoping I'd be heard. When that brought no response, I knocked a little louder and heard the volume on the TV go down.

Mia opened the door and looked at me suspiciously. She was a petite woman with dark hair and strong green eyes. The tank top she wore showed off her two full sleeves of tattoos. One arm featured unicorns and dragons, while the other had a darker theme of witches and occult symbols. These weren't cheap tats but works of art that had taken someone many hours to complete.

"What?" she asked.

I held up my ID. "I need to talk to you about your ex-husband. May I come in?"

She looked over her shoulder as if expecting to see one of her kids standing there.

"I guess." She waved me inside, then picked a clicker up off the couch and muted the TV. "What's he done?" she asked, as if not surprised to see a cop at her door.

"I'm afraid he's been killed."

It was clear from the look on her face that this wasn't what she'd been expecting me to say. She was obviously shocked, but didn't seem either happy or devastated by the news. "Killed? How?"

"Hit and run."

"Wow. I… I don't know what to say."

"Does he have any other family in the area?"

"No. There's extended family, I think. Maybe some cousins, but I don't think he ever met them." She put her hand to her mouth. "Oh… of course, there's our children. Wow. I…" She sat down on the edge of the couch.

"Sorry. I just realized that I have to tell them their father is dead. When you told me he was killed, I was just thinking about myself. We've been divorced for a couple of years and—this may sound strange—we weren't real close even when we were married. Since then, we've become like friendly strangers. Don't get me wrong though, he's great with the kids."

"I'd like to ask you a few questions, if you don't mind."

She shook her head. "Please, go ahead."

"Do you know if he had any enemies?"

"Col? That's a funny question." She looked at me and frowned.

"Why is it funny?"

"He didn't have a lot of friends *or* enemies. He stuck to himself when he wasn't working. He liked his job with Sunshine."

"So there's no one he had issues with?"

"Oh, don't get me wrong. He got mad at people. Especially, like, if a tool broke or maybe one of the kids' toys, and the store wouldn't make it right. He had a temper. Not that he, like, got into fights or anything. He'd just fume about it for days. I don't remember him ever talking about someone being mad at him."

"I want you to think about this next question carefully. I also want you to know that I'm not on the hunt for anyone but the person who killed Colson."

"You make it sound like whoever hit him did it on purpose. When you said he'd died in a hit and run, I figured you were talking about an accident?" she said, one eyebrow raised.

"We don't know exactly what happened. For the sake of the investigation, it's best if we assume that the person hit him on purpose. Has he ever been involved in anything illegal?"

"Like what? Are you talking about drugs?"

"Drugs or maybe a theft ring. He *did* have access to various homes and businesses."

She gave me a disdainful look. "If he did, then I don't know what he did with the money. He got by, but there were times he struggled to come up with the mortgage or insurance payments."

"Did you ever think he was hiding anything?"

She looked down at her hands.

"I'm not trying to get anyone in trouble or make your ex-husband look bad. All I want to do is find the person who killed him," I assured her.

"He had a second phone," she admitted. "By the time I found it, we were already in the process of getting a divorce, so I didn't see the point in rubbing salt in the wounds. I assumed he had a girlfriend."

"Did you look at any of the numbers on the phone?"

"I flipped through them. No one I recognized. In fact, there weren't any names on any of the numbers."

"Did he ever use drugs?" I asked.

"He smoked the occasional joint, but never anything more than that. Col liked to be in control."

"Did he ever talk about a man named Davis Briggs?"

"He worked with him. Oh!" Her eyes opened wide. "I heard he'd died and… the FBI thinks he was a serial killer. But if he's dead, how could he have killed Col?"

"He couldn't have killed Col," I said obviously. "However, with two suspicious deaths involving the same small business in less than a week, we have to consider the possibility that they're connected. Do you know if Col and Davis were friends?"

"We really haven't talked much about anything other than the kids in a long time. He probably mentioned Davis a time or two, but my memories are vague. I'm sorry." She was wringing her hands. "I don't know how the kids are going to take this. Do you think there will be much about it on the news?"

"Who can predict the news and social media these days? I think it's safe to say there will be some interest in his death. Was anyone else close to Col?"

"My kids, but they wouldn't know anything about his friends. They're only six and eight. Please don't question them," she pleaded.

"Only if it's absolutely necessary, and right now I don't anticipate that. Is there anyone else you can think of who might have known him well? Mother or father? Siblings?"

"I've already told you. There's really no one. His parents died when he was young, and he didn't have any brothers or sisters."

"We're going to want to search his house. Any chance you have a key? That will save us having to break through the door."

She nodded and walked over to a bookcase by the door. Picking up a set of keys, she took one off the ring and handed it to me. "How can I get it back?"

I gave her my card. "You can call me anytime. And if you need anything. We have victims' advocates that can help you line up counseling for yourself or your children, if you need it."

I left her trying to figure out how to explain their new reality to her children and went back to the Suburban. I texted Cara not to wait up for me, than checked on the request for a warrant to search Holloway's house that I'd submitted before leaving the accident scene. It had been approved, so I called Shantel and asked her to meet me at the house.

"If I'd have known how much trouble you were going to be, I wouldn't have coached you so much when you were a squeaky-clean new deputy," Shantel grumbled as she got out of her van.

We both donned full PPE before going inside the house. Even though this was not where Holloway had been killed, we still needed to take precautions since there was no telling what we might find inside. If, at some later date, we had a suspect who claimed he'd never known Holloway, but we'd found some of his DNA inside the house, it would poke a few holes in his story. One of the most important aspects of modern criminology was preserving evidence. We always had to assume that everything was important. No harm, no foul if we were wrong; but if we were right, a bad person went to jail and a victim's family got a taste of justice.

Holloway's house was dark and quiet. We walked up to the front door and knocked. I wasn't surprised when no one answered, and I used the key that Mia had given me to get in.

"Looks like it did when we were here before," I told Shantel as I scanned the living room.

"I'll fingerprint and bag up that Xbox," Shantel said, nodding to the gaming console that sat next to a sixty-inch flat screen TV with a small crack on one side.

"I remember the days when you couldn't communicate with someone through a game console."

"And you had to fight off dinosaurs to get to the Blockbuster video store," Shantel said with a grin.

"Exactly. The good old days."

I was opening cabinets in the kitchen as we talked. They were surprisingly well organized, stopping just short of looking OCD. The counters and cabinets were clean and dust-free, and there were no dishes in the sink or the dishwasher.

"He sure kept things neat," I said, finishing up in the kitchen.

"The living room doesn't say much about the victim. Plenty of toys for the kids, but not much for him," Shantel reported, meeting me in the hall.

The first bedroom belonged to his kids. There were two twin beds with colorful sheets and pillowcases. The walls were painted bright colors with stencils of various animals. We didn't find anything of interest and went to the next bedroom.

"Door's locked," I said, surprised. Not many people kept an interior door in their house locked. "We'll come back to this." I started to feel a little excitement at the thought of what we might find inside. Could there be an answer to why Holloway had been run down behind that locked door?

The next door led to the bathroom used by the kids. Brightly colored toothbrushes and tubes of toothpaste and shampoo were scattered on the counter, and a few toys lay on the bottom of the tub. We made quick work of it and moved to the door at the end of the hallway. As I'd anticipated, it was the master bedroom.

"Your average monk has a more interesting bedroom

than this," I said, looking at the sparsely appointed room.

"Had a boyfriend once who was a Marine for twenty years. His apartment looked like this," Shantel said.

The room had a twin bed with two pillows and tightly fitted sheets. At the foot of the bed was a neatly folded blanket. In the closet, we found several sets of work overalls, a few polo shirts, slacks, two pairs of jeans, a jacket and half a dozen pairs of shoes neatly lined up on the floor. There were no electronic devices in the room or any personal letters or papers. The master bath was as clean and orderly as the bedroom.

"I'd pay this guy to clean my house," Shantel said.

"Let's check out the locked room." I'd put a universal key in my pocket, anticipating a locked desk drawer or strongbox, but certainly not an entire room.

"Let me do it," Shantel said after watching me move the key back and forth a dozen times, trying to get the lock to move. "For goodness' sake, it's just a cheap interior door."

"I'm out of practice." As soon as I said it, I felt the gadget catch on the internal mechanism. "Aha!" I exclaimed and opened the door with a flourish.

Inside the room was a desk with a computer, a monitor and speakers. There were two bookcases against one wall filled with books and notebooks, and a chair pulled up to the desk. Everything was neat and tidy. Like the kitchen cabinets, the room spoke to a personality riding the edge of OCD. A small closet held several neatly stacked boxes. I opened a couple of them and found that they contained exactly what had been written on the outside: receipts and papers dating back ten years.

"Orderly guy," I observed.

"You sound disappointed."

"With the locked door, I was hoping to find something interesting. A drug lab, a counterfeit printing press or maybe money from a bank heist."

"You dream big, I'll give you that. The guy probably didn't want his kids messing around with the computer. I understand that. I got a couple of nieces and nephews that get into everything when they come over."

"You're most likely right, but maybe we'll find some incriminating evidence on the computer."

"You're making this guy sound more like the bad guy instead of the victim," Shantel said, giving me a quizzical look.

"Yeah, it's kinda funny. There's just something about the man that rubs me the wrong way."

"Did you feel like that when you interviewed him?"

"No. And I think that's what's bothering me. Padilla and I were in the front room, and everything looked normal. He was just a divorced guy who got his kids on the weekends. But now, he gets run down when it looks like he was meeting someone at night on a dark road. His ex-wife tells me he had a second phone with mysterious numbers in the recents. And his house looks like two different people live here: family guy and OCD monk guy."

"You don't like the fact that you might have missed something when you were talking to him."

"Bingo! Anyone who's that good at hiding his other side is worrisome."

"Your pride is hurt. Most people have two sides," Shantel said knowingly.

"Not me," I proclaimed in a firm voice as I watched her dust the computer for prints.

She chuckled. "Who are you trying to kid? You're both Mr. Investigator and your dad's son. And you're being your dad's son right now."

"What's that supposed to mean?" I felt irked at her suggestion that I acted like a kid sometimes.

"You get all worked up when you think that you made a mistake 'cause you feel like your dad is always looking over your shoulder."

"Since when did you get a degree in psychology?"

"Don't get touchy. We all have our issues. Now help me bag up this computer for Lionel."

We loaded the computer and Xbox into the crime scene van, then I headed for home. Cara gave me a grunt and a kiss when I finally crawled into bed, where I spent fifteen minutes thinking about the investigations before falling asleep to dream about cars coming out of the dark to hit me while Tina Knightly laughed and filmed it.

Over breakfast Saturday morning, I told Cara as much as I could about what had happened the night before.

"You seem to be monopolizing Julio's case," she said.

"I don't think he minds getting some help. Any investigator would need assistance with a case that has as many nasty angles to it as this one does, including the FBI and media attention. Dad's been fielding a lot of calls, even from the national media. Sad to say, serial killers are popular."

"I know you don't want to be hovering over Julio. Even though your dad is good about letting you run your own investigations, you always feel like he's looking over your shoulder and putting pressure on you," she said while buttering her toast. My spoonful of cereal stopped halfway to my mouth.

"Why does everyone think I have daddy issues?" I said it a bit louder than I'd intended.

"I didn't say that."

"Shantel said almost exactly the same thing last night. I don't feel like Dad's looking over my shoulder."

"Don't you?"

I thought seriously about the question. "I'll admit that occasionally I feel like he's judging me. He *is* my boss. I'm going to have to judge everyone under me in a month when I do evaluations."

"What do you think is going to happen to Tina?" Cara asked, and I was grateful for the change of subject.

"I'm more worried about what's going to happen to your parents if Tina finds out they were behind the video," I said, putting more cereal in my bowl.

"What can she do?"

"Sue. She could sue all of us. According to the lawyer Dad's talked to, she doesn't have a case, but you can sue anyone for anything."

"Mom and Dad have lawyer friends. They'll handle it. By the way, they've invited us out to the cabin tomorrow night for a fish fry."

"Can I spend the whole time giving them a judgmental glare?" I asked.

Cara laughed. "I might join you."

We spent the rest of the weekend doing various chores around the house and trying not to melt in the late summer heat. On Sunday, a thunderstorm rolled through the area right before Henry's fish feast, cooling the air and making for a pleasant evening. I tried hard to quell my various concerns about the cases and Tina Knightly for the sake of enjoying precious time with family.

CHAPTER SEVENTEEN

As we got ready for work on Monday, everything I'd tried hard not to think about came roaring back into my brain. At the top of the list were Cara's parents.

"I'm still worried they aren't taking the situation seriously enough," I told Cara.

"They think they've beaten Tina."

"There's also Tina's personal goon, Karter Greer, to worry about. I know I saw him at the softball game on Friday. I'm not sure if he's stalking us because Dad fired him, or because of Tina, or maybe both. What I do know is that he's a loose cannon. I'll feel better when your parents are back in Gainesville and out of his line of sight."

"They'll be fine. They've both dealt with weirdos in the past," Cara said confidently.

"You need to keep your eyes open too. Keep your head on a swivel when making deliveries or going from your car to the clinic," I said seriously.

"I'll be careful. He doesn't have anything against me."

"I'm not sure he'll make that distinction."

We left for work at the same time. I followed Cara to the vet clinic and watched her get out of her car and walk into the building. She gave me an eyeroll and blew me a kiss for my paranoia.

At the office, I scanned emails and the previous night's reports before heading for a meeting of all supervisors to discuss the upcoming Labor Day picnic at the park on Lake Loka.

I arrived five minutes early and had just gotten seated when Pete came over and held out a cookie toward me.

"Beth sent these up from records. Homemade dark chocolate coconut macaroons. I grabbed you one and almost got in a fistfight with Andy Martel when he saw me take two."

Knowing Beth Miller's prowess in the kitchen, I took the cookie and popped it into my mouth as Pete sat down beside me.

"Listen up!"

Captain Roy Grant had marched up to the microphone and was staring around the room. I knew he was taking a headcount to see if anyone had ignored his request for this mandatory meeting. Grant had been the head of patrol until his recent promotion to second in command. He was comfortable on the podium and was willing to take names and rap knuckles if needed.

"Sheriff Macklin has restricted leave this Labor Day weekend to emergencies only," Grant announced to a loud chorus of groans around the room. He ignored them.

"As you all know, we always need extra security at Lake Loka Park for Memorial Day, the Fourth of July and Labor Day. However, we have a special situation this year that requires us to double our efforts. Two groups of drug dealers have been battling it out for turf. We've managed to jail some of them, but they're able to recruit quicker than we can send them to jail. Two weekends ago, there was a shootout between these entrepreneurial young men at a cookout. Sadly, innocent bystanders were hurt and killed. Thanks to tight lips from everyone at the party, the bad guys are still on the loose." He took a deep breath. "Word on the street is that both groups are planning on attending the picnic. This is not good news."

"Why don't we just round most of them up and put them in jail for the weekend?" Phil Eccles asked. One of the reasons I liked working with him was his direct approach to problems, and I couldn't help but nod at the suggestion.

"Because it would make us look heavy-handed and worsen our relationships in the communities where these dealers are working. Also, it would disrupt a major multi-jurisdictional investigation. I'll let Sergeant Olson, who heads up our drug task force, speak to that."

Sergeant Olson was often kidded about looking like the TV character Steve Urkel. The jokes never crossed the line, however, because everyone knew he was capable of taking down a man three times his size. He held a black belt in at least two martial arts, and he would be the man I'd pick in any hand-to-hand fight. He stood up and looked around the room.

"You know how hard we've been trying to keep others from moving in and filling the void left by our successful prosecution of the Thompson family. Unfortunately, these two new groups come from outside our county and have spent months cultivating soldiers and mules within our community. They're already responsible for several murders in Adams County.

"Working with the DEA, we're close to making major arrests that will cripple both groups' efforts to secure our county as their new profit center. To answer Lieutenant Eccles's question, if we pick them up on minor charges and lock them up for the weekend, we'd disrupt the larger investigation and possibly miss the chance to uproot these bad guys and put them away for the major crimes they've committed. Like I said, they're based outside of our county, and they can just switch personnel on us if they think we're making moves to take them down."

Anyone could see how much Olson wanted this bust. I understood his point, but I wasn't sure it was worth the risk.

"Is your investigation worth getting someone killed at the

picnic?" Phil voiced my thoughts.

Olson held up his hands. "I understand your concerns and I'm not happy about our choices. I didn't make the final the call. Sheriff Macklin has discussed it with the lead DEA agent, and they've agreed to this decision."

Grant tapped the mic, bringing everyone's attention back to him.

"This meeting wasn't called so y'all could discuss a course of action that has already been decided. We're here to make sure that the picnic comes off without any incidents. I will also remind everyone that the media has their eye on us." I was sure that Grant's eyes lingered on me as he spoke. "No division is going to be on easy street this weekend. Seargeant Olson, your people will assist the deputies not involved in your task force in identifying persons who might pose a threat, is that correct?"

"Correct. This is an opportunity for your men," Olson looked around the room at each of us, "to become familiar with these two groups of drug dealers. Put eyes on them so your people will recognize them if they have any dealings with them in the future. They're dangerous.

"I'm going to be in charge of the assignments and will make sure that patrol deputies are partnered up with members of our task force. As an added measure of security, Sergeant Henley and the tactical squad will be present and ready to respond. Pete, do you have anything you'd like to say?"

Pete stood up. "We hope you won't see us. The plan is for us to remain discreetly posted in the woods around the picnic area, ready to respond if trouble breaks out."

"You don't have to hide," someone shouted.

"We don't want to raise tensions or scare innocent bystanders by standing around in tactical gear," Pete explained.

"How could y'all start shooting with the crowd that's going to be there?" someone else asked.

"I'll be the only person with a rifle. The rest of my squad

are going to be carrying frangible bullets in their handguns and will only move in if shooting breaks out. At that point, the best thing we can do is stop the threat. While there *is* a chance that one of our rounds could pass through a bad guy and hit a bystander, the public is in more danger with the dealers holding their guns sideways and blasting away at each other."

There were nods all around the room. Most gun-toting criminals couldn't hit the side of a barn, so their bullets often ended up hurting the innocent.

"What if we see other illegal activity going down?" Sergeant Toomey asked.

"Treat it like any other violation of the law," Grant responded. "Just remember that there will be a large crowd of people, some of whom will be intoxicated and others who would like nothing better than to see a riot. I repeat, the media is watching us. Keep in mind that everyone has a camera pointed at you. Tell your deputies to act accordingly."

After a few more questions and quiet grumbling, Grant dismissed us.

I went back to my office and drew up a schedule for everyone in CID to work the picnic, then sent it off to Sergeant Olson.

Lynn Lewis was the only one who complained when she saw the schedule.

"I'm not the picnic type. Can't I work traffic instead? I know we've got some guys teaming up with the highway patrol on drunk driver watch. I'm good at giving sobriety tests."

"Okay. I'll tell Sergeant Olson that you've volunteered to work the road on Labor Day. Though I'm not sure you've made the best decision. The picnic isn't going to be *that* bad."

"My boobs sweat a lot," Lynn said and walked out of my office, leaving me blushing.

Julio knocked on my door not long after she left. "What

did you find out from the ex-wife the other night?"

I slapped my forehead. "I meant to check with Lionel this morning about having Holloway's phone and computer analyzed."

"Don't worry. I just saw Shantel. She's already given everything to Lionel. He's hoping to get to it this afternoon."

I leaned back in my chair. "Mia appeared to be genuinely upset about his death. I think mostly because of the impact it will have on their children. When I asked her about Holloway's inner circle for the last couple of years, she said she didn't know who he hung out with. She made it sound like they weren't that close even before the divorce."

"Did you get the feeling she was hiding anything?" Julio asked.

"I think she never really knew her husband. After going through his house, I can understand why. It was a model of compartmentalization. He even had his office locked. I've searched his house, talked to his ex-wife and even talked to him, and I have no idea what to think about the man."

"He had a secret."

"Agreed. You don't have a burner phone unless you're hiding something. There weren't any signs of a sexual partner at his house. Maybe Lionel will get some hits when he goes through the phone and computer."

"He could have been using the burner phone for a hook-up app," Julio suggested.

"True. Any luck with the security cameras?" I asked him.

"None yet. I wish I could use Sanderson. She's great at finding them and checking footage."

"Not a good idea with her brother being involved, even if he is just a friend of the victim."

"I know. I've got some more places to check. At the time the accident happened, the footage won't be good enough for more than maybe the make and model of the truck."

"You never know. There could be an identifiable decal on the truck," I said encouragingly.

"Dr. Darzi's office said that the autopsy would be done

late this afternoon."

"You go."

"I'm getting better at them," Julio said proudly.

"I'm not sure that's a good thing."

"I can't complain since I was the one who wanted to investigate violent crimes."

I turned my full attention to him. "I'm not sure I ever asked you why."

"My family came from a tough part of Puerto Rico and moved to a rougher part of New York. I was five and can remember my brothers getting beat up by the local bosses. I hated seeing them bleeding and in pain, mentally as much as physically. When we moved to Orlando, things got better, but I never forgot the abuse. The creeps who beat up my brothers were never punished except by God. I wanted to be the like the cops I watched on TV, bringing justice to the bad guys."

"When did you figure out that it wasn't going to be like on TV?" I asked sardonically.

Julio shook his head. "You're wrong. It *is* like the TV shows. It just takes a lot longer. I still remember the first person I arrested for a felony. A guy who beat up his wife. He took a plea, but I went to court to see him sentenced. I felt like I was in an episode of *Law & Order*."

"I grew up watching the sausage being made. Dad would come home grumbling about all the injustice."

"So why did you follow in your dad's footsteps?" Julio asked.

"I wouldn't put it that way. I... What with my mom passing and not knowing what I wanted to do... Dad made me promise to go to the academy when I encouraged him to run for sheriff, and I just sort of fell into the job from there."

"You're a good detective."

"And that's why I'm still here. I discovered I have a knack for unraveling crimes. Which is good 'cause I wasn't that great on patrol."

"Really?"

"Took too long on calls and was always arguing with my sergeant and the watch commander. I wanted to investigate the crimes when I was supposed to just take the report and let an investigator follow up."

"But eventually you found your place," Julio said.

"Hey, you're layering on the butter pretty thick. Don't think you're going to get out of working the picnic. And evaluations aren't until next month."

"I didn't mean to sound like a suck-up," he said with a grin and stood up.

I waved him out of my office.

After spending a couple of hours working on reports and other cases, I found my mind still drifting to thoughts about Briggs and Holloway. Even though I knew I should have left it to Julio, I wanted to take a break and do some investigative work. I picked up my phone and buzzed him.

"Have you started on Holloway's victim profile?" I asked.

"Not yet. I've been following up on the traffic and security cams. I don't want to lose any footage."

"Mind if I dig into his background?"

"All help is appreciated," Julio said.

I started by pulling up Holloway's driver's license so that I had his date of birth and full name. Next, I did a basic online search. It helped that Colson Emerson Holloway wasn't a very common name. I found his birth certificate and discovered that he'd been born in Hershey, Pennsylvania to Grayson and Sylvia Holloway. Then, I searched their names, hoping to find out where they had died, thinking that might lead me to other states where Holloway had lived. Instead, I got a surprise. While Sylvia had died ten years ago, Grayson Holloway was still alive and well and living in Hershey.

I found a number for him and left a message. Ten minutes later, he called back.

"What's my son done now?" he asked by way of a

greeting.

"We don't know that he's done anything wrong," I said.

"Your message said you're with the sheriff's office. He must have done something to get your attention."

"Mr. Holloway, I'm afraid your son was killed by a hit-and-run driver last night."

There was silence on the other end of the phone for a few seconds, then: "Oh."

"I know this is hard. If you want me to call back later, that's fine. I have some questions I need to ask you."

"I don't know anything about my son for the last ten years." Holloway's voice was emotionless.

"Which is one of the questions I would like to ask. Why were you and your son estranged?"

"Estranged. That's a funny word. How can a father and son be strangers?"

There was more silence.

"I know this is tough," I told him.

"Everything about raising Col was tough. Now his momma and him, that was a different story. She loved that boy so much."

"So what happened between the two of you?"

"Good question. I just don't know the answer. We never connected, not ever. I know for a fact that he was my biological son, but it was like he had a different father. Got into trouble quite a bit when he was young, but as he grew, he seemed to get better."

"What sort of trouble?"

"The worst was when he hurt a young woman. Beat her up bad. I thought he'd be in jail for a long time, but the judge took pity on him. First offense, good record at school, that sort of thing. He was sent through a... what did they call it... a diversion program, that was it. He had to live in a cabin and chop wood for a couple of months. When he came home, his probation required him to get counseling and drug testing."

"Did he get into any more trouble?"

"I wondered. Nothing that they could arrest him for. He had a few girlfriends and, after a couple of months, each of them decided they didn't want to see him anymore. Sometimes we had stuff around the house go missing. Little valuable items, but never enough to call the police. Not that my wife would have let me call the police, even though she knew. We both knew. Colson always had money, even when he didn't have a job."

"When was the last time you saw or talked to him?"

"Ten years ago, when his mother died. Like I said, she loved the boy. But when she was gone, we had no reason to talk."

"I don't know if you're aware, but he had an ex-wife and two children. I've talked to her, and I don't think she'll be interested in claiming the body," I said, then gave him a minute to let all of this sink in.

Grayson was quiet for a while, then said, "I won't judge the boy in death. His mother would want him next to her, so if you'll let me know who I need to contact, I'll arrange for his body to be brought home." There was a deep melancholy in his voice.

"I'll let you know when the coroner is done with the body. I'll also keep you up to date on the investigation."

"I don't care about the investigation. Who killed him and why is part of a life we didn't share. And I don't want to know the children either. I'm sure he told them I was dead, and I'm fine if they believe that. Thank you for taking the time to call me," he said and hung up abruptly.

I found myself looking at the phone and thinking about fathers and sons. Dad and I often irritated each other, but I'd never doubted his love for me or felt like I could have ever disappointed him beyond redemption.

CHAPTER EIGHTEEN

"Our victim wasn't a very nice man," I told Julio when he came back from the autopsy. It was after five and I had just put my computer to sleep before getting up and heading home.

"Whoever hit him didn't want him getting back up," Julio said. "Darzi said that the damage to his midsection was remarkable. He said he'd have to check some statistics, but he figured the truck was going at least fifty miles an hour."

"Ouch!" I filled him in on what I'd learned from Holloway's father.

"My abuela would say that the man had a darkness inside him."

"I'd have to agree with her. The question is: what part did his own demons play in his death?"

"Beating up women," Julio said thoughtfully. "Do you think he could be the serial killer the FBI is looking for?"

"We need to let them know about his history. Anything's possible at this point. But how would that explain the burned-out van and the trophies in Briggs's house?"

"Holloway planted them there to shift the blame onto Briggs," Julio suggested.

"Why?"

"The witness found him, and he was afraid she'd expose him."

"So why not just kill her and dump the body like he did all the rest?"

"Maybe Briggs discovered that he was a killer."

I considered the possibility. "That would make some sense. So Holloway has to get rid of Briggs, which is too close to home. In order to get away with it, he kills Briggs and plants the evidence on him."

"How do you think Briggs might have found out?"

"He had a habit of helping the downtrodden, so it's possible that he met the FBI's witness and learned from her that Holloway was the killer. Still, if she knew Holloway's name then why didn't she give it to the FBI?" I wondered.

"Maybe she saw Holloway at Briggs's house. Or she rode to work with Briggs one day and saw Holloway at the shop or on one of the jobs."

"I like that better. But if she was hanging out with Briggs, you'd think someone would have seen them together. Witnesses saw him with Kelly Airlie and knew she was living in his house. No one mentioned seeing him with Kat Fergusson."

"So who killed Holloway?" Julio asked.

"And why?"

"An accomplice?"

I shook my head. "I doubt it. Not many serial killers have an accomplice. When they do, they're usually related, or at least close friends. We haven't uncovered any close friends for Holloway."

"Someone learned he was the killer, so they decided to kill him?"

"Why?" I asked. "Why not just turn him in and let the law handle it? Florida has the death penalty. It might take years, but eventually he'd either die in prison or make it to the death chamber."

"They could be a criminal themselves," Julio threw out. "You know, the type that will steal or sell drugs but draw the line at beating up women and children."

"An anonymous tip would have worked in that case."

"Regardless of what happened, Padilla and her crime scene team need to go over Holloway's van with a fine-tooth comb. If he put bodies in the back to transport them, then there will be evidence, even with all the paint and chemicals," Julio said.

He took his phone out and called Padilla. After a short conversation, he hung up and said, "She's going to have a team out there in a couple of hours."

"People don't realize how hard it is to get blood and other bodily fluids out of all the cracks and crevices in a van."

"The employees at the paint company *do* clean them out regularly," Julio said.

"It's worth a shot. I don't think they spray out the front of the vans. All it would take is for Holloway to have a spot of blood on his shoes or clothing to transfer it to the van's seat or floorboard."

"It will flip the script if he's their serial killer."

"Yep. Any word on the truck that hit him?"

"Marcus is working on the pieces of broken plastic found at the scene. I've also brought back Holloway's clothes from the autopsy, along with the debris that Darzi vacuumed off of them."

Before I could say anything else, both of our phones lit up with text messages. Julio read his first.

"I'll be damned. They just found a truck burning in the national forest. You want to come look?"

I called Cara and told her I'd be late for dinner.

A fire truck from the forestry service was still at the scene when we got there.

"At least we've had plenty of rain lately," the ranger told me as he rolled up a hose. "No chance of the fire spreading. This must be important to get two investigators out to look at it."

"The truck could have been involved in a hit and run," I said, following Julio over to what was left of the vehicle. The ground all around was wet and covered in tire tracks. There wasn't much chance of getting any evidence from this scene.

"When do you think you'll be able to tow it out of here?" the ranger asked.

"We'll get it out tonight," I promised.

It was already six o'clock. I got on the phone and called our preferred towing company. The woman who answered the phone said they were still busy cleaning up various issues from rush hour, and that it would be more than an hour before anyone could get out to us.

I looked down at my clothes and sighed. Clean clothes or not, I wasn't going to make the same mistake twice. Slowly, I got down in the mud and used my flashlight to look under the still-dripping remains of the truck. Filthy now, I stood back up.

"At least there isn't a body under this one," I told Julio. I tried to wipe off some of the mud from my pants, but all I did was smear it around and make it worse.

"I can't tell if this is the vehicle that hit our victim," Julio said, looking at the front end. The fire had melted all the plastic and even warped some of the metal.

"If they'd used a car, we might be able to see a dent in the hood. This truck is so tall that if you got hit with it, you'd go flying and not even touch the hood," I said. "We'll just go on the assumption that this is our vehicle until we're proven wrong. Still, keep the bulletin out there until we know for sure."

"I've got the VIN number," Julio said. "This truck hasn't been reported stolen."

"Interesting. Maybe we'll be lucky and the guy took it from the airport or somewhere, and we have him on camera. Who's the owner?"

"Dante L. Comacho. Lives in the north end of the county."

I watched him tap his phone screen repeatedly before putting it up to his ear.

"Mr. Comacho?" Julio asked, and that was the last thing I understood. The rest of the conversation was in Spanish, and not even slow, high-school Spanish.

Julio hung up and told me, "He's a truck driver and is currently on a job in Texas. Said that he thought his truck was at his house. Not a happy man to find out it's been turned into an eyesore."

"One of us should check his house," I said with a small smile.

"One of us needs to stay out here in the woods until the tow truck gets here."

I took a quarter out of my pocket, flipped it and managed to catch it before it hit the ground. I slapped it down on my forearm. "Call it."

"Tails," Julio said.

I lifted up my hand so he could see the coin. He muttered a few words in Spanish that *were* familiar to me, as I'd heard them come of the mouths of more than one suspect in handcuffs.

"I'll let you know what I find," I told him. When I saw the frown on his face, I pointed to my clothes. "Hey, I *did* save you from having to get down in the mud."

"True enough."

I found the house in a sparsely populated area of the county. Comacho lived in an old clapboard cottage. The grass in the yard was overgrown, which could easily happen this time of year if no one was home to mow on a regular basis. A chain-link fence surrounded the yard. I looked for a dog before entering through a creaky gate.

There were no toys or efforts at landscaping. Off to the side of the house, a partially restored Oldsmobile was up on blocks. The front porch was bare except for a couple of cheap plastic chairs. The door was locked.

I went around the right side of the house, checking windows as best I could since the house was on blocks two feet off the ground. The bottoms of the windows were at my chin level, making it difficult to see if they were locked. I tried to lift them and got resistance on all of them.

As I climbed up the cinderblock steps to the small back porch, I saw that the back door had been pried open. I took a deep breath. I could push the door open and enter the dwelling without permission and without a warrant, or I could write up an official request, submit it electronically and wait however long it took to get it back.

I settled for option three, calling Julio and asking him to contact Camacho to get permission to enter his house. There was no guarantee he'd say yes. Lots of people didn't want cops poking around their house, especially if they weren't there. Luck was with me, and I had permission within five minutes.

After taking multiple pictures of the pry marks, I slipped on gloves and booties and went inside. The back door opened into the kitchen, which was neat in a bachelor way. Nothing looked disturbed. A quick walk through the house told me that whoever had broken in hadn't been interested in ransacking the house. Everything screamed standard bachelor pad, with furniture and clothes that all looked serviceable and nothing more. The only things that Camacho had obviously spent money on were the large TV and gaming console in the living room, and both were untouched.

Back in the kitchen, I started looking at the walls and opening drawers until I found what I was looking for. In the drawer closest to the door were a few sets of keys, including one that held an old and worn Oldsmobile key. The key drawer was almost as common as a hook by the door, and bad guys relied on people doing common things.

I closed up the house and called Shantel, asking her to send out a tech to dust the door and kitchen for prints. As I drove home, I called Julio and brought him up to date. I could hear the tow truck working in the background, so I didn't feel too guilty about leaving him out there.

As I approached the driveway that led to our twenty acres, I saw a car parked on the shoulder of the road near our gate. It was sitting at an odd angle. As I slowly pulled up behind it, I saw a dark figure trying to climb the gate onto our property. The person clearly wasn't having much luck, then fell awkwardly to the ground. The figure stumbled to its feet and turned around. The headlights of my car illuminated the face of Tina Knightly.

Shocked and a little puzzled, I wasn't sure what I wanted to do. I should have backed out of the driveway and called dispatch to send a deputy to deal with her. I considered that for almost a minute, then looked on top of the dash to make sure the old SUV still had a dashcam and that it was working. I didn't want to confront Tina without a clear record of the encounter.

Once the camera was on, I opened the door. Tina stood in the blinding glare of the headlights, squinting at me. There was no way she could see me with the lights in her eyes. After observing her a little while longer, I didn't need a breathalyzer test to know that she was three, four or maybe even five sheets to the wind.

"Tina!" I said in a loud, clear voice as I stepped out of the SUV.

"Sonofabitch!" she screamed.

Hearing this, I almost changed my mind, crawled back in the Suburban and called dispatch. Instead, I took a step away from the vehicle so she could see me.

"What are you doing at my house?"

"You think I'm through!" she yelled. "I ain't through just 'cause some suck-egg TV station suspended me. This is the twentysomethin' century, and we got computers, Internet, cell phones and all kinds of shit. I've got my own YouTube channel." She seemed to think about this and giggled. "Like every other idiot. Doesn't matter. I'm going to beat you and your whole egg-sucking family." She went down to her knees. "Don't try and help me up."

I hadn't made a move toward her.

"I got this," she slurred, trying and failing to get back to her feet.

"Who can I call to come get you?" I asked.

"No one! I'm going to stake out your house and catch you and your rotten father in whatever game you're playing. You made me look like a crazy, mean bitch."

"I haven't done anything to you. I had nothing to do with that video."

"Don'tyoufuckinlietome." She was half sobbing now.

I wanted to tell her that she had started all of this with her unwarranted attacks on me and my family, but now wasn't the time. I wasn't going to kick someone when they were down. But with the camera on, I didn't dare go over and try to help her off the ground. I tried to think who I could call to help her. It wasn't like we had any mutual friends.

Finally, I called Darlene.

"Why are you calling me? I don't like the woman!" Darlene exclaimed after I explained the situation.

"I thought you might could get Hondo to come down and help get her home."

"Why Hondo?"

"He's an EMT. If she goes into, I don't know, some sort of medical issue, he can help her."

"He doesn't like her either."

"I can't leave her lying in a fetal position in front of my gate. If for no other reason, I can't get around her and I'm tired."

"Why don't you call dispatch?"

"I don't want to get the sheriff's office involved in this. She's liable to sober up and claim we kidnapped her."

I heard Darlene laugh softly. "Maybe you're not as dumb as you look. Okay, Hondo's working tonight. Maybe he can respond like they just saw someone on the side of the road. He'll have to fudge things a little to explain driving out there in the country. Hold on. I'll see what he says."

Darlene and Alejandro Valdez, one of the county's best EMTs, had dated for a while. Though they were no longer romantic, they'd remained friends and close colleagues.

I called Cara while I waited for Darlene to get back to me.

"She's what?" Cara asked, clearly appalled.

"Curled up in front of our gate and crying."

"Mom and Dad should see this," she said with a heavy sigh.

"There's Hondo. Got to go," I told her when caller ID told me that Hondo was on the line.

"Man, you could have called me direct. No need to involve the ex," Hondo joked.

"Can you help me?"

"On our way, compadre. I am taking a dinner break and might get lost in the woods." He chuckled. "ETA twenty-five minutes."

I hung up and sat down inside the Suburban, then called Dad. I tried not to look at Tina, who was half crawling back toward the gate.

It took a couple of minutes for Dad to stop laughing. "You're getting it all on the dashcam, right?"

"Watching her isn't as funny as it sounds," I said. "Really, she looks kind of pathetic."

"She's earned every second of her humiliation. But I won't release the video unless she continues to harass us." The humor had left Dad's voice. He warned me to be careful and to let Hondo take charge of getting her off my property, then hung up.

My headlights caught movement from the driveway, and I saw that Cara was coming down. I wasn't surprised. I climbed out of the vehicle and waved for her to stay back.

"Wow, she's really not in great shape," Cara said, stopping about ten feet from the gate.

Tina was crawling around on the ground, cussing at everyone and everything.

"Hondo is on his way."

"Where will they take her?" Cara asked.

"Icanfuckinearyouyouknow," Tina growled.

"You're a little drunk," I said.

"Aintalittleskunk," she responded, and went into peals of laughter. "IdongetchaGreergonnagetcha," she mumbled.

"What about Greer?" I asked, alarmed and stepping closer.

"Gonnagetcha. Onyatrail, cowboy." She started laughing again.

"You need to tell him to leave my family alone," I said before I remembered that I was talking to a drunk woman.

"Ihiredhim to getcha." She pointed her finger at me.

"I should warn you that this is all being recorded on the SUV's dashcam," I said, loudly and clearly enough that anyone watching the video later wouldn't have to strain their ears to make out what I was saying.

I heard the ambulance pull in behind my SUV. Hondo got out, followed by a young man with blond hair and tentacles tattooed up his neck almost to his face. They both went straight to Tina.

"You could have picked her up off the ground," Hondo chided me as he opened his bag and took out a blood-pressure cuff.

"I didn't want her to get upset and hurt me or herself." I wanted to get this on tape, as it was the God's honest truth.

"Idontneednoamblance." Tina swung her arm at Hondo.

"We want to check your vitals," he told her in the calm, commanding voice he used a hundred times a day.

"Damnyou." She halfheartedly struggled against him.

"Your heart rate is elevated and blood pressure ain't great. We're going to take you to the hospital."

"Nonononono!"

"We can't leave you out here on the side of the road," Hondo said, nodding to his partner, who moved in and took her other arm.

"I want to get him on tape," Tina said, her voice

suddenly clear.

"You can do that tomorrow," Hondo told her as they lifted her to her feet, "when you're feeling better. We'll give you an IV, and they can give you some coffee and evaluate you at the hospital. Great time, lady. Guaranteed."

Tina seemed to give up and went limp, as though she'd finally reached her limits. This lasted only until they got to the back of the ambulance, where she started acting like a cat that was being put into a carrier for a trip to the vet. Finally, they convinced her to climb in the back of the ambulance, and the man with the tentacles got in with her.

"Appreciate it, Hondo." I shook his hand.

"Always glad to have you owe me one, my friend."

"I'm sure I owe you more than one."

After Hondo left with Tina, I called dispatch and gave them an abbreviated version of events, asking them to send a tow for her car.

Cara opened the gate so I could drive through, then hitched a ride up to the house with me. Once we were inside, I gave her a hug.

"Just once I'd like to have a normal day," I groaned as I fixed a ham sandwich and dished up some macaroni and cheese that she'd left warming on the stove.

"I see what you mean about Karter Greer," Cara said, sitting down to watch me eat.

"We all need to be careful. You saw Tina tonight. If she can go off the rails like that, then Greer or someone else could do worse."

"I'm sorry that my parents have made this situation so much worse than it already was."

"They were trying to help. Who knows, maybe they did."

"It's kind of sad seeing Tina like that, crawling on the ground," Cara said.

"Go watch that first video she did where she crucified all of us, including Mauser. You won't feel so bad about her wallowing in the mud after that."

"Speaking of mud, what happened to you?"

"I had to get down and look under that truck."

"Don't tell me there was another body under it."

"If there had been, I wouldn't be home yet, and Tina would still be trying to climb our gate. We aren't even sure that this truck is our murder weapon. It was too badly damaged to be sure. Shantel and the folks at the lab will have to do comparisons of the plastic on Holloway's body, the evidence from the scene and the truck itself before we can be sure. There might even be some blood left under a fender or inside the wheel well that could confirm it."

After dinner and a hot shower, I was feeling human again. It was too late for me to do any work, so I lay on the couch to read. Cara came over, so I lifted my legs up so she could get settled. Instead, she started trying to tickle my feet, which was an open declaration of war. The war didn't last long and soon we were deep into peace negotiations.

The rest of the week went by fast with few new developments in the investigations of the deaths of Davis Briggs or Colson Holloway. By Thursday, however, enough evidence had been found to declare that the truck left burning in the woods had been the one that struck Holloway. Agent Padilla also let Julio know that they were still going over Holloway's van, and that they'd brought in some high-tech equipment to scour it for any evidence that could link it to the serial murders.

CHAPTER NINETEEN

On Friday, I came into the office thinking more about the picnic detail on Saturday than the Briggs or Holloway cases. I figured it would be next week before we made any more headway, so I was surprised when Agent Padilla knocked on my door.

"To what do I owe the pleasure of this visit?"

"Frustration," Padilla said, dropping down into a chair. I would have pointed out that I hadn't invited her to sit but decided I should be happy that she hadn't tried to take my own chair out from under me.

I told her about my encounter with Tina Knightly on Monday.

"Couldn't happen to a better person. That cheers me up a little. Thanks. Now, if you could give us evidence in our murder investigations, that would be lovely." She sighed. "Holloway's van was clean. But not too clean. No one had scrubbed it down or sprayed it out for a week or more. Our techs even found debris under the edge of the panels that showed no one had totally washed it down in a long time. Not what you would expect if it had been used by a murderer."

"You didn't want it to be Holloway anyway," I reminded

her.

"At this point, I would be glad if we had concrete proof that *anyone* was the murderer."

"So you've changed your mind about Davis Briggs?"

"Let's just say that you've sown the seeds of doubt. I'd like to have something more solid than the box of trophies." She looked unsettled.

"Holloway could still have used the van and just been careful."

"I know. We took the industrial vacuum to it so the lab boys and girls might find something to give us a DNA bingo, but we'll have to wait for them to run their tests. We picked up some stray hairs that could turn out to belong to one of our victims. Again, we'll just have to wait."

I told her what I'd learned about Holloway from his ex-wife and father.

"See, he fits our profile better than Briggs. I've given the lab some of Holloway's skin to pull DNA. If his DNA matches any of the souvenirs or the box they came in, then the needle will be pointing in his direction. Not that it would be conclusive, since Holloway worked with Briggs. It wouldn't be unreasonable to find some of his DNA in a co-worker's house."

"You got the DNA from Darzi?"

She nodded. "I had one of my agents go by his office and take a sample."

"I appreciate you keeping an open mind."

"Having an open mind is one of my weaknesses. Tell me where you are with the hit and run."

I filled her in on what we knew.

"If you need our help analyzing the truck, just let me know. This particular serial killer has turned us into quite the experts on firebombed vehicles."

"Is there any chance of finding out anything about the accelerant that was used?"

"Nice thought. Most of the time we can tell *what* was used, but we can't dig any deeper than that. I had the same thought. We have a similar MO, so what about materials? If we had liquid samples of whatever was used to burn the truck and Briggs's van, then we could tell you if they came from the same source. But with just watered-down, minute traces…" She shook her head and stood up. "Keep in touch." She gave me an ironic salute and was gone.

Later that day, Julio came running into my office as excited as a kid on Christmas Day. "I found something. I just don't know what it means."

"What?"

"Holloway's van. First, let me tell you how I figured it out. I was going back over his profile and decided to look at any contact he'd had with law enforcement. All I found were some traffic violations, and I was going to let it go at that. But I decided to look at all of them and compare their locations to the serial murders."

"And you found a connection?" I asked eagerly.

"No. What I found was that a speeding ticket he got two months ago was received when he was driving his Sunshine Industrial Paint van."

"So?"

"The tag number was different than the one on the van the FBI has been analyzing."

"The company gave them the wrong van?" I couldn't understand how that could have happened.

"No. They gave them the van that Holloway had been driving since Briggs died. I talked with Zavala and his employees this morning. What I discovered was that Holloway was driving the van that had originally been assigned to Briggs."

"But I saw Zavala pull the information from Davis's file."

"Exactly. Someone switched the registration cards in the two files. When Zavala assigns a van, he just takes the registration and title and drops them into the employee's folder."

"All someone would need to do to switch them would be to get into his office and move the registration and title from one file to the other."

Julio nodded. "Zavala's office is always unlocked. The vans were bought as a package fleet deal, so they're the same make, model and year."

"So Holloway could have just switched any personal items from Briggs's van to his and vice versa, and no one would know the difference."

"Right!" Julio was almost dancing with excitement.

"So it was actually Holloway's van that we found burned with a body underneath?"

"Bingo!"

"Well, that certainly changes things." My brain was working through all the additional questions that this revelation would create. "This means that Holloway probably was Padilla's serial killer, and he killed Briggs as a way to point the investigation toward someone else."

"But then someone killed him," Julio said.

"Why? And who?"

"Could it be someone else at Sunshine? Or maybe his ex-wife."

"We need to dig deep into alibis," I said. "The ex-wife seems like a longshot. Though, if she found out that he was a serial killer, would she have been willing to kill him to keep her kids safe?"

"Why not turn him in to us or the FBI?" Julio asked.

"She loves her kids. That was pretty clear when I interviewed her. Would you want your kids to know that their daddy was a serial killer? Maybe she decided that she could run him down and no one would ever know. She probably wouldn't lose much sleep over killing a dangerous person like him."

"You think that's the way the hit and run went down?" Julio asked.

"When I told her Holloway was dead, she looked shocked," I said doubtfully.

"What she'd done might not have sunk in until you told her. After all, we aren't talking about a hardened criminal.

We're talking about a momma bear protecting her cubs. She could have killed him to protect them, yet still felt bad about having to run him down."

"Or she has a brother, father, sister or lover who was willing to do it for her once she convinced them that Holloway was a killer." Even as I suggested it, I thought the idea had a lot of potential.

"I've got some more digging to do." Julio was coming down off of his high. "Are you going to tell Padilla?"

I picked up my phone and clicked her number. I put the phone on speaker and set it back down on my desk.

"This is Padilla. Speak," she said.

"That's how my dad talks to Mauser and me," I told her.

"And Mauser is probably more responsive."

"Actually, not true. Look, I've got Deputy Ortiz in my office. He's dug up an interesting tidbit." I waved my arm at Julio, who looked surprised that I was going to let him tell her the news.

Julio gave her the short version.

"No shit? I feel like we should have caught that. Nice work. So Holloway could be our killer. Fascinating." I could almost hear the gears working in her head. "You got any suspects for the hit and run?"

We went over the ex-wife theory.

"Mia Holloway, right? What's her maiden name?"

"Compton," Julio said.

"I like the idea that it was someone close to her who ran him down. We can help you with the backgrounds on the people in her life."

Julio nodded. "That would be helpful."

"What do you know about her?"

As soon as she asked the question, I started to mentally kick myself for not pushing for more information from Mia the night I'd talked with her.

"Let me follow up with her. The notification went well. If I come by to ask more questions, it shouldn't seem odd to her."

"Sounds good," Padilla agreed. "We'll go ahead and do a standard background check on Mia and her closest relations. Briggs's friends might have been right about him."

"You can cross-check everyone connected to Mia with Dante Comacho," Julio suggested. "Whoever took the truck knew where to find the keys."

"10-4."

Julio left to start checking the alibis of everyone who worked at Sunshine. I headed out to find the ex-Mrs. Holloway.

Irritated at myself for not having thought to ask where she worked, I went back to her house. There was no car in the driveway and a knock on the door went unanswered. I had the same result at the main house. Frustrated, I looked around at the neighborhood. There was an older man working in his flowerbed across the street.

"You look like a cop," he said as I approached, and he stood up with an effort. Tall and thin with sparse grey hair, he stared at me with sharp eyes, then glanced at the SUV across the street. "You don't look like a K9 officer."

"It's a loaner." I showed him my ID.

"You related to the sheriff?"

"His son," I admitted.

"Like him. Voted for him every time. Heck of a dog he's got."

"Mauser is quite impressive."

"Not too well trained though."

Trying not to laugh, I said, "I think Dad did a better job with me."

"Ha! I hope. So what are you doing over at the Comptons' house?"

"I'm looking for Mia."

As soon as I said it, his eyes got big. "That was her husband, I mean ex-husband, that was killed in that hit and run last week."

"I'm afraid it was."

"I didn't make the connection before now. I met him a

couple of times when he was picking up the kids."

"What'd you think of him?" I asked.

The man gave me an appraising look. "You sound like he's more of a suspect than a victim."

"And you sound like you've been in my shoes." I smiled.

"Twenty years in the military police. And, to answer your question, I didn't like him. Set off alarm bells. The eyes, I think, and the way he looked at me."

"How's that?"

"As a nuisance. Like anyone that interrupted his mission was in the way. He was here to pick up his kids and an old guy from across the street was a bother."

"We've talked with plenty of people who liked him."

"Sociopath. As soon as he looked at his kids, his eyes changed, he got all soft and friendly. But I wouldn't give you a nickel for those kids' chances if they got in the way of his happiness."

"You sound like you sized him up pretty quick." As I said it, I did a little appraising of my own. Did this man care enough about Mia and her kids to help her out with an ex who posed a danger not only to her, but to others? His eyes were cold steel.

"You know how the job works. You might only have a few seconds to take the measure of a man."

I couldn't argue with him on that point. I stuck out my hand in a friendly manner. "I'm sorry. I didn't get your name."

"Bart Rider." He took my hand, and the grip told me that he might groan while getting to his feet, but he could still put up a fight if he wanted to.

"Do you know if Mia is at work?"

"Should be. She drops the kids off at school and then drives to Tallahassee. She works for the state."

"You know where?"

"I've got her cell phone number, if that would help."

"Thanks."

He took out his phone and pulled the number up for me.

"Mia's a nice girl. I'm glad she divorced that guy. Guess now he's completely out of their lives."

I looked at him and saw those steel-blue eyes looking back at me. I thanked him and started back across the street. As soon as I was at my car, I called Mia.

"Truth is, I took the day off to be with the kids," she told me.

"I'd like to ask you a few more questions."

"I'm at the city park near the Anglican church."

"I'll be there in ten minutes."

I didn't have a hard time finding her. It was a hot day and school was in session, so they were the only people in the park. The two kids were happily running around the playground equipment while Mia sat on a bench in the shade of a couple of sycamore trees.

"I watch them run around like they don't have a care in the world and wonder how they're really processing the death of their father," she said as I walked up.

"I will be glad to give you the number of our victims' advocate. They'll help you find a qualified grief counselor."

"I may take you up on the offer. I have to do something to try and get through to them. I know what can happen if you bottle up your emotions. I had to have several operations when I was their age. Issues with my leg not being straight, a birth defect. I told everyone I was fine, even when I wasn't. Never wanted to talk about the operations or the pain. Now, I look back and see all the trauma and phobias that grew out of those hospital experiences."

"Children can internalize pain and grief," I agreed. "The problem is that all of those issues can be like an abscess. They fester under the skin and poison everything."

I watched her carefully. What was she hiding? Or was she hiding anything at all?

She sighed. "So, what did you want to ask me?"

"I'm interested in any of your friends or family who might have come in contact with Colson. How well they might have known him." I didn't want to sound like I was looking into her friends and family as suspects, so I'd come up with this half-truth to get the information I wanted.

"Almost everyone I know knew Colson."

"How did he get along with your friends and family?"

"Not well, honestly. Looking back, I can see how controlling he was."

"And how did they feel about him?"

"I think he purposefully made them dislike him. He'd snub them every chance he got. Argued with them. He didn't want us to have friends and family over to the house, or to go visit them. Worked well too. It got to where I dreaded us seeing my friends."

"I'd like to talk to some of them," I said.

"I don't know what they can tell you."

"This is background. I'm looking for connections. They know Colson and might know other people who have a problem with him. We're a small community."

"It's funny, I keep forgetting that you're looking for the person who ran him down. I've been so busy thinking about how my children are going to handle his death, I haven't had much time to think about what happened to him."

"His father is alive." I tossed it out to see how she would react.

"I always wondered."

"Why do you say that?"

"My family has a section in the Old City Cemetery. Once a year in the fall, we get together and clean around the graves and pick up any flowers or trash. Colson came with me a few times, and whenever I'd ask him about his parents' graves, he'd get defensive. I could tell he was being evasive."

"Your apartment. Is that your parents' house?"

"Yes. Since the divorce, I've seen a lot of them. They babysit the kids when school's out."

"If they didn't like Colson, they must have hated him still being in the children's lives."

She gave me an odd look, and for a second, I thought I might have tipped her off. Finally, she said, "Yes and no. My parents feel that children need a mother and a father. As much as they didn't like Colson, I think they wanted him to be in the kids' lives. They never ran him down in front of the kids."

"Your parents sound like good people. Was there anyone close to you that knew Colson well?"

"Craig. Craig Pressman. I haven't thought of him in years. He introduced us to each other." Mia looked off into the distance, remembering past events.

"Does he live around here?"

"No. Or at least he didn't. We met him in Tallahassee. I was going to Tallahassee Community College. He was taking accounting classes. Nice guy. I dated him for a few months before we decided we weren't compatible. It was mutual. He was a party guy; I was a go-to-the-park kind of girl. A few months after we stopped seeing each other, he called me and asked if I wanted to go on a date with a friend of his. I said sure. Now here I am."

"When was the last time you heard from him?"

"Why are you interested in Craig?"

"We're interested in anyone who knew your ex-husband."

Mia looked over at her kids, who were now playing around a trio of large plastic dinosaurs.

"I feel funny giving you people's names knowing that you're going to go talk to them."

"We have to investigate Colson's background in order to find out who hit him and why."

"What do you mean 'why,' if it was a hit and run? You think he was murdered? I can't believe any of this. Even though I couldn't live with Colson, I never wanted him hurt."

I thought that was an odd statement, but I let it go. "That's why we need to find the person who killed him. They need to be brought to justice."

"Sure, I guess." She didn't sound sure at all. "Last time I talked to Craig was a year or two after Colson and I got married. Craig was passing through Tallahassee and wanted to have dinner with us. Colson told him we had plans, even though we didn't. We'd gotten into a fight and he wasn't going to let me have any fun."

"Do you remember Craig saying where he was coming from or who he worked for?"

"Gosh, it was so long ago. Or at least it seems that way. Maybe it was Jacksonville or the beaches over there. He was on his way to Mobile. I do remember that much. He said it was for business, that's all I remember."

"Okay. Other friends?"

"Not of both of ours. He never wanted to meet any of my friends from work."

"Where do you work?"

"The DMV. I work with groups that want to have a specialty tag. I tell them what they need to do and make sure they get all the forms together, that sort of thing."

I took a deep breath. "I have to ask you a question that you might not like. But remember that I would ask this of anyone whose spouse or ex-spouse was killed. Where were you before I came to your house the other night?"

"Oh, you can't be serious." Mia looked like she couldn't decide whether to laugh or cry.

"We ask many people who are not suspects to provide an alibi. When we arrest the person who killed Colson and they go to trial, their lawyer is going to want to know if we looked at everyone else and cleared them."

"I was at home with my children. They went to bed around nine o'clock."

"You never left the house?"

"I would never leave my children alone." Her mood had changed swiftly from friendly to irritated. It was up to me to figure out whether she was experiencing honest emotions, or if she was irritated that I was getting close to her and a possible accomplice.

"Thank you. That's all I need to know right now."

As upset as she was when I left her at the park, she was

going to be even more angry when I talked to her parents and co-workers. Julio and I had no choice but to pursue this line of questioning. She had a legitimate motive for wanting to cover up Holloway's murderous personality.

I was also sure that Holloway's killer had a connection to Dante Camacho and his truck. Yes, Camacho had kept his keys in a predictable place. But I still I felt like whoever had stolen his truck must have known that he was a truck driver and would be out of town for a while.

As soon as I had a solid list of people close to Mia, I would run the names by Camacho to see if he recognized any of them. If he didn't, we'd have to dig deeper and see if he had any obscure connections to one of them.

CHAPTER TWENTY

I had just driven away from the park when my phone rang. The caller ID showed it was Tina Knightly. I let it ring as I considered whether I should answer it or let it go to voicemail. With reservations, I connected the call.

"What can I do for you?" I said, making an effort to keep my voice neutral.

"You have every right to ridicule me. Having said that, I'm calling to apologize." I could almost hear her chewing the crow.

"Are you apologizing because you know we have a dashcam video of your performance, or because you sincerely feel bad for making me deal with your drunken assault on my property?"

"The latter. I've been dragged through the mud so much lately that a little more wouldn't matter."

"Speaking of dragging people through the mud, are you also apologizing for the other times you've trashed my family and friends?"

"I might have stepped over the line… a little," she said grudgingly.

"Are you apologizing to Mauser?"

I heard a heavy sigh. "Sure. I'm sorry I disparaged the

mutt's reputation."

"Why the change of heart?" I asked, genuinely curious.

"Waking up in the hospital was a red flag. Plus, I got a good dressing down from my parents that stung because they were right. I don't know if you're aware of my father's career, but he was a reporter in Cincinnati for years. One of the warnings he gave me was that a journalist can't use their power as a personal weapon against people they perceive as enemies. They should simply tell the truth."

"Okay. Though you'll understand if I don't immediately embrace you in friendship."

"I'm good with that." She took a deep breath. "There's another reason I called. My parents weren't the only ones to visit me in the hospital. Karter Greer came by. He's off the chain. I thought you should know that he was talking pretty crazy about you and your father. Before this latest drinking binge, I might have said stuff to him that didn't help."

"We figured that he was feeding you inside information about the sheriff's office," I said, hating to have our suspicions confirmed.

"And to keep him pumped up, I said stuff that fed his paranoia. I'm not proud of what I did. I'm just sorry that it took a total breakdown to make me see it."

"I've been concerned with Greer's behavior for a while. How dangerous do you think he is?" I asked.

"On a scale of one to ten, I'd give him an eight."

I winced. "Has he made any specific threats?"

"No. He ranted about making you and your father pay for firing him and humiliating him. Oddly, he was angrier about the video with the old lady than I was. Which reminds me: do *you* have anything you'd like to apologize for?"

"I can say with all sincerity that I had nothing to do with that video. But in the interest of maintaining honesty, I'll admit that I have suspicions about who was behind it."

"I'll let it go. It was kinda funny, actually. Luckily, the Internet generation has the attention span of a hyperactive squirrel on crack."

"Do you know where Greer is now?" I asked.

"No. Look, there's something you need to understand about him. His life is falling apart. This whole starting-a-detective-agency thing, it's just fantasy. He tried to borrow money from me to get it started and I refused. His marriage is on the rocks. He brought a lot of his problems on himself by being an asshole, but he doesn't have enough self-awareness to know that. He just blames you and your father."

"And his only purpose in life now is to destroy us," I said, realizing that I might not have been taking the threat Greer posed as seriously as I should have.

"Exactly."

"I appreciate the heads-up. If you hear anything more from him, let us know."

"I really don't want anyone to get hurt."

We mumbled awkward goodbyes.

Karter Greer was a boil on my butt that needed to be lanced before the situation turned ugly. The trouble was, I had no idea how to find him. I headed for the sheriff's office. Dad needed to know about Greer.

I had to wait outside his office while he finished interviewing a prospective recruit. Dad took an interest in all of our new hires, starting at the lowest level. When the door finally opened, I was pleasantly surprised to see Jessie Gilmore smiling and shaking Dad's hand.

"Now I'll have to go in there and tell him all the reasons he shouldn't hire you," I kidded her as she came to the door.

"Don't you dare! I've worked too hard for this."

"Rumor has it that you're tops in your class."

"You better run a little faster in your hamster wheel if you don't want me taking your job." She gave me a playful punch in the arm that could have left a bruise.

"You've been taking this academy stuff too seriously," I said, rubbing my arm.

"Toughen up or wash out." She laughed and practically danced out of the office.

"You want to see me?" Dad asked, a smile on his face. Jessie had that effect on people.

"Serious business," I said and followed him into his sanctum. The temple beast rose from its mattress in the corner and came over to drool on me.

"Tina Knightly wishes me to extend her apologies for besmirching your reputation," I told Mauser as I ruffled his ears and sat down in a chair across the desk from Dad. The moose drooled some more on my shoes and made happy snuffling sounds.

"You talked to Tina?" Dad asked skeptically.

"I did indeed. She was quite contrite. Seems that being transported to the hospital, bombed out of her mind, and then being chastised by her parents might have made a dent in her ego."

"That's something."

"She apologized all around."

"She must know we have a dashcam video of her rolling around on the ground." Dad clearly wasn't ready to take the apology at face value.

"In my opinion, it goes deeper than that. She sounded sincere. And she also wanted to warn us that Greer is off the chain."

"Isn't that old news?"

I told him exactly what she'd told me.

"And you *did* say you saw him at the ball game last week." Dad looked down at his hands, mulling over everything I had told him. "Our hands are tied until he commits a criminal act. He's filed a lawsuit against us for unlawful termination. If we do anything that could be interpreted as retaliatory, he gets more ammunition for the suit."

"There has to be some way of warning people without sticking our necks out too far." Even though I understood Dad's caution, I didn't think it would help the guilt we'd feel if Greer hurt someone we cared for.

"Warn everyone you trust and tell them not to spread the

word beyond our friends and family," Dad finally said.

Mick Klein was waiting for me when I got back to my office.

"I'm worried about the picnic at Lake Loka," he said, settling down in a chair.

"Most of the department is going to be there," I said encouragingly.

"I wish we could set up a security point and search everyone who comes in."

"I talked to Dad about that when the question of manpower and overtime came up. He pointed out that the park includes fifteen unfenced acres and half a mile of shoreline. Even if we fence off access from the road, people could still come through the woods or from the lake."

"I know."

"This turf war can't be that bad."

"We have a few moles in the groups. Word is that both sides smell blood."

I rubbed my forehead and sighed. "Any suggestions?"

"I don't know. I don't think either side really wants to start anything crazy for fear of the heat that would come down on them. My concern is that if some idiot starts a fight, all hell will break loose."

"That's why most of the department is going to be there," I reminded him. "The instructions are for everyone to be calm and deliberate. If there's a minor violation, we're to keep it localized to a small part of the park and make sure it doesn't spread."

"I'd like to speak to our people," Mick said. "Tell everyone to watch those of us involved in the investigation and the members of the drug task force. We'll signal everyone if we see members of the opposing groups starting to interact. At that point, we'd need to get between them and let them know we're aware of the situation and plan to shut it down."

"Talk to Pete. I know he's scoping out the grounds today with an eye to how his men will be staged. He's also running over different scenarios with them."

Pete and Mick didn't always see eye to eye, so I was a little surprised when Mick nodded.

"I will. Pete's done a good job with the tactical squad." He shrugged. "I guess there isn't much we can do except prepare for the worst and pray for the best."

"Dad could get with the county commission and try to shut the picnic down, but there would be howls of protest from the vendors selling food and the commissioners whose constituents look forward to the celebration every year."

"I'm not suggesting we knuckle under and let the bad guys win," Mick said, standing up.

"Everyone is going to meet tomorrow morning at nine. I'll make sure you have a chance to talk."

"I'm not one to give speeches. I just think this is a delicate situation. Plus, I really want to catch the shooters from that party. I don't mind so much when the bad guys square off as long as they make sure no innocents are in the line of fire."

I could tell by the look on his face that he was taking the shooting investigation personally.

Once he left, I looked at my computer. There was more work I could have done, but it was late, and I was ready to call it a day. I thought about Labor Day. It was meant to be a carefree time when we looked back at summer fun and forward to fall temperatures and holiday cheer. But this year felt different.

As if to emphasize the point, my phone rang as I was walking through the half-empty halls to the front of the building.

"I thought you should know that Karter Greer was just here talking crazy," Albert Griffin said when I answered.

"Why would he be at your house?" I asked, furious.

"He wanted to know where Eddie was."

"Why?" I couldn't imagine what beef Greer would have with Eddie. He'd been just a rookie at the department when Eddie had acted as my confidential informant.

"He kept saying that he needed to talk to him."

"What did you say?"

"I didn't tell him anything," Mr. Griffin answered.

"Good. You said he was acting crazy. What kind of crazy?"

"Like he was on drugs or hadn't had any sleep in the past week. Wired would be a good word for it. He was hyper, shifting his weight from one foot to the other and talking fast, barely coherent."

"Damn it! This is just what I need," I cursed. "Where is Eddie?"

"He'll be getting off work at the library in about thirty minutes."

"Have you warned him that Greer is looking for him?"

"I called him first."

"Good. I'm heading to the library. I'll figure out what to do next once I have eyes on Eddie."

I didn't know if Greer planned to hurt Eddie or not. All I knew was that I wanted to get there first. I'd known that Greer could be lazy and incompetent, even vindictive. Now I was realizing that he might be dangerous.

The library parking lot was almost empty when I pulled in. Chances were that my marked SUV would scare Greer off if he had plans to attack Eddie, though I couldn't imagine why that should even be a possibility. Of course, crazy people didn't have to make sense. The more I was learning about Greer, the more convinced I became that he was unraveling.

"You have ten minutes to find a book," Eddie said when he saw me come through the door.

"I'm here to check you out, not a book." I grinned. "That didn't come out right."

"If you're a weirdo, then I'm calling the police," Eddie said, playing along.

"No, we'll keep our traditional roles. You're the weirdo and I'm the cop."

"I guess Albert called you," Eddie said seriously.

"Let's get you off the front desk. Is there anyone else who can finish checking people out?"

"Albert's probably overreacting. I've never done anything to Greer."

"I'm not sure that matters. He's targeting my friends and family."

"I'd be pretty far down on the list," he scoffed.

"Can we talk about this somewhere that doesn't make you such an easy target?"

"I'm not going to leave Julie here alone if Greer is going to cause a problem."

"We aren't leaving," I assured him. "But I don't want Greer to be able to see you."

The library's checkout desk was directly in line with the glass front doors. Greer could take a shot through the glass if he was in a particularly violent mood.

"Okay," Eddie finally agreed as a woman walked up to the counter, carrying a handful of novels. He disappeared through a door behind the desk, causing the woman to glare at me for sending Eddie off to the back without letting her check out first.

One of Eddie's co-workers came out and smiled at the woman, who gave me one more stab in the chest with her eyes before sliding her books across the counter.

"You can come into the back office with me," Eddie said from the doorway.

"No. I want to see Greer if he shows up."

"He doesn't even know where I work."

"Let's hope not. He was at a ball game the other night watching me and my family. Avoiding him is the best thing you can do."

Eddie looked thoughtful for a second. "I wonder if he saw me with Kat Fergusson."

I'd been looking out the front windows but abruptly whipped my head toward Eddie. "The woman whose body was found under the van? How the hell did you know her?"

"She passed through here several years ago, back when I

was still using… We used to hang out. She's been gone for ages but showed back up about two months ago, and I saw her once or twice. I felt horrible when I heard she was dead."

"Why do you wonder if Greer saw you together?"

"She was his CI for a hot minute," Eddie said.

"You're kidding." I was having a hard time processing this new piece of information. Did it fit into the bigger puzzle of Briggs and Holloway, or was it nothing more than an odd tangent?

"No. I don't think it lasted very long."

"Maybe he was jealous that you were a friend of hers," I said, thinking out loud. "And maybe the fact that you'd been *my* CI enraged him." It didn't make a lot of sense to anyone sane, but I didn't think we were dealing with a sane person anymore.

I waited while Eddie closed up the library, then drove him home. But once we were in the driveway of Mr. Griffin's house, I had second thoughts.

"You shouldn't stay here if Greer is looking for you," I told Eddie.

"I'm not going to leave Albert all alone." Eddie snapped his fingers. "Hey, I'll call Jessie. We were going to hang out this weekend anyway. She can come over and we'll all stay in Albert's house."

I thought about this for a minute and then nodded. "That should work. Keep the doors locked."

Eddie was on the phone with Jessie before he was all the way out of the car. I stayed in the driveway until he was safely inside the house.

As I drove home, I couldn't help thinking that I had enough to worry about this weekend without Greer causing trouble. I wished there was some charge that we could have brought him in on, but I knew Dad was right. Anything we did to him had to be solidly grounded in probable cause, or Greer's lawsuit would bite us in the ass for sure.

I was too restless to settle down and watch TV or read

with Cara. I went outside and organized the back of the Suburban, where all my tactical gear and extra equipment was still jumbled up from when I'd transferred everything from my wrecked car. To calm myself, I tried to think about all the elements of the Briggs and Holloway murders, wondering if we'd ever know for sure who'd killed Holloway. But I couldn't keep my mind on the facts. It kept playing through all the crazy scenarios that could happen at the picnic the next day, with an added dose of worrying about Greer.

Once I had the SUV as organized as it was going to get, I went back inside to find Cara reading a fantasy novel on the couch and looking like she was about to doze off.

"Have you heard from your parents today?" I asked

She thought for a moment, then looked a little surprised and reached for her phone. "You know, I don't think I have."

After letting her mother's number ring and go to voicemail, she called her father's phone. When it also went to voicemail, she looked at me with concern in her eyes. I felt a rush of adrenaline.

"I'm heading over to the cabin. I'll call Dad on the way."

Cara was putting on her shoes before I finished talking.

"I'm going too."

I knew better than to argue.

CHAPTER TWENTY-ONE

I called Dad as I drove. "Have you been to the cabin today?"

"No. Anna has been driving me crazy trying to push a whole list of herbal medicines on me," he said grumpily.

I explained the situation.

"I'll walk over and meet you at the cabin," he said and hung up.

We made the drive in record time. As I slowly drove up to the cabin, the only vehicle I saw was the Laursens' old Volvo. The cabin was dark and quiet. I didn't like the fact that the lights were off, but as soon as I had the thought, the lights came on. Dad had arrived before we did.

"Stay in the car," I said in a tone that must have convinced Cara that I was serious.

As I walked to the cabin, I heard noises from inside and an occasional gruff bark that I recognized as Mauser's. I opened the front door and saw Dad in the living room, untying Anna and a bruised Henry. It didn't escape my notice that Dad removed the gag from Henry's mouth before doing the same for Anna. Mauser came over and leaned against me.

"He'd never have gotten the upper hand if he hadn't hit me with a piece of firewood," Henry said, then added, "Or if

Mauser hadn't been asleep in the bedroom." He sounded embarrassed on the dog's behalf.

"Who did this?" Dad asked as if we didn't already know the answer.

"A young guy, strong. He was raving about you two. He looked through our phones." Henry was breathing heavily as he spoke.

"He's crazy," Anna added. "He's got some connection to Tina Knightly. That's what he wanted to know about."

I pulled up a picture of Greer on my phone and showed it to them.

"That's him!" Anna said, and Henry nodded.

Dad took Henry and Anna over to the small dining table and offered them both shots of whiskey from a bottle in a cabinet against the wall. "Call dispatch and put out a stop-and-hold on Greer, with a note to contact me immediately," he told me.

I made the call, then turned to see Dad giving Anna and Henry hard stares.

"We need to know everything," he said, using his sheriff's voice. "That includes all about your shenanigans with Knightly and the video."

Henry and Anna looked at each other, then down at the floor.

"We were trying to help," Henry said guiltily.

"You can blame me," Anna said.

Before she could continue, Cara appeared in the doorway. Mauser welcomed her to the scene of the drama, and I waved her over to join us.

"I have a good friend… I'm not going to tell you her name. She's not to blame," Anna said.

"We need the name. If Greer looked at your phones, than he already knows it," Dad pointed out.

Henry and Anna exchanged more looks.

"Mom!" Cara said in a menacing voice.

"Salem Potts. Her name is Salem Potts," Anna said.

"That sounds made up," Dad said.

"That's her stage name. The truth is she has a… well, a bunch of names."

"They're called aliases," I said dryly.

"You might call them that," Anna admitted. "She's a stage magician who earns extra money doing slip-and-fall routines."

"You mean slip-and-fall scams." I was having a hard time hiding my irritation.

"Whatever." Anna dismissed the accusation. "We had just seen her perform at the co-op so we… sort of came up with an idea to get this Knightly woman back for what she did to all of you."

"Wonderful," Dad growled. "Where is she now?"

"I don't know! I swear. She had her assistant make contact with the guy who posted the video."

Henry nodded. "Anna's telling the truth. Salem was heading out west, but that's all we know. We made sure she didn't give us any details."

"In case you were caught." Dad rolled his eyes.

Mauser came over and placed himself between Dad and Cara's parents.

"Don't protect them, you Bendict Arnold," Dad said. "Okay, I'll assume you're telling the truth about this Salem woman. What exactly did Greer do and say when he was here?"

"I was out back cleaning the grill," Henry told us. "I started to come back into the house when I saw this guy rush over and clout me on the head with a piece of wood. I was staggered by the blow and, before I could do anything, he swung the log into my stomach. I went down on my knees, then I felt him poke me with a gun barrel. He told me to get up. Once I was up, he told me to go inside."

"How was he dressed?" Dad asked.

"Black cargo pants and a black T-shirt. He had a tan rag wrapped around his forehead."

"Did you see the gun?" I asked, wondering what sort of half-assed Rambo impersonation Greer had been doing.

"Semi-auto of some sort. Black, but I don't think it was a Glock. I was going to fight him rather than let him come inside where Anna and Mauser were." He gave Mauser a soft pat on the head. "Trouble was, Anna had already looked outside and Greer locked eyes with her."

"I couldn't do anything. He had a gun on Henry." Anna took up the story. "This guy looked at me and waved the gun at Henry, making it clear he'd shoot him if I didn't do what he said. Next, he waved the gun at the sliding door, wanting me to open it."

Anna suddenly stopped talking. I think she was considering how bad the situation could have turned out. She wasn't one to normally worry about consequences, but she wasn't stupid either.

"What happened when you opened the door?" Dad prompted.

"Greer pushed Henry inside and came in right behind him. He stood there and kept pointing the gun back and forth between us. I've seen enough strung-out people to know that if he wasn't on drugs, he was at least sleep deprived to the point of being almost delirious. He started screaming about our phones."

"It was confusing," Henry said.

"It was," Anna echoed. "I couldn't figure out why a guy would be this crazy and violent just to get a couple of cell phones."

"That's when he started ranting about you guys and Tina Knightly. He claimed y'all fired him and had a vendetta against him because he was friends with Knightly," Henry said, rubbing at his head, where I could see a fair-sized knot and clotted blood.

"Did he know you two were involved with the video?" Dad asked.

Henry shook his head. "He wasn't real clear about that, but he kept going on about how we were all against him. That he knew we'd been involved with the Internet assault against Tina. It was funny how he talked about her. Like she was a queen up on a pedestal."

"I got the phones and, after I'd handed them to him, he made me tie up Henry before he tied me up too. Then he… just left."

"Don't forget about Mauser," Henry said. "He was barking up a storm by this time because of all the shouting."

"Earlier I'd closed the door to the bedroom so the sound of my cooking wouldn't wake him up," Anna said, and I may have rolled my eyes.

"Good thing you did 'cause that maniac might have shot him," Henry said, giving Mauser another pat. For his part, Mauser looked happy to be getting accolades without having actually confronted the gunman.

Dad's mood was getting darker by the minute. I knew he was thinking about the picnic the next day and how much manpower he didn't have for a manhunt.

"Y'all are coming up to the house," Dad told Anna and Henry, then he called Genie to warn her about the incoming houseguests.

While Cara helped Anna and Henry load their things in their car, Dad pulled me aside.

"Greer needs to be found and brought in. You know we can't afford to be short any deputies for the picnic tomorrow. Suggestions?"

I managed not to look too surprised at the question. I was becoming more at ease with the concept of Dad asking for my opinion.

"Let me and a couple of handpicked deputies look for him tonight."

"Can't be you," he said with a firm shake of his head.

I knew he was right. The hunt for Greer needed to look professional, not personal.

"Pete?" Even as I said it, I knew what his objection would be.

"No. I need him at his peak tomorrow."

"Julio, Mick and Matti Sanderson," I said, knowing we could count on all of them to do the best job possible.

"Not Mick."

Of course. Mick was important for tomorrow's security detail too.

"How about Lynn?" I suggested.

"Call them. But first call dispatch and get a deputy out here to take a report from Cara's parents. Once there's a report, I'll swear out a warrant for Greer's arrest. We'll also need to get crime scene techs to go over the cabin, but it doesn't have to be done tonight. I'll lock up carefully so Shantel can come in and look for evidence later." Dad turned to Cara's parents. "Was Greer wearing gloves?"

"Yes," they said in unison, and I could see Dad's hopes of finding any evidence in the cabin going out the window.

Once a deputy had been dispatched our way, I called Julio, Lynn and Sandy. All three were eager to help when they heard what had happened to Cara's parents.

"I'm going to meet them at the office after I drop Cara off at home," I told Dad.

"You don't need to drop me off," Cara yelled over her shoulder.

I thought about it for a second. "You're right. I'd rather have you close by. If Greer is on the hunt, then we all need to stay in groups."

"Agreed," Dad said. "Remember, don't go into the field hunting Greer. Leave that to the others."

"Pinky swear. I just want to give them some suggestions, then I'll head home."

"I'm shaking," Cara said later as we drove to the office. "To think what might have happened to Mom and Dad." I could hear her fighting back tears.

"We'll get him. Poor Dad. With everything else he's got to worry about, there's this maniac that he has to tiptoe around because the crazy guy has filed a lawsuit. Did I tell you he was stalking Eddie?"

"Why Eddie?" Cara asked, shocked.

"Same reason as any of us. Probably because he looked like an easy target. Most of the rest of our friends are law enforcement. Also, Eddie knew the woman whose body was found under the van."

"What's that got to do with Greer?"

"According to Eddie, Kat Fergusson was Greer's CI at one point."

"Could there be any connection to the murder?"

"You mean between Greer and the murder? I don't see how. What motive would he have for killing an old CI? Most likely, it's just a coincidence. The underbelly of Adams County is a small, interconnected world. Greer worked the streets and was even involved with some drug stings. I'm not surprised that he knew Eddie and Kat Fergusson."

We pulled into the parking lot of the darkened sheriff's office. Lynn, Julio and Sandy were parked together and leaning on the hoods of their cars, talking in the warm night air. I parked near them and got out while Cara stayed in the Suburban.

"I can't believe that Greer would go that far," Sandy said. She'd spent more time on patrol with him than the rest of us had. They'd been hired about the same time.

"He's dangerous. Dad's sworn out a warrant for his arrest on aggravated assault. We could also charge him with kidnapping. I don't have to tell you that he's armed, and while he's a mediocre shot... still, he's armed and better than the average street shooter."

"Where do you think he's going to go?" Lynn asked.

"Think about anyone close to Dad or me. Particularly ones that aren't active LEOs. I texted Shantel and Marcus while we were at the cabin. Eddie's already been targeted. Try and find out where Greer is staying and check out his wife's house. She could be in danger. Warn her that he's got a warrant out on him and that she should take precautions. If she can stay with someone else, that would be best. Even better if she can leave the area."

I stopped to think for a minute, then held up my hand.

"Never mind. I'll talk to his wife. Y'all handle the other targets. Sandy, you know him as well as any of us. Does he have any particular haunts?"

"He spent a lot of time eating junk food in his car. One of his usual parking spots was by Rose Hill Cemetery. Another was behind the Fast Mart on the southside of town."

"Check them out and talk to any other deputies you think might have insights into his whereabouts."

"I know your dad wants them rested for tomorrow, but if we spot him, can we call in other resources like the tactical team?" Julio asked.

"Only if it's necessary. Don't call them if it's a questionable sighting. You can also use the highway patrol to back you up. Dispatch is putting the word out, so another officer might find him before one of y'all do."

"Oh, I hope not," Sandy said menacingly. "He's made all of us look bad. I'd like to be the one to put the cuffs on him."

"Remember to tread softly. We don't want to make a martyr out of him," I warned.

"This is when you long for the old days. When we would have taken him out back and beat him senseless with sacks of potatoes the first time he screwed up," Lynn said.

"You've been watching too much TV. Even you aren't old enough to remember those days," I told her.

"Yeah, wishful thinking." She smiled. "We'll treat him like the delicate flower his mother thinks he is."

I went back to the SUV.

"One more stop," I told Cara. "I'm going by Greer's old home and warn his wife."

"Were they mad that you're going have them out all night hunting Greer?"

I shook my head. "I think they're looking forward to catching him. This is personal for them too."

I got Greer's old address from dispatch and headed over there. The lights were on in the small, midcentury-style home. I drove by and circled the block, looking for Greer or any vehicle that he might have been using. Satisfied, I pulled into the driveway.

"You'd better come in with me," I told Cara. "If he comes by while I'm inside and sees you, I don't want to think about what he might do."

With my head on a swivel, we went up to the door and knocked. I heard someone moving on the other side of the door and felt myself grow tense.

"Who is it?" a soft female voice asked cautiously.

"It's Sergeant Larry Macklin. I want to have a word with you about your husband."

The door opened and a woman I vaguely recognized from some of the department's family events stood there, looking at us with concern in her eyes.

"Has something happened to Karter?"

"Not yet. This is my wife Cara. Could we come in and talk?"

"Sure. I'm Rita." She nodded to Cara and backed away from the door, closing it behind us once we were inside. "We can sit in the living room. I know that Karter hasn't been too... stable lately. He's taking the separation hard. I told him to take some time to find a new job and put the trouble with the sheriff's office behind him. I really thought that some time apart would give him a chance to reassess his life."

I was having a hard time seeing this sweet, softspoken woman with the brutish boar I knew as Greer.

"He's wanted for committing an assault this evening. And, frankly, several people who have interacted with him are concerned about his mental health."

"He's had a hard time lately," she said apologetically. "All that trouble with the sheriff's office. Oh, I know y'all had to do what you did. Still, being fired has been an ordeal for him. Also, I saw where a person he'd worked with had died. Murdered."

"You mean Kat Fergusson?" I asked.

"That's her name. Horrible what happened to her. I saw Karter at the store yesterday and told him I was sorry to hear about it. I knew they'd been close."

"How did he react?"

"He didn't say much. Seemed… I guess you'd say shutdown. Not that he's ever been one to be emotional." She paused. "Anger. He expresses his frustration and fear through anger."

"Right now, he seems very angry," I told her. "Do you have someone you could stay with until he's arrested?"

Rita looked at me like I'd started to sprout wings.

"Karter would never hurt me," she said firmly.

"You're separated. Which suggests there have been… marital tensions. It would not be the first time that a distraught spouse took it out on their partner. Even if he's not mad at you, he might decide to bring harm to himself and you."

"I doubt that. If he's as upset as you say he is, I'd want to be here if he comes back. I'm sure I could talk to him."

This woman had one of the worst cases of savior complex that I'd ever seen.

"I know I can't *make* you take precautions to protect yourself. All I can do is warn you that the last time your husband was seen, he was threatening people with a handgun."

"I appreciate your concern. Trust me, I'll be fine."

"Can you help us locate him?"

"I don't know how."

"Are you paying any of his bills? Like his cell phone bill?" I asked.

"No. He pays that. He even refused to let me pay for his apartment."

"He has an apartment?"

"It's more of a motel room. The Roads Best Motel out by the interstate will apparently rent rooms by the month."

"And he has a room there?"

"At least he did when he first moved out."

I took out my phone and texted Julio to check out the motel. Then I asked, "Does he have any close friends?"

"I think that's part of his problem. Most of his friends were his fellow deputies, and with the way he was fired…"

"Did you know that he was spending time with Tina Knightly?"

"Oh, yes. He's been trying to get his private detective agency started. The state has been dragging their feet on his permits, which has been another sore point with him. You see, he's had a difficult time."

"Has he taken on any clients?" I didn't bother pointing out that if he didn't have a license, then he couldn't legally have clients.

"I think there was a guy he was working with. I haven't met him, so I can't tell you much."

"Did Greer tell you anything about this guy?"

"Just talked about meeting a guy he was working with. Oh, he did say it was a murder case."

"No name or other details?" I pressed.

"I can't remember. You can ask him," she said, acting like I could just pick up the phone and call Greer.

Then I had a thought. "Would *you* mind calling him? If he answers, tell him that he needs to give himself up. If he doesn't want to come in to the sheriff's office, he can surrender to the Florida Highway Patrol or any other law enforcement agency."

"I'll try. To be fair, he doesn't always answer my calls on a good day." Rita picked up her cell phone and called him. "See," she said, turning the phone toward me. I could hear his voicemail message.

I motioned for her to leave a message.

"It's worth a try. If you do see or talk to him, let me know immediately and urge him to surrender." I took out one of my cards and handed it to her.

With nothing else productive left to do, Cara and I drove home. I tried to relax into our pre-bedtime routine of walking Alvin and making sure the cats were fed, but I knew it was going to be a long night. I left my phone next to me on the nightstand, knowing I'd be checking it constantly, with no hope of sleep before tomorrow's big day at the lake.

CHAPTER TWENTY-TWO

I dropped Cara off at my dad's so that she could spend the day with her parents. She'd tried to talk me into letting her come to the picnic until I'd explained about the potential for a drug war. After that, she was content to spend the day with her folks, Genie and Mauser.

Genie told me that Dad had left the house at dawn. He wanted to scout out the park before others started arriving. I knew he would also want to be at the morning briefing, especially in light of the warrant that was out for Greer.

I made it to the lake just in time for the briefing and, sure enough, Dad filled everyone in on what had happened the night before.

"I know that most of you have worked with Karter Greer for quite a while. I'm sure that some of you still look on him as a friend. I want to speak to those deputies. The best way to be Karter Greer's friend right now is to help bring him in safely. From the recent eyewitness accounts, I don't believe that he is thinking straight.

"We had to fire him because he made a mistake that led to a person's death. There was no malice in the actions the department took. Even though he's threatened members of my own family, I still want him brought in unharmed.

Custody is where he's going to find safety and help. Having said all of that, if there is anyone here who doesn't think he can do what is necessary to stop Greer from committing more acts of violence in our community, I will give them a pass for today. If you chose to go home, you won't be punished. We just need everyone to be clear on their priorities. And, of course, if you go home, you won't get any of that sweet time-and-a-half holiday pay." Dad smiled and there were a few chuckles in response.

No one left.

Following Dad were multiple reports from Mick, Pete and the tactical team, Sergeant Olson with the drug task force, and an agent from the DEA. Emphasis was placed on not letting any incident escalate and get out of hand. There were lots of nods all around, and everyone seemed pumped to make this a safe event. Even the weather was cooperating, with the temperature expected to top out just below ninety with only sixty percent humidity. With everyone wearing protective vests, the less heat and humidity we had to deal with, the better.

Next, we all received our assignments from Captain Grant and Lieutenant Phil Eccles. I was stationed on the south side of the park near the shore of the lake with five other deputies, including Julio. Due to his familiarity with the suspects in the party shooting, Mick was going to be roving through the crowd and advising other deputies.

By ten o'clock that morning, the crowds were growing. A band started to play on a portable stage that had been set up by the county's parks and recreation department.

"I can't believe that two people have already been put into Ubers for being intoxicated," Julio said, shaking his head as we stood side by side and watched the crowd.

Through our earbuds, we heard Mick pointing out various persons of interest in his murder case, but none of them were near our position.

"Greer's wife is a trip," I told Julio. "She seems more like his defense attorney or his counselor."

"One of my cousins had a girlfriend who took it upon herself to save him from the streets. She worked like a drill sergeant to get him on to the righteous path. A year after he'd gotten clean, found a good job and learned how to be a man, she left him. Said he was boring."

"People are strange. It's odd that the body we found was Greer's old CI," I mused.

"You can understand how he probably felt knowing she'd been killed. If it was anyone else, I might even think he felt guilty that he wasn't able to protect her," Julio said.

"I get that. A CI can become like a partner. They're out on the street giving you tips. Some of those tips could save your life, or help you get a step up in the department if it's a big bust." Something about our conversation was niggling at the back of my mind, but I couldn't clarify the thought.

A call came through our earbuds asking who was wandering off into the woods. This was pretty typical chatter. If you needed eyes on a suspect and couldn't make out the identity of the deputy closest to that spot, you'd ask them to identify themselves.

"If Holloway murdered Briggs in order to set him up for the serial murders, what made him think that the authorities were on to him?" Julio asked idly.

"I guess the fact that Kat Fergusson was a witness. She must have been able to identify him."

"So why hadn't she told the FBI who he was, or done something to point the finger at him?"

As we watched a multi-generational family group of about fifteen people, one of the younger women stood up and started an argument with the oldest woman. It went back and forth until a man about the same age as the younger woman tried to take her hand and pull her away from the older woman. At that point, the younger woman kicked dirt at the older woman and everyone in the group started fighting.

Julio and I had already started to move toward them when the dirt went flying. Fifteen minutes later, the younger woman and her two children were heading toward the family car while the man was apologizing to his mother and the rest of the family.

With peace restored, Julio and I returned to our observation spot, which provided us with shade and a tree to lean against when we needed it.

"You must be exhausted after last night," I said.

"Once we'd looked everywhere we could think of, we took turns sleeping while staking out the motel. The clerk said that Greer hadn't checked out, but he also hadn't seen him in the last twenty-four hours."

"What were you saying before that episode of *Family Feud*?" I asked.

"I don't remember. Something about the Briggs and Holloway cases." Julio snapped his fingers. "I was just wondering why Kat Fergusson hadn't told the FBI if she knew who her attacker was."

"I don't know how many informants you've worked with. A lot of them have mental issues and tend to be paranoid. They may trust the one deputy they have a relationship with, but not any other LEOs." As I talked, my mind was working its way through a mental maze.

"I get that. There was a guy who hung out at the Fast Mart for about a year. Heavy into drugs and not quite right in the head. Chief Marks was the only one he'd talk to. I mean, even if all you wanted to know was the color of a car that had driven by, you'd have to get Darlene to come ask him about it."

My mind was buzzing. "You've hit on the answer. I think."

"What?"

"Who would Kat go to? Who was her handler?"

"Greer! She went to Greer rather than tell the FBI or any of the other officers. Let me think this through." Julio was literally vibrating with excitement.

There was constant chatter in our earbuds, but we'd tuned it out as I came up with our new trail to follow. If we hadn't been distracted, we would have been paying more attention to our surroundings.

"Kat went to Greer and told him who the killer was, or at least gave him enough information to figure it out," I said. "But at that time, all he could think about was embarrassing Dad and the department."

"So he decided to pin the serial murders on a person who was living here and was close to some of our people." Julio looked stunned at Greer's audacity.

"He might have even planned on revealing the real killer later, after we'd admitted that Briggs was the murderer. Getting two jabs in. Greer could always claim that Holloway killed the witness because he knew she could identify him."

"So he went to Holloway and told him that the Feds were closing in on him, and gave him the idea to use Briggs, his co-worker, as a patsy," Julio said.

"It's sort of brilliant," I admitted. "In a mad-as-a-hatter sort of way."

"He's not one of us," I heard Pete's voice say into my ear.

"Whoever it is, they're wearing a deputy's uniform," said another voice that I didn't recognize.

"Greer!" I said loud enough that I almost didn't need to key the mic.

Julio's head started swinging right and left.

"Where is he?" I asked.

"Your side. He keeps fading back into the woods. I can't get my glass on him to give a positive ID," Pete responded.

"Everyone swing south through the crowd. Let's push him away from the picnic," Dad instructed. "DEA and the tac team, stay in place and keep an eye on our dealers."

I saw Dad moving quickly and smoothly through the crowd, which was starting to look confused at the march of a dozen deputies toward the woods on the south side.

"It's possible that Greer killed Kat Fergusson and Colson Holloway," I informed everyone over the radio. "A man who's already committed murder doesn't have much to lose."

I saw my dad react a second later as a shot rang out from the woods. He looked surprised more than hurt as I ran toward him.

The shot created panic and overreactions from our drug-dealing friends. Guns quickly appeared in the hands of more than a dozen men in the crowd.

I reached Dad, who was waving me off. The bullet had hit his protective vest. Through my earbuds, I heard Pete saying that he couldn't get eyes on Greer. Now that people were running every which way and threatening voices were screaming at each other, it was hard to keep track of what was happening.

The hero of the moment was Mick, who went striding fearlessly between the two factions, telling them to put up their guns and go. The drug dealers were utterly confused by this reaction from a deputy. Mick told me later that two of the drug lords were practically hopping up and down with their guns in hand, with no idea what to do. Finally, one of them swore loudly and waved his minions toward their cars.

"I'm fine," Dad assured me, rubbing the spot on his chest where the bullet had hit. "I made eye contact with him before he fired."

Dad headed toward the woods again, with half a dozen of us following him like soldiers storming a beach. The underbrush was thick at the edges of the clearing by the lake, then gradually the woods became more open.

We were a hundred feet into the woods when Pete's voice came over the radio. "He's doubled back and heading for the parking lot. I've got a shot." A split second later: "No, I don't."

"Don't fire unless he turns back toward the lake. Let him go if you have to. We don't want him shooting again in this crowd." Dad was already moving up through the woods in the direction of the parking lot, with the rest of us on his heels.

"No one would question your judgment if you gave the

order to shoot," I told him.

"He could have aimed for my head. Though I'm sure he knew I had a vest on." Dad was breathing heavily as he stomped through the woods.

A dozen feet ahead, I could see the parking lot and cars, lots of cars, many of them already heading for the exit. As we burst out of the woods, two more shots rang out, and the crowd in the lot hunkered down behind the parked cars.

On our side of the parking lot, I could see a car with a flat tire stalled in the grass. Julio stood on one side of the car with his Glock pointed into the front seat. On the other side stood Pete, rifle in hand and breathing heavily through a huge smile.

Pete's voice went out on the radio telling everyone that the suspect was secure. The entire time he was talking, Pete kept his eyes focused on Greer.

Dad and I reached the car at the same time. Greer was inside, his forehead against the steering wheel and his hands held up. A rifle lay in the seat beside him, and there was glass all over the backseat from the shattered rear window.

"Sorry," Pete said to Dad, who was frowning at him. "I saw a chance to shoot out the tire and figured a second round in the back window would give us time to get up next to the car."

"I'm going to want a very thorough after-action report," Dad said with a stern glance at all of us. "Get him out of the car and cuff him. And throw a blanket over him so the photographers don't get a picture of him wearing one of our uniforms."

Two days later, we were all laboring, even if the judges and other parts of the justice system weren't. Greer hadn't been willing to talk on Saturday afternoon or on Sunday, but Monday morning found him willing to be interviewed. His lawyer kept advising him to be quiet, but he just ignored her.

"Greer can't stop talking," Julio said, grinning as he met

me outside the interview room at the jail.

"Has he confessed to killing Davis Briggs?"

"Yes and no. He admits he's responsible because he pointed Holloway to Briggs. He's also denying that he murdered Kat Fergusson, which I find less believable."

"I agree, though I'm not sure how we can prove it. How does he explain Holloway's death?" I asked.

"He admits to killing him. Good for the world, eliminating evil. Basically making himself out to be a hero."

"We'll see how well that plays out in front of a jury. I've got Lionel working on all of Greer's electronics with help from the FBI."

As if summoned by the acronym, Agent Padilla came out of the interview room.

"He's the worst type of murderer. Full of himself and just smart enough to get away with a few tricks."

"And he has the sweetest, most trusting wife you could imagine," I told her.

"The worst ones do."

"I've been talking to the State Attorney. He's confident that we have enough evidence to make sure that Greer never sees the outside of Raiford again." The state prison at Raiford, with several maximum-security wings, was the place that the worst of the worst murderers in Florida called home.

"I think the reason he asked for me is that he's hoping to get some federal charges," Padilla said.

"He's thinking that a federal prison would be safer for an ex-deputy than Raiford. He's probably right," I said.

"We won't charge him with a federal crime unless he isn't charged or found guilty in the state courts."

"What about Colson Holloway?" I asked.

"We're putting together a full dossier on him. Being dead gets him a bye on being formally charged, but I've met the families of his victims. They deserve to have answers. My boss wanted me to cut our losses and close the cases without a full follow-up. I told him I'd resign first. We've spent years on these murders. A few more months of interviews and reports isn't going to break the bank at the FBI."

The interview ended when Greer got tired and angry because we wouldn't bring him a full meal from the Palmetto restaurant. If I'd thought we needed more of his lies, I'd have paid for the lunch out of my own pocket, but we didn't. Six hours of him running his mouth while downplaying the horrible acts he'd committed, and making himself out to be a hero for killing Holloway, was enough.

I hurried home and got cleaned up, then made it out to Dad's place in time for a cookout. Anna and Henry would be going home on Tuesday morning, so this would be our last meal together until the holidays.

"Everyone is out back," Cara told me as she met me at my car. "Mom and Dad are still feeling awful about what they did."

"As they should." I pulled her in close as we walked around the house. "Don't worry. I won't give them a hard time."

She turned and gave me a kiss as we walked.

Mauser and Jimmy came trotting around the corner. Jimmy was wearing his softball jersey and Mauser was all wet. The dog waited until Cara and I were close enough to enjoy the full effect, then shook himself, sending water everywhere.

"I ran the hose over him 'cause he was hot," Jimmy told us with a smile that suggested he enjoyed seeing Mauser spray people with water.

"Day like this, the water feels good." I smiled and Jimmy laughed.

The breeze shifted and the smoke from the grill caught us as we came around the corner.

There were two round tables with umbrellas over them, and Cara's parents and Genie were in the shade of the nearest one. Dad was tending the grill.

"We'll be ready to put the hamburgers on soon." He gave us a wave with an old piece of rebar that he used to stir the coals.

We rearranged the tables so that Cara and I could sit at the other table in the shade of the umbrella while still facing Cara's parents and Genie.

"I know Cara told you not to bring up our stupidity, but I want to personally apologize," Anna said, shocking me. She wasn't one to admit mistakes. "I pushed Henry to go along with me. I did it because you've done so much for us. I felt like I needed to give back."

One thing about Anna was that you never had to wonder if she was being sincere.

"It was crazy, but sweet," I allowed. "Oddly, I think you helped Tina more than us."

"The department hasn't caught too much bad press for the shootout at the picnic. Luckily, no one was hurt," Dad said from the grill. He rubbed the spot on his chest where he still bore a bruise. "Well, except for me."

"Do you think he knew you had the vest on?" I asked.

"I do. Not that he couldn't have missed and hit me somewhere else. The man wasn't the best shot in the department. Still, Pete returned the favor. He had several opportunities to take him down."

"You'd ordered Pete not to shoot," I pointed out.

"A weak moment."

"How could Greer think that teaming up with a serial killer was a good idea?"

"I talked to Tina Saturday evening," Dad said. "She thinks she might have put the idea into his head. Seems they were strategizing a month ago when she brought up the idea that if she could uncover a major crime that was going on under our noses, it would show us up as incompetent. She wanted Greer to help look for possible crimes going on under the radar in Adams County. When Kat Fergusson came to Greer, wanting his help to expose Colson Holloway as the serial killer, he saw his opportunity."

"Is there any possibility that Greer told Tina about Holloway?" I asked.

"I doubt it. Tina, even at her craziest, still comes across

as law-abiding. As far as we know, she's never crossed the line from legal to illegal, even when she was posting crap about us. I think Greer knew she wouldn't go along with the worst parts of his plan. I do think that if the box of trophies hadn't been found, or if no one realized what they were, then Greer would have found a way to play the hero-slash-brilliant detective and shown Davis out as the serial killer."

"So when Holloway wasn't useful anymore, he ran him over?" Anna asked.

"He posed a threat to Greer. As long as he was alive, he could implicate him," I explained.

"Greer willingly admitted to killing Holloway?" Henry asked.

I nodded "And making himself out as a hero. A clue we missed was the truck that was used in the hit and run. Greer had responded to a burglary at Dante Comacho's house a year ago. He'd walked through the house with Shantel and seen that Camacho kept the truck keys in the drawer."

"Let me get this clear in my head," Anna said. "Colson Holloway was a serial killer that the FBI was looking for. There was a witness…"

"Kat Fergusson. He'd tried to abduct her but she was able to get away."

"So Kat tells Greer about Holloway instead of the FBI. How does that make sense?" Anna asked.

"It does when you factor in Kat's paranoia," I explained. "She had a relationship with Greer and trusted him."

"We've worked with some addicts and folks with mental issues. Paranoia is standard issue with those poor folks," Henry said.

Genie got up and brought the hamburgers from the house. An hour later, with a full stomach, I watched Jimmy try to convince Mauser to return a softball when he threw it. Mauser looked as interested in playing ball as I did. I leaned back in the lawn chair and sighed contentedly, hoping that fall and the holidays would bring quieter times.

Larry Macklin returns in:

Halloween's Haunt
A Larry Macklin Mystery—Book 22

ACKNOWLEDGMENTS

As always, thanks to my wife, Melanie, for her editing skills and support; to H. Y. Hanna for her inspiration, assistance and encouragement; and to all the fans of the series. Larry never would have come this far without all of you!

Original Cover Concept by H. Y. Hanna
Cover Design by Florida Girl Design, Inc.
www.gobookcoverdesign.com

ABOUT THE AUTHOR

A. E. Howe lives and writes on a farm in the wilds of North Florida with his wife, horses and more cats than he can count. He received a degree in English Education from the University of Georgia and is a produced screenwriter and playwright. His first published book was *Broken State*. The Larry Macklin Mysteries is his first series and he released the Baron Blasko Mysteries in summer 2018. His most recent series, the Mortician Murder Mysteries, was launched in 2022.

The first book in the Macklin series, *November's Past*, was awarded two silver medals in the 2017 President's Book Awards, presented by the Florida Authors & Publishers Association; the ninth book, *July's Trials*, was awarded two silver medals in 2018. Howe is a member of the Mystery Writers of America, and was co-host of the "Guns of Hollywood" podcast for four years on the Firearms Radio Network. When not writing, Howe enjoys riding, competitive shooting and working on the farm.